WINNERS AND LOSERS

The eagerly-awaited third novel in the Family Feud series

When Sarah Jenkins meets Connor Searles she is truly attracted to him. But Connor has just joined a rock 'n' roll band, and Sarah can't help feeling jealous when she sees newspaper pictures of him with other girls. Connor's band proves to be a major success and his fame increases until he is blamed for an assault on a woman. Can he prove his innocence and will Sarah believe him?

Recent Titles by Linda Sole from Severn House

The Family Feud Series
THE LIE
A PROMISE MADE
WINNERS AND LOSERS

The Sarah Beaufort Mystery Series
MISCARRIAGE OF JUSTICE
JUSTICE IS SERVED
A DIFFERENT KIND OF JUSTICE

The Country House Series
GIVE ME TOMORROW
A BRIGHT NEW DAY
WISH DOWN THE MOON

The London Series
BRIDGET
KATHY
AMY

THE TIES THAT BIND
THE BONDS THAT BREAK
THE HEARTS THAT HOLD

THE ROSE ARCH
A CORNISH ROSE
A ROSE IN WINTER

FLAME CHILD

WINNERS AND LOSERS

Linda Sole

Severn House Large Print
London & New York

This first large print edition published 2012
in Great Britain and the USA by
SEVERN HOUSE PUBLISHERS LTD of
9-15 High Street, Sutton, Surrey, SM1 1DF.
First world regular print edition published 2009 by
Severn House Publishers Ltd., London and New York.

B000 000 007 8035

British Library Cataloguing in Publication Data

Sole, Linda.
    Winners and losers. -- (A family feud saga)
    1. Domestic fiction. 2. Large type books.
    I. Title II. Series
    823.9'14-dc23

    ISBN-13: 978-0-7278-9939-2

Severn House Publishers support The Forest Stewardship Council
[FSC], the leading international forest certification organisation. All
our titles that are printed on Greenpeace-approved FSC-certified paper
carry the FSC logo.

MIX
Paper from
responsible sources
FSC® C018575

Printed and bound in Great Britain by the
MPG Books Group, Bodmin, Cornwall.

One

'Where are you going?' Sarah turned as she heard her mother's voice. 'If you're meeting friends at that youth club again, just be careful – and don't talk to strangers on your way home, especially men in cars or vans.'

'Mum!' Sarah's laugh was a mixture of affection and frustration. 'Anyone would think I was fourteen. I'm nearly nineteen. You don't have to treat me like a child.'

'You think you're grown up and in some ways you are,' Mrs Jenkins said. 'But you are still very young, Sarah. You don't know what some men are like – and you read about dreadful things these days...'

Sarah kissed her mother's cheek. 'Don't worry. I'm always careful. I shan't be late so don't watch the clock.'

She went out of the front door, closing it carefully behind her. Her mother and father were stricter than her friends' parents were, but they spoiled her, buying her pretty clothes and anything else she wanted. The only problem was that they treated her as a little girl – her mother in particular – and she wasn't a child any more. Several of the girls she'd gone to school with were already married and had started families of their own; others had gone to university or had moved away to find better jobs than were available in their small market town – or city, as it ought to be called.

Sarah had once asked why Ely was called a city, when it was really only a small town. Her father, who was a member of the council, told her it was because they had a wonderful cathedral and that she should be proud to live in such a quiet, respectable place.

Sometimes she thought she would like to go far away. She liked shopping in Cambridge when she could, because there were a lot more shops and it seemed more alive than her hometown, but she could only manage to get there now and then, especially now that she had left school and found herself a job. She was lucky to have been taken on by a smart dress shop, which had recently opened in the High Street. Her wages were not generous, but she earned more than some of her friends did.

She walked past St Mary's church and the Cathedral green, where the old cannon stood guard as it had for years, heading for Cambridge Road. As she approached the youth club, she saw some of her friends gathered outside and waved to them, her spirits lifting. There was always something to do at the club, because she liked playing darts or table tennis, and even though she couldn't play she enjoyed watching the young men playing snooker. Sometimes one of the members would bring a new record and they would dance.

'Janice ... Phyllis,' she called to her friends. 'I

was afraid you might not be here.'

'We were thinking of going to the jive club,' Phyllis told her. 'I went last week and it was good fun, Sarah. You should join.'

'I should like to,' Sarah replied. 'I'll see what Mum says and let you know.'

'Surely you don't have to ask?' Janice stared at her as if she were mad. 'I stopped asking my mother years ago.'

'Mum likes to know where I am,' Sarah said. 'Oh, don't let's talk about it. I know what you think, but Mum is so good to me. I don't like to upset her.'

Sarah saw the look that passed between her friends. She knew what they thought of the way she always tried to respect her parents' wishes.

'How do you like working in Woolworth's, Phyllis?' she asked to change the subject.

'I'd rather work where you do,' Phyllis said. 'You lucky thing. How did you manage to get a job like that?'

Sarah laughed. She had been lucky to get the job. She suspected the fact that she was Ron Jenkins' daughter might have had something to do with it, but she wasn't going to confess that to her friends. Her employer's husband was a Mason and Sarah's father had met him at the lodge meeting. He'd told Sarah there was a job going. She knew she wasn't the only one who applied, but she was the one chosen.

'I suppose I was just lucky,' she said. 'Have you been to see *Gone with the Wind* yet? I went on Monday with Mum and Dad.'

'I saw it ages ago, the first time it came here,'

Janice said.

'Oh yes, so did I,' Sarah agreed. 'But I loved it so much I wanted to see it again – I could watch it over and over. Rhett Butler is gorgeous, isn't he?'

'You mean Clark Gable,' Janice said and grinned. 'I go to every film he stars in...'

The girls smiled at each other as they discussed their favourite film stars and the new clothes, make-up and records they had bought. When they entered the large set of rather dingy rooms that were used for the youth club, a round robin game of table tennis was going on, and a group of young men were playing darts. One of them called out to the girls and they drifted towards them, smiling and nudging each other as they accepted the invitation to play. The smell of cigarette smoke was strong, mixing with the pungent odour of hair cream and the strong, cheap perfume some of the girls wore.

Sarah took the set of darts and smiled at the young man. She knew him as Phil Burton. His father was a local shopkeeper and very respectable, but Phil was known to be a flirt and he was all hands. Sarah thought that if she took him home her mother would think him very suitable, but then she had no idea that he had already tried to get Sarah to go with him in his car up to the deserted aerodrome. Sarah was well aware what would happen if she did, and so far she'd said no and meant it. She was aware that some of the men thought she was stuck up or frigid, but she didn't particularly want to end up having to get married in a hurry the way some of her friends

8

had.

She liked Phil, as she liked some of the other men, but she hadn't yet seen anyone who made her heart beat faster.

Connor Searles sat in his car eating fish and chips and watching the girl walking towards him in the driving mirror. There was something different about her; she dressed more stylishly than most other girls did in the small market town of Ely, and she held her head high. He had seen her about the town a few times but he didn't know her name. He wound down his window as she drew level and grinned when she turned to look.

'Hello, darling,' he said confidently. 'Where are you off to this evening?'

She gave him a slaying look and walked on without speaking. Connor let out a piercing wolf whistle but she didn't glance back.

'You don't want to bother with her,' his mate Tiddy Jones said from the passenger seat. 'Stuck-up bitch! I asked her for a dance down the church hall last Saturday and she told me to get lost.'

'Why would she bother with you?' Connor asked and laughed as Tiddy aimed a blow at his head. 'She'd have to be mad to go out with a loser like you!'

'Now who's talking?' Tiddy scowled. 'Face it, mate, we've neither of us got a chance with the likes of her – our wages wouldn't pay for the clothes she was wearing, let alone buy her the kind of house she would expect.'

'Speak for yourself. I've got prospects,' Con-

9

nor said, though he was lying. He worked on his brother's farm for little more than his keep – a comedown from the days when his father, Robert Searles, had been one of the richest farmers in the district.

'Oh yeah? Tell me about it,' Tiddy drawled. 'You're like me, mate, stuck in a dead-end job. Worse off, if you ask me. At least my father owns his smallholding – your brother has sons of his own. When he dies you'll get nothing.'

'Wouldn't want it,' Connor told him. 'I'm only hanging around until Dan gets on his feet and then I'm off.'

'Where to?' Tiddy asked and laughed, as Connor couldn't answer. 'Forget it, mate. You'll never make the break.'

'What is her name?'

Tiddy stared at him, then made a mocking face. 'Sarah Jenkins. Much good it will do you. Her father owns a part share in a local building firm. They've got money. She went to a boarding school and thinks she is worth ten of the likes of us.'

'I haven't found a girl yet who said no when I asked,' Connor said. 'She'll fall like all the rest when I'm ready.'

'Yeah and pigs might fly,' Tiddy retorted. 'Let's go to the jive club. Jean Bates goes there and I fancy her...'

Connor obligingly started the engine. He was lucky to have the small Austin and knew that Tiddy hung around with him mainly because of it. Dan had bought the car cheap and done it up for him, giving it to him for his last birthday. He might not earn enough to court a girl like Sarah Jenkins, but he certainly wasn't interested in a slut like Jean Bates. Tiddy could have her and welcome.

Sometimes Connor wondered why he hung out with Tiddy, who wasn't really a friend – not like Peter Robinson. Peter was Alice's brother and they had been friends all their lives, but Peter had got tired of working on the land. He'd surprised everyone by joining the navy when he was twenty.

'Why don't you come too?' Peter had asked. 'It will be more fun than hanging around here all our lives.'

Connor had made the excuse that he couldn't leave his brother in the lurch, which was true but only a part of the truth. Dan had come home from the war a hero, but there had been too many problems waiting for him, not least the fact that their elder brother Henry had let things go and the farm was facing bankruptcy. Despite that, he had taken his youngest brother to live with him and his wife, and Connor felt he owed him something for that at least. Sometimes he felt trapped working on the land with no prospects for the future, because things had moved on in the few years since the war ended. Gradually the country was becoming more prosperous, putting the years of hardship behind it. Connor knew he wanted more out of his life, but as yet he didn't know what he wanted to do.

Tiddy was right about the girl, though. There was no way he could afford to give her the things she expected from life.

11

Sarah let herself into the house and went straight up to her room. She looked at herself in the mirror, brushing her thick hair. It had been cut to collar length recently and she'd had an ends perm to put a little bounce into it. She supposed the colour of her hair was quite pretty, because it had sort of reddish lights in it and a slight natural wave. Her mother had said she didn't need a perm at all, but Sarah liked the extra bounce.

She'd had fun at the youth club, but she'd left earlier than she needed to because she had got bored with the darts and her friends had gone off to the pub for a drink. Sarah had been asked along but she'd refused; her mother didn't like her to go into pubs. She didn't like Sarah to smoke either, but she had that evening.

Undressing, Sarah thought about the man in the car. She hadn't answered when he spoke to her, because her mother had told her she shouldn't – but she had noticed that he was rather good-looking. He had very dark, almost black hair that looked a bit wavy. She hadn't been able to see the colour of his eyes in that quick glance, but she thought they might have been grey.

Sarah sighed as she slipped into bed and switched off the lamp. Phil had tried to grope her when she went outside to the toilets at the club, but she had managed to avoid him.

'Mummy's girl,' he had called after her.

The jeer stung a little, because she knew that one of her friends must have been talking about her behind her back. She was pretty sure that

12

neither Janice nor Phyllis was a virgin. They didn't say it openly, but she had heard some whispering going on at the youth club and she wondered if they knew what the men said behind their backs.

Sarah didn't want them to talk about her like that; she would rather they laughed and called her a mummy's girl – although she wasn't, not really. She did lots of things her mother wouldn't approve of, but some of the advice she was given made sense to Sarah.

She saw her friends wheeling prams and looking washed out, as if they were tired and fed up with struggling to make ends meet. They hadn't had much chance to have fun. Sarah wished she could find someone she really liked enough to do it with – she wouldn't mind getting married then – but so far she hadn't met the right one.

As she fell asleep she was still thinking about the man in the car. He had such bold eyes and his grin had nearly made her smile despite her determination to ignore him.

'Connor,' Alice Searles said as her brother-in-law came down to the large farmhouse kitchen the next morning, yawning. 'There's a letter for you – and a card from Peter. I had one too. He says he is in Gibraltar and he will have leave in a couple of months. He is going to visit when he gets back.'

'Great,' Connor said and smiled at her. He had always liked his brother's wife. She was a little plumper than she had been when she first went out with Dan, but still attractive. 'I was thinking about Peter last night...'

'Do you miss him? I do.' Alice sighed. 'I'm glad he joined the merchant navy, though, because it has been a good life for him. I think he hoped you would join too.'

'He asked me to,' Connor admitted. The kitchen was warm and smelled of dogs, babies, herbs and frying bacon. It was a familiar smell and comfortable, but sometimes he would rather have been alone, away from all the hustle and bustle in the mornings as the children scrambled for their breakfast before leaving to walk the three miles to school. 'I thought about it, but I don't think the navy is for me. Besides, I couldn't just walk out on Dan – he needed me.'

'Yes. He still does...' Alice looked thoughtful. 'You shouldn't let that stop you, though, Con – if there's something you would rather do with your life?'

'I wouldn't if I knew what would suit me,' Connor said truthfully. 'I sometimes think I ought to do something but I don't know what I want...' He grinned at her. 'Do you want me out of your hair, Alice?'

He had lived with them since his brother came back at the end of the war. It hadn't occurred to him that Alice might enjoy having her home to herself.

'No, of course not, daft,' Alice said and smiled. 'I just think you don't have much fun tied to the land. Don't let the years slip by and then regret it, Con.'

'I've got a holiday coming up, remember. I'm

off to stay with Emily in a couple of days.'

'Yes, that will be nice for you. Emily has such a lovely home and she always makes us all feel welcome.'

'That house is lovely, but she has a hell of a time to keep it going.'

'Yes, I know. Everyone thinks she is rich, but in a way she is no better off than we are...'

'That bacon smells good.' Connor grinned. 'Any chance of a bit of fried bread to go with it?'

'Lady Vane,' Emily's housekeeper called as she entered the study where Emily was working at the beautiful Georgian partners' desk. 'You asked me to remind you that your brother is coming to stay tomorrow. I think you wanted to clear any appointments for the next few days?'

'Yes, Sheila, thank you.' Emily smiled at her. 'I did remember. The vicar had arranged a meeting of the Church Friends Association for tomorrow afternoon, but I told him I would not be able to attend so he has moved it to the sixteenth of next month.'

'I've given Connor his usual room and Cook is preparing a list of menus for you to approve.'

'Connor isn't that fussy about what he eats.' Emily's expression was amused, because there wasn't a female member of her staff at Vanbrough who didn't have a soft spot for her youngest brother. 'Do you know, it's six months since he visited, because Dan can't spare him for more than a few days now and then.'

'Will Mr Daniel and Mrs Alice Searles be coming for Christmas this year?'

'Oh, I'm not sure. Christmas is months away yet. Dan is always so busy on the farm. I've asked him and his family, and Frances too, but I doubt if my sister will come. She is wrapped up in that hotel of hers in Cornwall.'

'Well, I suppose it takes up a lot of her time.'

'I am sure it does.'

Emily sighed as her housekeeper left the room. Frances expected her to visit her at the hotel, because she didn't – or wouldn't – understand how much work was involved in running an estate like Vanbrough. She seemed to imagine that all Emily did was sit around and be waited on – or pretended to! Frances had no idea of the work that went into keeping up the traditions here.

Getting up from her desk, Emily walked to the window and glanced out at the beautiful view of smooth lawns and ancient trees. There was a mist drifting through the park, giving everything a slightly murky feel, but it would clear by mid morning. She loved this place, loved it as much as her father-in-law had, and was as much a prisoner of duty as Vane had been for the whole of his life. Sometimes she felt trapped by her surroundings.

When Simon had brought her here as a young bride for the first time she'd been overwhelmed by the magnificence of the house and grounds. She'd been nervous of Vane and his wife, Amelia, but she had learned to love this place – and to love Vane.

Her marriage had been such a tragic mistake. Simon had never loved her. He hadn't been

16

capable of loving any woman – his tastes lay elsewhere – and he'd married her to please his father and to get an heir. Vane had loved her, though, loved her with a passion he had controlled, keeping it secret until he was on his deathbed. After Simon's death, Vane had found ways to keep Emily here, setting up a convalescent home for badly injured men towards the end of the war and putting her in charge. He had left Vanbrough to Emily's son Robert, along with part of the money. Vane had wanted Emily to run the estate, because he knew she loved it. Amelia had been very angry, because she knew that Robert wasn't really Simon's son.

After the funeral she'd gone off in a rage, vowing to contest the will and tell Vane's cousin the truth about Robert's birth – but she had never carried out her threats. Seven years had passed since Vane's death but Emily had heard nothing from her. She thought that Amelia must have decided the estate was more trouble than it was worth, and perhaps she was right. It was certainly hard work, and finding the money to keep going was more difficult than when Vane was alive.

He had left Emily ten thousand pounds for herself. Robert had four times that amount but it was tied up in a trust. The income came to Emily until her son was old enough to look after his own affairs and the money was used to pay the running cost of the house, which were ridiculously high. She was as careful as she could be while maintaining the standards Vane would expect, but money was tight.

'What do I do next?' Emily looked up at Vane's portrait. 'I can't put up the rents for the tenants and I can't stretch the income from Robert's trust. We need at least another thousand a year if I'm to keep supporting all those charities.'

Vane's image stared down at her unmoved. Once upon a time he had seemed to answer her when she talked to him, but that had stopped happening a long time ago.

'I made a promise and I've kept it – but I'm not sure I can continue for much longer, Vane.'

Vane made no reply. Why should he? He had carried the burden during his life and the problem was hers now. She had accepted the burden and grown into her position. A beautiful, poised, elegant woman, she was admired by many but remained slightly apart, giving everything she had except herself. Emily had a deep well of love within her, but she had learned that it was unwise to love because it ended only in pain.

She frowned as she thought about her problem. There was really no one she could go to for help. Her sister Frances was rich, of course. She'd inherited a lot of property after her husband died – or had blackmailed her father-in-law for it, if you told the truth. Sam Danby had made her suffer for that, but in the end Frances had come out of it a wealthy woman. Money that had come from a dubious source, but enough so that Frances would never have to think twice about paying a bill.

Most people thought Emily was rich, because she lived in a house that everybody admired and many envied. She was always being asked to sit on this or that committee and to contribute to a new charity. Vane had been a charitable man, but he had divided his money in half when he died and that meant Emily's income was far less than her father-in-law had enjoyed.

'Damn you, Vane!' Emily said. 'I should sell everything and go off and live in Spain!'

It was an empty threat. She would struggle to keep going for as long as she could, but she might be forced to sell one of the farms. Before she did that she would need to take advice – perhaps from Vane's cousin, Alan Leicester. They had met at the funeral but not since, although Alan had phoned a couple of times and sent cards at Christmas.

Emily felt the niggle of guilt at the back of her mind. Alan should be Lord Vane. The estate hadn't been entailed and Vane was entitled to leave it where he chose, but the title should by rights belong to his cousin. Robert had been Vane's beloved grandson as far as the world was concerned – but it was a lie. A lie he had accepted and compounded by leaving his estate to Emily's son.

Shaking her head, Emily thrust the doubts to the back of her mind. She still missed Vane like hell, but she was perfectly capable of managing. She would find the money she needed, though something would have to go – either some land or one of the pictures. In the meantime she would forget her problems and enjoy Connor's visit. She didn't see nearly enough of her family.

* * *

19

'Have you got everything you want?' Alice asked as Connor came downstairs carrying his battered old suitcase. 'Clean shirts, pants, socks?'

'Don't fuss, Alice,' he said but he was grinning. At twenty-four, Connor was a tall, strong, good-looking man with dark hair and bold eyes. Everyone said he was much like Daniel had been as a young man, but at his age Dan had already seen the horrors of war.

'Emily won't think much of me if I let you visit her without the things you need.'

'Emily wouldn't blame you. She knows what I'm like.'

'Are you ready?' Daniel asked as he came into the kitchen. He was wearing stained cords and a shirt in a green and brown check that had seen better days, his cap pulled over his eyes. 'I'll run you to the station, Connor. You don't want to leave your car standing there while you're away.'

'Thanks,' Connor said. He kissed his sister-in-law's cheek. She smelled of babies and cooking. There had been a time when she always carried the scent of flowers. He noticed how tired she looked and said impulsively, 'Don't work too hard, Alice. You should make Dan take you for a holiday.'

'What did you want to say that for?' Daniel asked as they went out to the yard. A couple of mongrel dogs were sniffing round but ran to him, barking eagerly as he opened the van door. He shooed them away. 'You know I can't afford to take time off, let alone pay for a holiday.'

'I'll look after things here when I get back,' Connor offered. 'I can ask Jack Mullins to give me a hand with the cows and there's not much else needs doing until we lift the potatoes. Why don't you take Alice to visit Frances? She is always asking for one of us to go down. It wouldn't cost more than a tank of petrol and a few flowers for Frances.'

'Alice wouldn't go if I suggested it. It would mean taking the children and that's too much bother.'

'She looks tired. The children wear her out.'

'You don't need to tell me how to look after my own wife!' Daniel glared at him. 'Four kids are a lot. I've told her she needs help in the house but she won't listen.'

'You should put your foot down – and you need a holiday too. It's not my business but what happened to your ideas for a garage of your own?'

'Bankruptcy and lack of time,' Daniel growled. 'When we lost everything after the war I had no choice but to put those fields into Alice's name. I've struggled to clear my debts. Clay owed me money. I got some of it but he never finished paying me back and I've given up bothering.'

'Clay!' Connor's mouth twisted with disgust at the mention of their elder brother. He had been the only one to survive the bankruptcy with any amount of money, though both Frances and Emily had come into money. 'He couldn't lie straight in bed! The bastard cheated us all when Dad died! You and Henry let him get away with

21

murder.'

'I was away fighting a war,' Daniel reminded him. 'Henry had no head for figures. He did his best but the worry killed him, poor devil. You don't remember but we had to pay Margaret out of Dad's estate and there were other things...'

'I remember Clay raped Margaret – his step-mother! You paid her to keep quiet. You should have let him go to prison!'

'Maybe. Forget it,' Daniel muttered. 'I haven't forgotten the garage. One day I'll get there.'

'Yeah...' Connor took out a packet of cigarettes and offered them to his brother. Daniel shook his head but Connor lit up. 'One day I'll be rich and famous. Pigs might fly!'

Daniel laughed. 'You'll have to marry into money, Con. There are plenty of girls after you. Janice Baker's father is loaded. He owns the carrot factory over at Manea. Marry her and you'll be in clover when he goes.'

'Only trouble is that she looks like a horse,' Connor replied. 'Thanks, but I'll keep looking for now.'

'It's money or looks,' Daniel said. 'You rarely get both in this life. It's not fair that you ended up with nothing from Father's estate. I meant you to have the fields on Stretton Road, but it didn't work out the way it should. When I can afford the garage you can take over the land.'

'I'm not sure I want it,' Connor said. 'There must be something more out of life than slog-ging your guts out to scrape a living, Dan.'

'I wish I knew how to get it.'

'Yeah, me too.' Connor grinned at him. 'I'll

22

ask our rich sister for money for the garage.'

'You say one word to Emily and I'll have your guts for garters!'

'I meant Frances. Emily lives in that damned barn of a house but she hasn't got a penny to spare.'

'I know. Emily would have lent me the money for the garage if she had it. She asked me once when she had some money going spare but I turned her down. I've sometimes regretted it,' Daniel said. 'But you won't get a penny out of Frances. She blames me because the land was lost. I wouldn't ask her for anything if I were you – that money has blood on it if you ask me.'

'Money is money,' Connor said. 'But I wouldn't really ask either of them. It was a joke ... you should know better.'

'Yeah, right,' Daniel said as he brought the van to a halt. 'Have a good time, then – and give Emily my love.'

'Yes, of course. You should think about what I said, Dan – about a holiday for Alice. Mary might have the kids for a week or so...'

'Mary has enough to do,' Daniel said. 'Frances asked her to help run the hotel but she wouldn't leave Stretton. Most of her kids are grown up now, but she stills works part-time in the packing factory.'

'Mary has had a rough time. She came out of things badly when Henry died, but you don't hear her complain. I still think she would have the kids if you asked – or Emily might.'

'I'll think about it,' Daniel said. 'Go on or you will miss your train.'

'Right – see you in a week or so, then.'

Connor left his brother and went into the station.

Daniel sat where he was in the van, staring into space. He had tried hard to put all thought of the garage out of his mind, because it was a dream he had given up after the bankruptcy. He was struggling to clear his name because the shame of bankruptcy was something that didn't sit well with him. Damn Clay for forcing them to take decisions that had led to the crushing debts that had caused the bank to foreclose on them. It wouldn't have happened if Daniel had been home to help Henry run things, but he'd been stuck in a German prisoner of war camp and his eldest brother had struggled alone until his heart gave out.

If Marcus Danby had been alive, Daniel might have asked his brother-in-law for a loan to get back on his feet, because Marcus had been approachable, but there was no one else. He couldn't go cap in hand to Frances – though she had more money than she knew what to do with – and Emily was struggling. If he were Emily, he would sell that damned great mausoleum of a place, bank the money and enjoy life, but she loved the estate and refused to move out.

Shaking his head, Daniel started the van again and headed for Ely. It was market day and he liked to visit the cattle market and then have a drink in the pub afterwards. It was his one chance to get away from the farm and Alice.

Connor had annoyed him by saying he ought

to take Alice for a holiday. He was well aware that his wife was looking tired and washed out. She never seemed to have time for anything but the kids these days, and sometimes Daniel wished that he hadn't married so young. He hadn't meant to get married at all until his business was up and running. If he had stuck to his word, he would have had the garage by now, but they had four children and it took every penny he could earn from his smallholding to feed and clothe them all.

Alice had been lovely when they were courting. Daniel hadn't been able to resist making love to her, and when she'd fallen for a baby there had been no hesitation. He had married her straight away, and he didn't really regret it. He loved Alice but sometimes he wished that they were back at the start of their marriage. His children were precious, of course, but it would have been better if they had come later, once he'd got a bit of money in the bank.

Daniel drove round past the Lamb Hotel and into Market Street, heading for the parking lot behind the cattle market. He could smell the pungent smell of animal excrement as he got out of his van, leaving it unlocked as he strode towards the pens. The nervous bleating and bellowing of the animals added to the general noise. The auction was already taking place, though they hadn't got to the livestock yet. They were still selling bits and pieces of machinery, tools and other items that were often put into the sale. Sometimes you could find a box of china that someone had discarded. Alice collected blue and white and he bought the odd piece for her if he saw it going cheap.

'Not a bad day for it,' a voice remarked and he turned to see Bill Henderson, a neighbouring farmer who had a lot more acres than Daniel had these days. 'I've got my eyes on a couple of Herefords – need to build up my milking herd a bit.'

'I'd like a couple of Jerseys if I could afford it,' Daniel said. 'But I saw a few good Herefords in the pens.'

'Your father had Jerseys once, didn't he?'

'Yes, before the war,' Daniel agreed. 'Henry sold them. He preferred Herefords.'

He nodded to the man and walked on. There was nothing he wanted in the sale and he fancied a drink before he went home. He might take a look in the shop that sold television sets; he couldn't afford a new one, but now and then they had one going cheap. Alice and the children had watched the coronation of the young Queen Elizabeth at Alice's parents' house and he knew she would like a set of her own, though he wasn't sure what the reception would be like in the Fen. He ought to get her something, though the TV was probably more than he could afford; it would need setting up and an aerial. No, forget it, he'd find something cheaper.

Connor's words kept echoing in his head. Maybe he *should* find the money to take Alice away for a few days. Mary might have the kids over a long weekend...

Absorbed in his thoughts, Daniel didn't see the woman watching him as he strolled under the

arch into the pub yard. Even if he had, he probably wouldn't have recognised her. Daniel had
long forgotten the woman he'd known so briefly
in Liverpool during the war.

Maura watched as the man walked into the
public house. She was certain it was Daniel
Searles and for a moment her heart stood still.
She'd come to Cambridgeshire in the hope of
seeing him, even though she'd wondered if he
had moved on. She hadn't even known if he'd
survived the war. Seeing him so unexpectedly in
Ely had driven her breath away. She wasn't
ready to confront him just yet. She needed to
think about what she was going to say.

Would he even believe what she had to tell
him? She'd visited Stretton once during the war
when she discovered she was pregnant, hoping
to find him and explain, but she'd met his young
brother Connor instead and he'd made it plain
that Daniel wasn't around. Maura hadn't bothered too much then, because she'd had a job and
prospects. Things were different now. Recover-
ing from the break-up of her marriage and with
only a few pounds in her purse, she needed a
helping hand.

The Searles had land and money. Daniel owed
her something. It was time he started to help
keep his son. She'd managed alone since her
husband walked out, but she was down on her
luck and she needed money.

It was more than likely that Daniel would
disown his son, though if he looked at him, he
would see that she wasn't lying. David looked

just like his father. If he'd been with her now, Maura might have followed Daniel into the pub, but that could be a mistake. She needed to plan this carefully. Find out how the land lay before she approached him.

Maura knew that the one night they had shared during an air raid in Liverpool had meant nothing to Daniel. She had been on the brink of suicide, so desperate that she had begged him to make love to her when they ended up sharing a bed, because she was too drunk to look after herself.

But Daniel could have refused her! Maura hardened her heart. She was sick of working for poor wages and going without. She wanted her own hairdressing business, and Daniel Searles could buy it for her. He had plenty of money and if she got it right, he would be glad to pay her to keep his secret.

She imagined he had married the girl he'd been engaged to when he spent that night with her. Maura wasn't above blackmail if need be, but perhaps he would simply give her the money. She would take the bus to Stretton another day and ask some questions. Once she knew a bit more about his life, she would approach him.

Smiling, Maura walked in the opposite direction. It looked as if things were turning her way. She hadn't even been sure Daniel Searles had survived the war, but now she knew that he was alive and still living in the area she could make plans for the future.

Alice spent the day washing, cooking and looking after her two youngest children. When Daniel came in she was so tired that her head had started to ache. These days she never seemed to have a minute for herself and she was conscious of the fact that she had vomit all over her blouse. She'd meant to change and smarten herself up before Daniel came home but little Sally was teething and she hadn't stopped crying all afternoon.

'What's for dinner, love?' Daniel asked. 'Something smells good.'

'I've got a steak and kidney pie in the oven,' Alice said. 'Sally has been crying all day. I haven't had a minute to sit down!'

'You work too hard. You should have someone in to help you for a few hours a day, Alice. You look tired...'

'That's right, rub it in,' Alice snapped. 'I know I look a mess but I haven't had time to change – anyway, I don't have anything worth wearing.'

'You should say if you want a new dress...' Daniel frowned as he walked towards her. He reached out for her but the stink of the baby's vomit made him change his mind and move back. 'I know things are tight, but you have the egg money.'

'That goes on the children,' Alice said. Tears started to her eyes but she dashed them away angrily. 'I don't have help because we can't afford it, Daniel. You know we can't.'

'We can afford a few bob,' Daniel said. 'I've almost finished doing up that roadster I bought cheap. When I sell it I'll give you half the money. You can get your hair done and buy some new clothes – and I'll find someone to come in for a few hours a week.'

'You don't have to do all this just because Connor told you to take me on holiday.' Alice looked at him angrily.

'You know that isn't the reason,' Daniel said and took her into his arms despite the acrid smell that hung about her. 'I love you, Alice. I may not always remember to tell you, and I know things haven't been easy since I came back, but I'm doing my best and I've nearly cleared my debts. Once I'm out of that, things will get better.'

'I'm not complaining,' Alice said. 'I know you do your best. I'm not bothered about the new clothes, but perhaps we should have someone in to help a couple of mornings a week. If I had help with the washing and ironing, it would make things easier.'

'It's hard work for you with that old mangle and the copper,' Daniel said. 'One day I'll buy you a washing machine!'

Alice shook her head. 'Ma has always managed with the copper and a mangle,' she said. 'I think I'm not completely over Sally's birth yet; it pulled me down and I get so tired.'

'Of course you do, love,' Daniel said. 'Go up and change before Danny gets home from school. I'll put the kettle on and make us a cup of tea.'

'Thank you.' Alice hesitated as she prepared to leave the room. 'Did you buy anything in the market?'

'Just a few plants for your garden. I thought about getting you some flowers but decided you would rather have the plants. I'll put them in for you after tea if you like?'

'And I was moaning at you,' Alice said, looking rueful. 'I'm sorry, Daniel. It was thoughtful of you to buy me plants. I would much rather have them than cut flowers.'

'I thought you would.' He ran his fingers through his thick hair. 'I do love you, even if I don't always show it.'

'You work too hard yourself. You will have all the milking to do yourself now that Connor has gone away.'

'I might get someone in to give me a hand,' Daniel said. 'How would you feel about a couple of days at the sea somewhere – just you and me? After Connor gets back, of course.'

'I couldn't leave the children,' Alice said. 'Perhaps when Sally is a bit older, it would be nice. We haven't had much time just on our own, have we?'

'It was the bloody war,' Daniel said. 'Everything changed because of the war. Go on up and get changed, love. I'll make the tea and we'll have a cuppa before the lad gets home...'

Connor saw the car waiting for him when he left the station. Emily opened the door and got out, waving to him, her face wreathed in smiles. She came to greet him, throwing her arms about him as he set his case down.

'Connor! I'm so glad to see you!'

'It's great to be here.' Connor gave her an affectionate hug. She was dressed in something light and summery and she smelled of an expen-

31

sive perfume. 'How are you, Emily?'

'The same as always,' Emily replied. 'I seldom have time to think about how I am – but that's a good thing, isn't it? How are Dan, Alice and the children?'

'Dan is just the same. Alice looks tired. I think she needs a break from the children, but Dan says he can't afford to take her on holiday.'

'He knows they are welcome to come here – and they can bring the youngest children. Mary would look after the older two so they could stay in school.'

'Danny is shooting up,' Connor told her with a grin. 'Very grown-up. I think he will be taller than Dan when he's a man.'

'It's several months since I've seen them all,' Emily said. 'It isn't easy for me to get away, but I really should pop down. Perhaps I can persuade them to get away for a few days.'

'Just don't tell Dan I said anything. You know how proud and stubborn he is – like a prickly hedgehog when it comes to borrowing money. I think he has almost given up on that garage he wanted so badly.'

'I would have lent him the money when Vane was alive. I had money to spare in those days, but I'm afraid I don't have much now – though I could afford to give Alice some money for a little holiday.'

'She is as bad as Dan,' Connor said as Emily drove away from the station. 'I sometimes wonder which of them is the worst.' He looked at his sister. 'Anyway, how are things for you? I suppose you still put every penny you get into that house of yours?'

'It isn't really my house, it's Robert's. I am the custodian and he will take over from me when he's older. He may decide to sell. I can't pretend it isn't a liability – but Vane asked me to carry on for as long as I could.' A little sigh escaped her. 'Take no notice. You know I love the place.'

'Vane should have left you more money. He split his property up and then expected you to carry on as before. How did he think you would manage?'

'Vane was too ill to think clearly. Besides, he had Amelia and his daughter to think of. He couldn't give us everything. I feel guilty enough as it is.'

'I don't see why you should. If Simon had lived, it would all have come to him – and he would have had the burden of running the estate instead of you.'

'I think Simon would have sold,' Emily said, an odd look in her eyes. 'He intended to live in America, you know. I made Vane a promise and I'm doing my best to keep it – though I may have to raise funds by selling something. I hate to part with land and I can't take anything important from the house, but I've found some pictures that Vane had stored away because they needed restoration. I've sent them for valuation and I may sell them if they're worth anything.'

'You need a steady source of income. Something ongoing that would bring in the money regularly.'

'Tell me about it.' Emily laughed as he made a wry face. 'I can manage to keep my head above water as far as the house is concerned, but Vane supported a lot of charities and I may have to cut down on them a bit, though I don't want to...'

'What about the convalescent home? You told me that closed last year. Have you done anything with the dower house yet?'

'I considered letting to a tenant, but it is in a bit of a mess. It might cost too much.'

'Well, I'm a dab hand with a hammer and I can decorate. I did the parlour and stairs for Alice last spring. I'll take a look while I'm here – see if I can help get it into shape for you.'

'You're here for a holiday, not to work!'

'It won't hurt me to do a few hours in the mornings. I shall know what you need to get done and I might have an idea of what it ought to cost. Besides, I'll enjoy it.'

'Thanks, Connor.' Emily smiled at him. 'It is really nice having you here, love.'

'I like coming. I know how much you love this place and it is pretty special – even though it must be such a lot of work for you.'

Emily shook her head and he grinned. Emily had always been a fighter. He didn't mind doing a bit of decorating for her, but he wished he could think of something that would make a real difference.

Connor walked down to the dower house that evening after dinner. It was a warm, soft night and the scents of lavender and jasmine were in the air. He could understand why anyone would find these surroundings intoxicating; beautiful specimen trees made the park a peaceful and inspiring place to walk. It was, of course, an outdated way to live. Vane had clung to the old ways while he was alive, but two wars had changed England beyond recognition, and estates like Vanbrough were more of a liability than a privilege these days. You needed outside money, because the rents from farmland and cottages were not enough to support a lifestyle that belonged to the eighteenth century.

Emily had given him the key to the much smaller – though still substantial – property that had traditionally been used for the dowagers in past years. By rights, Amelia should have lived here, but she had gone off somewhere after Vane died, because it had still been a convalescent home then. Emily had kept it going until the last residents had been moved on, and since then it had stood empty. Gathering cobwebs and spiders, no doubt – and probably damp.

Connor went inside. Immediately he caught the sour smell left behind. It had been home to badly wounded soldiers for several years and there was plenty of evidence left behind. He turned up his nose as he visited the toilets and bathrooms, of which there were five in all – too many if it was to become a private house again. He thought that two of them could go, and the partitions that had been erected to make them could be torn down. The bedrooms that had not been partitioned were a good size and most were in reasonable condition. Some of the furniture was still here, but most of it looked fit only for the bonfire. Downstairs the back parlours had been used as bedrooms and there were toilets and other facilities that needed to come out.

Connor made a mental note of the jobs that needed doing. If he had a couple of months to spare, he could have done most of it himself, just calling in electricians and plumbers as necessary. Unfortunately, he had just one week. In that time he could only scrape the surface of what needed doing. However, he might be able to make a clearance, which would make it easier for Emily to have the professionals in to give her estimates.

Once the place was in reasonable condition she could rent it out and that should help her a little. He knew it would cost her several hundred pounds to put the house right. She might not have the money to do it, of course. If she could not afford the outlay, Connor would come back again and do what he could. He was torn between wanting to help his sister and Dan, but Emily was managing and in his heart he knew Dan couldn't do everything alone.

Sighing, he closed up and walked to the local pub he favoured. He had made one or two good friends over the years and he might get one of them to give him a hand.

Two

Sarah tried on the dress she liked. Her boss had gone out and she'd locked the door because it was her lunch hour. She didn't often bother to go to a café in the middle of the day. Her mother packed her a sandwich and she was able to make a cup of tea in the back room.

Twirling in front of the mirror, Sarah admired the dress from all angles. It had a full skirt and stiff petticoats underneath, which made it stand out. The bodice was tightly fitted, and the neckline was a deep scoop, but at the back it had a big stand-up white collar and it was tied with an orange bow at the front. The main colour was black with little floral motifs of orange and green all over it. It really suited her, made her feel special, but it was expensive.

She looked at the price ticket as she took it off. Seven pounds and ten shillings – more than twice what she earned in a week – but she would get a discount and she loved it. She had wanted it the moment it came out of the large brown box with all the other new stock. Sarah knew she had to have it. She would ask if she could put down a deposit and pay the rest over the next few weeks.

She smiled as she hung it up in the back room.

She was being extravagant, but it was her birthday soon and if her father knew she wanted the dress, he might just buy it for her.

He was away on one of his frequent business trips at the moment. Sarah wondered why he had to go so often – sometimes it was every weekend. However, her mother didn't seem to mind too much. She had been talking about taking a few days in Clacton – just Sarah and her mother. Mr Jenkins was too busy. He was always too busy to go on holidays. Sarah couldn't remember when he had last taken them away. She couldn't have been more than nine or ten. She supposed it was because he had to travel so much himself.

She went into the back room to eat her sandwich and drink her tea. She was allowed to have the radio on during her lunch break, and she liked to listen to music. She liked the new stuff they called Rock 'n' Roll, though it was really just rhythm and blues with a different beat. She would ask her father about the dress when he came home. He was usually in a good mood when he got back from one of his trips.

Maura got off the bus from Ely and stood outside the shop in Stretton High Street, wondering what to do next. She knew where the Searles family had lived before the war, but she'd already discovered that the house had been sold. Where would Daniel live now? She could ask around but she didn't want people looking at her and starting to gossip, so she would have to be careful. His name wasn't in the telephone direc-

38

tory but that didn't mean anything: a lot of people didn't have telephones.

Seeing an old man walking towards her, she hesitated and then approached him. Her mind worked swiftly as she tried to remember what Dan had told her about the girl he was courting. She needed to get the name right ... Alice ... yes, her name was Alice.

'Excuse me, sir,' she said in the soft Irish accent that most men seemed to find fascinating. 'I wonder if you could tell me where Alice Searles lives, please?'

'I could,' he said, gaze narrowing. 'Why would you be wanting to see her, miss?'

'It is Mrs Jacobs. I used to know Alice and Dan – but I moved away when I married and we lost touch.'

'You're not a Stretton person.'

'We lived in Ely,' she smiled as she lied. 'I knew she had married but I don't know where they live.'

'I'm not sure I should tell you,' the man said. 'Dan drinks in the King's Arms sometimes. You might find him there, though he only drinks on a Friday night.'

'Oh ... thanks...' *for nothing*, she added under her breath. It was Sunday and her day off from work so Dan wasn't likely to be at the pub this afternoon. It wouldn't be easy for her to come over on a Friday night. She worked hard and she had her son to take care of when she got home.

She frowned as the man walked off. Suspicious old devil! She should have known what village folk were like. Dan's brother had been the same when she'd visited during the war, almost warning her off. The man had been the only person in an otherwise empty street. Where was everybody? It was a lovely day – why wasn't anyone out enjoying the sunshine?

She had an hour or so to kill until she could catch a bus back to Ely. While she was here she might as well take a walk along the street. The Searles' old house was opposite the church. If she walked that way, she might see someone in the garden or the churchyard ... Perhaps a child might not be as suspicious as the old man.

As she walked along the street, she heard the sounds of music and laughter. Then she saw the notice advertising the village fête. Maura smiled. So that was where everyone had gone. She followed the sounds of voices and laughter, her spirits rising as she discovered that what looked like the whole village had turned out. Most people had obviously come on foot, though there were a few cars and vans parked in the field.

She looked about her at the various stalls. There were all kinds of games and competitions, from throwing balls at coconuts and counting how many beans in a jar to shooting arrows at a target. Hearing a roar of approval, Maura wandered towards where a tug-of-war was taking place. She saw a notice that said the Stretton team was taking on all comers. Her eyes went over the men lining up to take part and saw the very man she was looking for.

Dan had his shirt sleeves rolled up, his head bare. He looked every bit as attractive as he had during the war, and so like her son that her heart

40

turned over. She loved her son, even though it had been a struggle to bring him up alone. Maura smiled inwardly as she watched the tug-of-war begin. It was impossible to approach Dan for the moment, but her son was being looked after for the afternoon and she had plenty of time.

Alice stood with some of the other women, watching as the tug-of-war began. She was proud of Dan as he took his place in the line-up, because he looked strong and she knew the other members valued him. It wasn't often that he got a chance to take time off for something like this, because he worked so hard for his family. Alice knew that he wasn't happy struggling to wrest a living from his fields. He wanted more – he wanted that garage he'd set his heart on before the war – but money was tight and he had to content himself with doing up a few cars when he got the chance. The extra money came in handy, and things were better at the moment because he'd got a hundred pounds for the last car he'd sold. True to his word, he had given Alice half of the money, which she suspected was the whole of his profit.

Alice knew he meant her to spend some of it on herself, but as yet she hadn't felt able to buy anything. She really did need a new dress, but her mother had promised to buy some material from the market when she visited Ely next. Alice could make a couple of dresses for herself and also her daughters, Sally and Jean, at half the cost of ready-made. She wasn't bad at sewing and she could borrow her mother's sewing machine. Her hair needed cutting too. Alice was lucky enough to have a natural wave and she managed it at home most of the time, but it was looking dull and she was wondering if she should have a rinse or something. She wasn't sure where to go. She had asked Mary about the local hairdresser, but Mary said she always went to Ely.

'There's a place in the High Street,' Mary said. 'I had a permanent wave there last month. I hate the way they string you up on those things, but my hair is so straight. You're lucky – all you need is a good cut. There's a man there who cuts really well.'

'A man?' Alice looked uncertain. 'I'm not sure I should like a man doing my hair, Mary.'

'He is really nice,' Mary told her. 'If you want to make an appointment, I'll ring up for you – and I'll have the children while you go.'

'Thanks, that's good of you,' Alice said. 'I'll think about it and let you know.'

'Your hair could do with a beer rinse to get rid of the grease and put some life into it,' Mary said. 'If you don't want to go to a hairdresser, I could get you a special rinse.'

Alice had agreed to try it. Mary was meeting her here this afternoon and had promised to bring the sachet with her. Seeing her sister-in-law, she waved and walked over to meet her, pushing Sally's pram. Danny had the younger two with him. Her eldest son had taken the others on the swings. He had two shillings and sixpence in his pocket to treat himself and his siblings, and he wouldn't be back until it had all gone.

Turning away from the tug-of-war, Alice met her sister-in-law who was standing by the toffee apple stall.

'I want to get a few of these before I go home,' Mary said. 'Jimmy is here with his friends, but he loves these – and so does Vera. The older ones don't bother these days. They all used to come to the feast but they grew out of it after they left school.'

'Danny is looking after my two. I might buy some toffee apples later, but I don't want them just yet. I could do with a cup of tea – how about you?'

'Just the ticket,' Mary said. 'You look nice today, Alice.'

'I thought I would make an effort, but this dress is a bit tight on me now. I've got bigger up top since I had the children. I'm going to make a new dress when Mum gets the material next week.'

'Why don't you buy one? I saw some lovely ones on the market this week. You should have a trip into Ely, get your hair done at the same time.'

'The shop in Stretton High Street has some pretty ones, too,' Alice said. 'I look every time I come up the village, but they are expensive – twenty-five shillings is the cheapest. I could get two and one each for Sally and Jean with that sort of money if I make them myself.'

'I saw a lovely one for ten bob on the market,' Mary told her. 'It would really suit you, Alice.'

'It will probably be gone,' Alice said. 'It

sounds cheap, though. I should like a dress that was ready made for me, though I've made my own since I got married.'

'You're good at it,' Mary said. 'But you've got enough to do – and the dresses I saw on the market are lovely. There were several at that price when I looked.'

'Well, I might...' Alice turned her head as there was a burst of cheering. 'It sounds as if the first tug has been won. Oh, look, it was our men who came out on top!'

'They will be at it for ages. Men! They are more like small boys if you ask me,' Mary said scornfully. 'Come and look at the flower-arranging tent and then we'll have that cuppa...'

Dan laughed and joined in the general celebrations as the Stretton men won the second bout. They were the champions again this year, and it was a satisfying feeling.

'Coming for a beer?' Jack Gregson asked. 'I think we deserve it after that, don't you?'

'Yes, I think we do.' Dan looked round for Alice. He was a bit disappointed to see that she hadn't waited for the end of the competition. Most of the wives, sisters and mothers had been cheering them on all the way through, but it seemed Alice had got bored and gone off somewhere. 'I'll see you in a minute, Jack.'

Dan had seen his three youngest children. They were eating candyfloss and looked as if they were having a good time. He felt in his pocket and found a half-crown. He knew that Alice had already given them money, but the feast only came once a year and he had the rest of the money from that car. He needed to keep most of it so that he could buy another car to do up, but he could afford a few bob.

He walked up to Danny and ruffled his mop of dark, curly hair. 'Having a good time, son?'

'It's great, Dad. I've spent all the money Mum gave us.'

Dan produced the coin from his pocket and smiled as the boy's eyes lit up. 'Here you go, then. Don't tell your mum I gave it to you or she will have my guts for garters.'

Danny grinned and grabbed the coin. He called to his sister and brother and they all ran off, back to the swings or the coconut shy. Daniel stood for a moment in the sunshine, thinking how good life was. Maybe he didn't always have enough money to go round, but he was blessed with a loving family and that was what really counted.

'Hello, Daniel. Long time no see...'

Dan turned in surprise as he heard the soft Irish lilt of the woman's voice behind him. It took him a while to make the connection in his mind, but it was a memory he had deliberately buried. He didn't like to remember that he had been unfaithful to Alice that night during the air raid in Liverpool. He hadn't meant it to happen and now, as he looked at Maura, he wished it hadn't. She was an attractive girl, but there was something in her eyes that made him run cold.

'Maura...' He tried but couldn't recall her second name. 'Sorry, I'm not sure...'

'Maura Jacobs. I got married.'

'I didn't know. But wait, I remember ... you had been drinking because you couldn't bear what had happened to your fiancé.'

'I married someone else,' Maura said, her mouth hard. 'I didn't have much choice after that night – the night we spent together, Dan. You do remember what happened, don't you?'

Dan looked at her warily. A little pulse was flicking at his temple and he was afraid he knew what was coming next. 'It was down to you,' he reminded her. 'I told you I wasn't free...'

'I'm not asking you to marry me,' Maura said. 'I have a son – *you* have a son, David; your eldest son. It was all right while I had a husband, but he ran out on me last year. I have to work long hours and it isn't fair on David...'

'Are you saying he's mine?' Dan looked at her hard, praying that she was lying. 'Why should I believe you? Our Danny is my eldest son.'

'Alice's eldest,' Maura said. 'My son has a prior claim on you.'

'Why should I believe you? If you did have a child, why have I never heard about it before now?'

'I came here during the war to bring your handkerchief back. Your young brother told me you had gone away. I gave it to him instead.'

'Connor never told me.' Dan's gaze narrowed. 'What do you want, Maura? If you are going to make trouble...'

'I want money – two thousand pounds should do it,' Maura said, giving him a hard look. 'If you pay up, that is the last you will hear of me. If not, I might have to tell your wife. Or even

46

your son ... do you think he would like to know he has an older brother?'

'Damn you! Breathe one word of this to either of them and I'll—'

'Break my neck.' She threw him a look of scorn. 'Do you imagine you would get away with it? A dozen people have already noticed us, Dan. Just think of what you could lose.'

Dan scowled at her. 'Where the hell do you imagine I can get two thousand pounds from – and why the hell should I?'

'You're the son of a rich farmer. It should be easy for you. Besides, isn't your sister a lady or something?'

'Emily couldn't afford to lend me that sort of money, and I can barely keep my family these days. It is impossible!'

'Well, it's your choice,' Maura told him. 'Either you pay up or your wife will receive a letter in the post.'

'You're a cold bitch! I didn't want you. I just tried to help you out.'

'That's not quite as I remember it,' Maura said. 'I should say you were pretty desperate at the time. Maybe Alice wouldn't sleep with you...'

'Shut your filthy mouth or I'll shut it for you!'

'Threats don't scare me,' Maura said. 'If you lay one finger on me, I'll make certain the whole world knows what you are, Daniel Searles. I'm not greedy. I'll take fifteen hundred pounds but I want it soon.'

'I can't raise that sort of money.'

'A thousand pounds is my last offer. Either I get the money within a month or...' Maura smiled. 'You know what to expect.'

'Where will I find you?'

'I shall be in touch,' she said. 'Enjoy the fête, Dan. I'll see you around.'

Daniel watched her walk away. She was a cheating, lying bitch, just like Margaret had been. He had paid his father's second wife to stop her telling the police what Clay had done to her and it had cost him his dreams. He had almost finished paying his debts off so that he could clear his name of bankruptcy and now he was going to have to borrow money again.

Daniel frowned as he saw Alice and Mary walking towards him. He prayed that his wife hadn't seen him talking to Maura. She would certainly be curious if she had and he hated lying to her. He loved Alice and he'd always felt guilty about that night, but he had never entertained the possibility that he might have another child.

Damn Maura! She was lying – she had to be. Even as he denied it, he was remembering that night and realizing that she could easily be telling the truth. Alice had fallen for their first child on their wedding night. Why shouldn't Maura have conceived that night? He just wished it were a lie.

'You won, then.' Alice smiled at him. 'Why aren't you celebrating in the beer tent with the others?'

'I was looking for you. Do you want a drink or have you had enough?'

'I'm ready to go home when the kids are. Is something the matter, Dan? You look bothered – angry.'

48

'No, I'm not angry,' he lied as he ran his fingers through his hair. He didn't want to have to borrow money to give Maura. If there was any money to spare, it should be for Alice and his children.

His children ... Daniel felt the sickness in his throat. If Maura wasn't lying, he had another son. One he had never even seen.

'Daddy, you're home!' Sarah ran to her father and put her arms about him, hugging him. 'I miss you when you're away.'

'I miss you too, sweetheart,' he told her and kissed the top of her head. 'You're getting taller. I shan't be able to do that soon.'

'Where is Mum?' Sarah said, glancing round the kitchen. It was all neat and tidy, nothing out of place, but there was no sign of tea or her mother. 'Are you hungry?'

'Yes,' he said and grimaced. 'Your mother is lying down with a headache. How about I run you to the fish shop? I could just eat fish and chips.'

'Me too,' Sarah said. 'They are doing chicken and chips too at the shop near Paradise football ground. Mum likes that. Shall I ask her if she wants some?'

'I think she has one of her migraines. Just leave her to sleep it off, Sarah. She will be better in the morning. I think we should have fish and chips in the café on the market place and then I'll take my little girl to the pictures – what do you say to that?'

'I should like that, Daddy.' Sarah hesitated.

'Are you sure I shouldn't just tell Mum where we are going?'

'She told me she didn't want to be disturbed. Leave her to rest, Sarah. You know what she's like. She will be quieter with us out of the house for a few hours.'

'Yes, I know she feels awful when she has a migraine,' Sarah agreed. She smiled at her father. 'It will be really nice – just you and me.'

'I've been thinking about my little girl while I was away,' her father said as they went out to the car. 'What do you want for your birthday, sweetheart – some money or a surprise?'

'I've seen a pretty dress I like at the shop, but it is a lot of money.'

'Is it well made – a quality thing?' Sarah nodded. 'Then I'll give you the money to buy it and perhaps there will also be a little surprise on the day...'

'You spoil me, Daddy.'

'That is what fathers are for,' he said. 'You know I love you, Sarah. I always have. Whatever might happen in the future, that will never change...'

'Is something the matter?' Sarah asked, feeling a chill at the nape of her neck.

'No, of course not,' he replied. 'I just wanted you to know. I can't wait for those fish and chips. I'm starving!'

Sarah smiled, but she was thoughtful. She had begun to wonder lately what was causing the blinding headaches her mother was having more and more frequently. It was odd but they always

50

seemed to happen when her father came back from one of his business trips.

'You've made a really good start; it even smells better,' Emily said as she looked around the bedrooms in the dower house. Connor and his friends had taken down partitions of wood and plaster, broken up old toilets and basins and thrown them into a cart to be taken off to a tip somewhere. They had even made good some of the holes in the walls. 'I feel awful, because you've spent the whole of your holiday working – and I haven't even paid you.'

'You gave my mates something for their trouble and that is all that matters. You should get at least three estimates for the restoration work, Emily. If they are all too expensive, I'll do a bit of decorating next time I come.'

'You have already done more than I could ask or expect,' Emily said. 'It depends on those pictures I told you about. The gallery has agreed to sell them, though they say nothing is worth more than a hundred or two.'

'If I were you, I would put them in an auction. You might do a lot better that way – perhaps twice as much.'

'Do you think so?' Emily looked thoughtful. 'Well, I did think a couple of them ought to be more valuable. Perhaps I shall sell those at auction, but they may go for nothing – like the farm sale.'

'That was a bankruptcy sale. Dan had no control – but you have. Put a reserve of one thousand pounds on each and see what happens.'

'That is a lot of money!'

'If they don't sell, you can let the gallery have them at another time. You can't lose either way.'

'I suppose not...' Emily laughed. 'You're a bright lad, aren't you? Why do you waste your time on the farm?'

'Because Dan needs me. It won't be for ever. As soon as he has paid his debt I'm off. He told me he should be clear in another few months.'

'I wish I could help more. I have some of the money Vane left me...'

'You need to keep something in reserve. I'm in no real hurry. I'm not sure what I want to do yet.'

'You could go into building – or decorating,' Emily suggested. 'You're good with your hands, and you could run a business. You are clever enough, Con. You're not like Henry.'

'Poor devil,' Connor said. 'It was too much worry for him, Emily. He should never have had to carry all that through the war. Clay should have helped him.'

'Don't talk to me about Clay. The last time I saw him we had a row. He treats poor Dorothy like dirt. I do not know why she puts up with it. I wouldn't stay if I were her.'

'Dan should have let Margaret report him to the police. He would have had the money for his garage then – and Clay deserved it after what he did.'

'It would have upset Frances. I shouldn't have liked the scandal either, but Frances had to live in the village – and she worried about what her mother-in-law thought.'

'Much good that did her. Sam Danby tried to

rape her and then had her shut up in a mental home. If it hadn't been for you, she might still have been there.'

'Dan had too much on his plate to think about Frances, but I am sure he would have got round to it in time.'

'I'm not certain he would.' Connor frowned. 'He gave Sam a bloody nose when he found out, though. If Sam hadn't killed himself, I'm not sure what might have happened.'

Emily nodded but didn't answer. The official line was that Sam Danby had taken his own life while in an unstable state of mind, but Emily had always suspected that his wife might know more than she had let anyone guess.

'Frances came out of it with a lot of money. Not that it has made her happy, as far as I can see. She works so hard at that hotel of hers. I keep inviting her to stay but she never comes.'

'I suppose she feels the way you do about this house.'

'I'm not sure she does. I don't think she is happy, Connor. Not truly happy.'

'Are you happy?' Connor asked.

'Yes. Yes, I am. I have my problems, but I wouldn't change my life if I could.'

'What will you do about the dower house? I suppose you could sell...'

'No, I shall have it done up and let it if I can,' Emily said. 'I shall see what the pictures bring – but there is a house in the village I might sell when it comes empty. The tenant is getting rather elderly; I dare say it will be empty in a couple of years or so. It is a good house and should

53

fetch a few thousand pounds.'

'Let me know how you get on. I'll come again when I can, but that may not be until nearly Christmas. We shall have the harvest soon and then the potatoes. We only have one field down to barley so that won't take long, but I usually take piecework once we've got Dan's crops out of the ground. It's the only way I can earn a bit more money.'

'Well, have fun,' Emily said. 'Don't work all the time.'

'I shan't do that, believe me. I belong to a club – it's jive and jazz, and the lads wear those thick crêpe soles and long jackets with narrow trousers.'

'Are they the ones they call Teddy Boys?' Emily raised her eyebrows at him. 'I've seen photos in the newspapers. I didn't know it had caught on where you live. You don't wear clothes like that?' Her eyes went over him. He was wearing jeans, a shirt and leather slip-on shoes.

'I would if I had the money.' Connor grinned. 'The fashion is catching on fast. I listen to jazz when I can, but I have to be careful because the kids are asleep by the time I get in. I'm saving for a portable radio I can take to work with me. I've seen something about them being produced abroad and they should soon be available here. We have a band at the club most weeks. We can't afford the top guys, but it is fun. Sometimes I sing with the groups.'

'I had forgotten that you can sing,' Emily said. She leaned forward to kiss his cheek. 'It doesn't seem five minutes since you arrived. You've been working so hard that I have hardly seen you.'

'It was interesting. Maybe I'll go into the building business for myself one day.'

'If you want to make a change, come here,' Emily said. 'I could use some help on the estate. I don't mean land work; there are various projects I may think about if I can get a little money together.'

'I'll think about it when the time comes, but I can't let Dan down,' Connor said. 'I had better get on the train now. The guard is closing the doors.'

'Off you go.' Emily stood back to wave him off. 'Write to me, Connor.'

'Of course – when I get time.'

Emily sighed. Connor would send a card for her birthday and at Christmas, but he was unlikely to write unless something was wrong at home.

She stood waving until the train steamed out of the station, then turned and walked back to her car. She would miss him even though he hadn't been around all that much. Emily missed the other members of her family, but she doubted that either Dan or Frances would visit her, which meant that she had to find the time to visit them.

It really ought to be Frances. She hadn't heard from her sister for almost a month, which was unusual; Frances normally wrote regularly. Emily would have to find the time to visit her, even if only for a few days.

* * *

'I am sorry, Mrs Danby – but you made the second booking yourself,' Tara Manners said. 'I know I wrote Mrs and Mrs Saunders in the forward booking register.'

'It was my fault,' Frances agreed and nodded to her receptionist. 'I am not blaming you. I didn't consult the forward bookings when I took Mr and Mrs Jones' booking. I'm afraid it means we shall have to give Mr Saunders an upgrade to the penthouse suite – at the same rate as his usual room, of course.'

'You will lose fifty pounds, Mrs Danby.'

'Yes, I know – but it is my fault. I was careless and it is all I can do. Will you explain to them when they arrive, please?'

'You won't tell them yourself? I imagine they will be delighted to get an upgrade for free.'

'Yes, I dare say.' Frances smiled oddly. 'I have an appointment this afternoon. I don't think I shall be back by the time they arrive.'

'Yes, well, I can explain,' Tara said. 'Are you going somewhere nice?'

Frances glanced at herself in the wall mirror. She was dressed in a plain navy suit with a cream silk blouse and navy court shoes. Her soft hair was dressed back in a pleat. She thought she looked older than her years but preferred to dress severely. Looking attractive encouraged men to flirt and that was the last thing she needed or wanted. She had learned not to trust anyone – except perhaps Emily.

Frances sighed inwardly. She didn't see her sister often enough. Emily was always asking her to visit, but Frances wasn't sure why she didn't take more time off. Her staff were perfectly capable of running the hotel, perhaps more so than she was herself these days. She had been feeling so tired recently and she wasn't sure why. Yes, she worked long hours, but the work was not hard labour. She was still a young woman, but sometimes she felt years older – and she looked it. Especially when she'd had one of her bad nights.

She picked up her bag, a smart navy leather two-strap that matched her shoes. Both bag and shoes were expensive. Frances could afford the best, but she didn't find much pleasure in shopping these days. She supposed that she was still bitter over what Sam Danby had done to her – and the way Marcus had let her down.

She had thought herself the luckiest woman in the world when she'd married. Her husband's father, Sam, was one of the richest men in the district, and she and Marcus seemed to have a glittering future, but it had all gone wrong when her husband came home from the war. Marcus had changed. He drank a lot and quarrelled with his father. When he died in a car accident Frances had believed it was because he was drunk, but when she discovered what had been haunting Marcus she had begun to understand why he had simply given up: he had survived the war only to discover that most of his father's money came from prostitution.

Sam was a bully and he'd tried to force Marcus to work for him. Marcus refused, but then his drinking had got so much worse. Frances had come to blame Sam for her husband's death, and to hate him. She knew that she had made him turn against her by blackmailing him over his secret, but he had done such awful things to her.

Frances could never forgive and she couldn't forget either. Sometimes there was such a terrible darkness inside her. She had wild rages that she tried desperately hard to hide from everyone around her. She had found that the best way to cope was simply to shut herself away until she was feeling better. Emily expected her to put the past behind her and get on with her life. Frances had tried, but she didn't have her sister's resilience. She brooded on the past too much.

Frances couldn't help envying Emily her life. It was the reason she refused to visit, even though she missed Emily. If Emily came here, it was all right, but Vanbrough was such a wonderful place and she envied her sister's feeling of peace, of belonging. Emily had been loved. Vane had loved her and so had Robert's father. She might have suffered an unhappy marriage but she had got over it quickly, because she was in love with someone else.

Frances thought she had loved Marcus when she married him, but now she wasn't sure – she wasn't certain she knew what love was about. She knew about loneliness – that aching, empty feeling that had set in after her son died in hospital and everyone thought she had neglected him. She would never have done that ... although she *had* been drinking too much because she was grieving for her husband.

Emily had believed in her. Dan had apologized after he realized what was going on, but he had thought she was at fault in the beginning. Perhaps he still did. He hadn't brought his family to visit for ages and she knew he had been to Emily's once or twice.

She looked at her receptionist, realizing that she hadn't replied. 'Nowhere special,' she said. 'It is a business matter.'

Frances wondered why she'd lied as she left the hotel and got into the taxi, giving the driver instructions. She leaned back against the seat, trying to keep calm and not worry. There might not be any need to worry, because she didn't know if there was anything really wrong with her yet. It was just that she hated hospitals. She had ever since little Charlie had died and the nurse had looked at her as if she were a murderer.

She had been desperate when Dan drove her to the hospital. She had never ceased to regret that she hadn't taken her son to the doctor sooner, but she'd thought it was just a chill – just as she'd put off seeing a doctor when she started to feel unwell herself.

She couldn't really be ill. She wasn't even thirty-seven yet – wouldn't be for ages. It was stupid to feel so nervous of these wretched tests...

Daniel finished loading the milk churns and watched as the lorry trundled off down the road that led back to Stretton. The trouble with living miles down a drove was that he had to start milking half an hour earlier in order to get the milk to the pick-up point on time. As he climbed back into the seat of his tractor, Daniel was wondering what it was all about, the struggle to survive and keep his head above water.

He hadn't planned it this way! If he'd done things differently, he might have had his own garage now. He knew he could have made a reasonable living from that and then he could have handed the smallholding over to Connor, as he'd planned. A scowl settled on his face as he realized that his dreams were vanishing like early-morning mist. If he had to pay that scheming hussy for keeping her mouth shut ... But he wouldn't, damn her! He would tell Alice the truth ... But as he saw the smoke rising from the chimneys of his home, Daniel realized he could never tell her the truth.

Alice worked so hard and got very little in return, except a handful of children and more work. It wasn't the life he'd promised her or himself. He was caught in a trap and he couldn't see a way out.

'Damned if I do and damned if I don't,' he muttered to himself as he shut off the tractor and headed towards the kitchen. What was the worst that could happen? Alice wouldn't leave him...

As he entered the kitchen the smell of vomit hit him. Alice was pacing up and down, looking worried to death, and Sally was obviously ill again. All thought of telling his wife about Maura fled as he saw the red patches in his youngest child's cheeks.

'I think she is really ill this time,' Alice said. 'I don't know what to do, Dan. I have to get the others off to school and—'

'What's wrong?' Connor asked, walking into

the kitchen. 'If you want to take Sally to the doctor, I'll look out for the others. Danny will help, won't you?'

'Yeah,' Danny replied, looking at his screaming sister. 'Is she going to die?'

'No, of course she isn't,' Alice said. She thrust the child at Daniel. 'Hold her while I get ready – and then you can take me to the doctor's.'

'The surgery won't be open for another hour...'

'Take me to his house,' Alice said. 'She has been screaming ever since you left the house this morning. I can't stand it, Dan. It's different this time and I want the doctor to look at her. You know what happened to Frances's son...'

'I took Fran straight to the hospital. If you think it is that serious, perhaps...'

'I trust Doctor Parks,' Alice said. 'I don't like hospitals. They put poor Mr Giles outside and left him because they said it was healthy and he died of pneumonia three days later.'

'He had consumption,' Dan reminded her. 'Fresh air is supposed to be good for people with tuberculosis.'

'Not when it is freezing cold. I want to see Doctor Parks.'

'All right, love. Go and get ready, then. I dare say he will give you something to help with the fever. She's burning up, poor love.'

He kissed the top of Sally's head. She was hot and sweaty and she smelled of pee and vomit. Alice was a good mother but she couldn't cope with Sally's constant crying and sickness. Maybe they should have taken her to the doctor weeks ago when all this started...

61

* * *

'Sally has chicken pox,' Doctor Parks said after examining her. 'The rash is coming out on her body, Mrs Searles. You just need to keep her quiet and leave her to rest.'

'She keeps crying all the time,' Alice said, feeling tired. 'I know Danny had this when he was two but after the first day he was fine and I had a struggle to keep him indoors. The other two haven't had it yet.'

'You will probably find they catch it this time,' the doctor told her. 'I can give you a soothing lotion to smooth on her body, and you can give her a little of this medicine. Only a teaspoon in water, mind – and be careful not to give more than one dose every six hours.'

'Will it ease her?' Alice asked anxiously. 'She has always been one for crying right from birth. My other children were happier. I'm worried that she has something wrong with her.'

'I assure you she is a perfectly healthy young lady.' Doctor Parks smiled. 'Some children do cry more than others, and it is very worrying for the mother. You look worn out, Mrs Searles. I'll give you a tonic for yourself. It would do you good to get away for a bit of a break. Is there anyone who could look after the children for you?'

'My sister-in-law would have the elder three, but I couldn't leave Sally; she cries if I'm gone for more than a few minutes.'

'Perhaps that is because she knows you will pick her up. Sometimes it may be a good thing to let her cry it out – but that is up to you, of course.'

'Frances told me I should let babies cry, but I've always worried that there might be something wrong. I don't want one of my children to die because I didn't notice he or she was ill.'

'I am sure you would never do that.' Doctor Parks handed her a prescription. 'Take this to the chemist, Mrs Searles, and come to see me again if you are still tired in a month's time.'

'Thank you, Doctor.' Alice picked up Sally, who had stopped crying the minute the doctor had started to examine her and was now sucking her thumb, her eyes wide.

Daniel was waiting for her when she went out to the van. He jumped out and opened the door for her, looking anxious.

'What did he say?'

'Sally has chicken pox. He has given me some lotion to smooth on her skin and medicine – and he has given me a tonic. He says I need a break from the children...' Alice was thoughtful as Daniel took the baby while she got in and then put the child into her arms. 'I was thinking that perhaps we should try to get away, Dan. I had another letter from Frances yesterday, asking us to go down. If Mary and Connor could manage the others, I would like to take Sally – when she is over the chicken pox, of course.'

'Chicken pox.' Daniel frowned as he got into the driving seat. 'Thank goodness it wasn't anything worse, love. I'll talk to Connor and you ask Mary, then I'll give Frances a ring.'

'Yes, you do that. It's years since I saw the sea. I'm looking forward to it now, Dan.'

'Good,' he said, and smiled.

Daniel had made up his mind that he couldn't tell Alice the truth. It would upset her too much, and if the doctor had given her a tonic, she was obviously under the weather. He would have to borrow the money, though he wouldn't give Maura as much as she wanted. If he borrowed from Frances, she wouldn't charge as much interest as the bank. He could pay that scheming bitch and perhaps finish off his loan at the bank – and then perhaps he could begin to save for the future.

Daniel would pay Frances back, of course, but perhaps she would let him repay over a long period. She was a rich woman and she wouldn't worry about lending him a thousand or two. It would cost him to ask, because he had always sworn he wouldn't, but he was at the end of his tether. If he didn't pay Maura something, she would tell Alice that he was the father of her son. He would see what kind of a mood Frances was in and if he felt able he would tell her he needed money to start a business.

In the meantime he would let Maura stew. If he left her long enough, she might just give up and go off somewhere...

Three

Emily read the letter from Alice, her brow furrowing as she discovered that three of Alice's children were down with the chicken pox – and then Dan had taken it too.

He was the worst patient of them all. He was covered in spots and Doctor Parks thought he might have smallpox, but it wasn't and he is getting better at last. Connor had all the work to do, the milking and everything, but he got someone in to help and Dan is going to keep the lad on for a while. Now that he is feeling better we are taking Sally to stay with Frances for a week. Mary is having Danny, Jean and Rob to stay with her. Connor would have done his best to cope but it wouldn't be fair on him...

Emily laid her letter aside as the telephone shrilled. She was thinking what a rough time poor Alice had been having and wishing that Dan would bring all his family to her as she answered. 'Emily Vane speaking...'

'Lady Vane – Emily?' a man's deep voice said. 'I'm sorry it has been such a long time. I always meant to keep in touch, but you know how it is – we lead such busy lives.'

'Alan?' Emily was shocked as she heard the voice of Vane's cousin, but surprise was followed swiftly by guilt. 'How are you? It must be two years since you last telephoned...'

'Nearer three, I should think,' Alan said. 'How are things with you? I expect you run the place seamlessly, carrying on the traditions in Vane's name.'

'I do my best,' Emily laughed. 'Like you, I'm busy, but I like that – don't you?'

'I suppose I must or I wouldn't do it,' Alan said and his laugh was husky and warm. 'Anyway, I've just pushed through a sale of some of my businesses, which will mean that I am going to have a little less to do in the immediate future. My doctor has told me that I should slow down – take a bit of a rest.'

'I'm sorry. Nothing serious, I hope?'

'I had a scare. A slight heart attack, they say. I am told that I was lucky and was warned to take things easier, which means I have to learn to delegate.'

'I suppose we all have to do that in the end.'

'Yes ... well, I was wondering if I could come and stay for a few days? I have always found Vanbrough a peaceful place to be and it would be nice to see you and young Robert.'

'Of course you can,' Emily said instantly. She sensed that he was lonely. He had married soon after Vane died but his wife had died in a car crash a few months later. The verdict of the inquest had been that she had been driving while under the influence of alcohol. 'We would love to have you – and you can stay for as long as you wish.'

'You are a love,' Alan said. 'I'm not surprised Vane fell for you, Emily. Simon didn't deserve you. I was thinking of coming on a Saturday two weeks from now – if that will suit you?'

'Yes, of course. I shall look forward to it.'

Emily smiled as she replaced the receiver. She enjoyed having visitors to Vanbrough. Her family didn't visit often enough for her liking, but she had quite a few friends who came for long weekends. She wouldn't invite anyone else while Alan was staying, though. He obviously needed some peace and quiet.

Emily smothered her feelings of guilt. Alan ought to have been Vane's heir, because neither she nor her son was blood-related – but Vane hadn't seen it that way. He had known that Emily would carry out his wishes for Vanbrough to the best of her ability. Alan had his own life. He was wealthy, a successful businessman, and although he had just confessed to thinking Vanbrough a peaceful place, he would probably not have had the time or the desire to devote his life to it as Emily had.

She reached out for the letter from Alice, wondering how Frances would feel about the impending visit. Frances had been a bit irritable when Emily paid her a flying visit a couple of weeks previously. She had looked tired and older, but when Emily suggested she take time off and come back to Vanbrough for an extended stay she had snapped her head off.

'I have a hotel to run if you hadn't noticed. Just because you lead a life of leisure, it doesn't mean that we all can, Emily.'

'That's ridiculous and you know it.' Emily felt annoyed because she had cancelled a charity meeting to make this visit to her sister. 'I have as much and more to keep me busy as you do, Fran.'

'Sitting on the board of charities and drinking coffee,' Frances scoffed. 'You don't have to worry whether your bookings are up or down – or whether your suppliers are cheating you.'

'Neither do you,' Emily replied. 'You have staff to help you, just as I do – and you don't really need to work. You could sell this hotel and live off your investments.'

'What would I do then? Sit staring at the wall and go off my head with boredom,' Frances retorted and then shook her head. 'Sorry, Emily. I shouldn't take it out on you. I do miss you, you know.'

'You could live with me if you wanted. I could find you something to do if you felt bored.'

'I can't do that. Sometimes I wish I were there with you, but then I start to feel bitter and angry and I know it wouldn't be fair. I don't want you to suffer my moods.'

'Oh Fran, can't you put it behind you? I know what Sam did to you was awful, but it is over now.'

'It will never be over. I still have nightmares about being locked up somewhere...' Frances broke off. 'I love you, Emily, but I don't want to live with you. I need my independence.'

'You could have the dower house if you like. I'm going to do it up – as soon as I get the money together.'

'Don't tell me you're short of money. You have thousands in pictures and silver – Vanbrough is a treasure house!'

'Yes, but I don't own it – Robert doesn't either. It is a trust to be handed on to future generations.'

'Rubbish,' Frances said. 'Vane brainwashed you, Emily. If I were you, I should sell everything, invest the money and do something with your life. If you don't, you may wake up one day and find it is too late.'

'Is something wrong, Frances?' Emily felt chilled as she saw the expression in her sister's eyes.

Frances got up and walked to look out of the window at the garden. The window was slightly open and the smell of roses wafted in on a slight breeze. Emily shivered suddenly, feeling the goose pimples rise.

'No, nothing is wrong,' Frances said at last and turned to face Emily. 'I just think you are wasting your life there...'

Emily had a vague feeling all was not well with her sister, but, whatever it was, Frances hadn't wanted to tell her. Emily hadn't pushed her, but now she was wondering if she ought to have asked more questions. Her hand strayed to the phone, hovering as she thought about ringing Frances, and then the door opened.

'The Vicar is here, Lady Vane. He doesn't have an appointment but he says it is important.'

'Show him in, Martha.' Emily placed Alice's letter in her leather folder and stood up to greet her unexpected visitor. Frances was fine. She was worrying for nothing...

Connor watched as Dan, Alice and Sally drove off in his car. It would be more comfortable for them on the long drive down to Cornwall, and the van was better for farm business. Connor didn't mind taking it when he went into Ely. It wasn't as nice as his Austin, but it didn't matter.

It was surprising how empty the house felt with all the kids gone, and now Dan and Alice were on their way with Sally. He had the place all to himself for a whole week. Alice had been worried about how he would mange, but Connor could fry a bit of bacon or boil an egg – and he would buy fish and chips in Ely after he'd been to the club. He was looking forward to the meeting that week, because there was a new band performing. It was the first time they had booked the Bad Boys but Connor had been told they were good. They were a Rock 'n' Roll group who sang rhythm and blues, which was Connor's favourite music. He had been a huge fan of jazz and blues when he was growing up, but Rock 'n' Roll was the latest big thing in America. In England, a journalist had shortened the name Edward to Teddy and now the fashion for Edwardian-style clothes that the young men were wearing had branded them as Teddy Boys.

Emily had laughed when she'd asked if Connor was a Teddy Boy, thinking it funny. He had said that he would be if he could afford it, because no one knew that he had one of the narrow-fitting jackets and a pair of black drainpipes

70

in his wardrobe. Somehow he'd never found the courage to come downstairs wearing them when Alice and Dan were around, but he would wear them this evening – as well as the 'brothel creepers', which were his pride and joy and were hidden in a box at the top of the wardrobe.

Connor was whistling as he went outside to start mucking out the cowsheds. Tonight he was going to dress the part and 'strut his stuff' at the club. He grinned as he imagined himself doing the Lindy Hop with the girl of his dreams – even though it was very unlikely that she would be there. He doubted very much if Sarah Jenkins had ever been to a jazz club in her life, which was a pity because he really liked her. He couldn't afford to get married for years, but he thought he would like to marry a girl like Sarah when he did. He often wished he could meet her somewhere, though she probably wouldn't look at him. As Tiddy had said, it would take six months' wages to pay for one of the dresses she liked to wear.

Connor thought about what he might do if he left Daniel. He would have to give his brother time to find another man to take his place, of course, but he ought to think seriously about it. He had enjoyed working on the dower house and he thought it might be more interesting than working on the land. At least he would get to meet different people and he might earn more money.

He was going to need more money if he wanted to marry, because he didn't want to end up like Daniel. His brother was forever worried about paying the bills and Connor had no intention of living that way.

'I'm not sure that I like the idea of you going to that club,' Millicent Jenkins said as she looked at her daughter dubiously. Sarah was wearing a circle skirt with short white ankle socks and flat black shoes. Her long hair had been pulled back into a short ponytail and tied with a black ribbon. Her top was pink with a stand-up collar and pearl buttons, and she was wearing a pale pink lipstick. 'Your father would have a fit if he saw you dressed like that, Sarah.'

'He won't see me, Mum. His meeting at the Masons' lodge won't end until nearly twelve.' Sarah kissed her mother's cheek. 'Please don't worry. I'm going with Phyllis Brent and Ann Jones. I shall be home by half past ten and I won't do anything I shouldn't.'

'I wouldn't let you go if I didn't trust you to behave,' her mother said. 'But Mrs Harris was telling me that that club is where the Teddy Boys hang out and some of them have a bad reputation.'

'That's in big cities. You haven't heard of cinema seats being torn up or damaged in Ely, have you?'

'No, I haven't,' Mrs Jenkins admitted. 'You are nineteen and I suppose we can't keep you wrapped in cotton wool for ever – but please be careful and don't get involved with any nasty types, love.'

'I expect we shall dance with ourselves most of the night,' Sarah told her, crossing her fingers behind her back. 'Phyllis has been to the club several times and Ann went last week. They told me that a lot of the girls just dance together. They said the group this week is really great.'

'Do you know how to do these dances?'

'I learned some of them at the youth club, Mum – and Phyllis showed me how to do the Lindy Hop at her house. Her parents were out so we had the gramophone on and danced. It was fun.'

'I expect it was,' her mother said and smiled. 'Go on, then, you mustn't keep your friends waiting, Sarah. Have a good time.'

'Thanks, Mum. I won't be late.' Sarah grabbed her coat from the peg in the hall, pulling it on as she left the house. She had arranged to meet her friends outside the club and she was afraid they might go in without her if she were late.

Sarah blocked the odd sense of unease she'd felt as she left her mother. Something had made her wonder if she was feeling ill. She hoped her mother wouldn't have one of her migraines while she was out.

Connor and Tiddy walked into the club together. Tiddy was also wearing his drainpipes and a black and white striped shirt; he had the heavy crêpe-soled shoes that were so popular but he hadn't got the right jacket so he wasn't wearing one at all. He'd stared at Connor when he came out wearing his gear earlier, but hadn't said much.

Connor felt a bit self-conscious despite the fact that most of the young men present were wearing something similar to his outfit. The girls wore full skirts with several layers of petticoats underneath so that they stuck out and flared prettily when they jived or did the Lindy Hop. He had seen most of them here before, but he hadn't bothered to ask many of them for a dance, even though he was pretty good at the Lindy Hop. Usually, he was content to hang out near the bar and listen to the music, but this evening he felt like joining in – perhaps because of his new clothes. Connor grinned as he admitted to himself that he wanted to show off. He knew that he was attractive to girls and, if he chose, as the evening wore on, he could take the girl he fancied outside and kiss her. Some of them would let him touch them, and he was sure a couple of the girls here this evening would allow him to go all the way if he wanted. He wasn't interested in any of them, though, and it didn't look as if anyone new had turned up. He was about to head for the bar as usual when he saw three girls come in together. They were giggling and looked excited, as if they were new members.

Connor's breath expelled in a gasp as he saw her. Sarah Jenkins – at least that was the name Tiddy had given her. He said she was stuck-up, because she wouldn't dance with him at the church hall. Connor didn't attend the old-fashioned dance at the hall on Saturday nights, because he wasn't interested in that kind of dancing. He came to the club for the bands rather than the dancing, but it might be different this evening – if she would get up with him.

'I'll get the first round,' Tiddy said. 'Half of

bitter do you?'

'Don't get me one yet,' Connor said, not bothering to look at him. 'I'm going to ask someone to dance.'

He walked over to where the three girls were standing together. They looked nervous and excited, but as one of them noticed him approaching they went still and one of them nudged the other, whispering something. Connor almost turned tail. He wasn't usually apprehensive of approaching girls, but this one was special and he felt a spasm of nerves inside.

He stood a few paces from her, his mouth feeling unaccountably dry as he said, 'You're new here, aren't you?'

Sarah hesitated, unsure if he was speaking to her at first, and then nodded her head. 'Yes, it is my first time. I wanted to see the Bad Boys – they're good. At least, Phyllis says so.'

The lead singer stepped forward and announced the next number. Connor jerked his head towards the floor. 'Fancy trying this with me?' he asked. 'It's a Lindy Hop.'

'Oh yes,' Sarah answered. 'Phyllis taught me how to do it at home, but I'm not sure I'm any good...'

'Don't worry, I'll help you,' Connor said and offered her his hand. 'I like this dance. It's better than jive – more fun. Some people call it Rock 'n' Roll, but it started before that, in the thirties and forties.'

'You sound as if you know a lot about jazz and stuff?' Sarah looked at him shyly. Connor was sure she hadn't recognized him from the time he tried to pick her up in the street.

'I know a bit,' he said. 'I've got a lot of blues and jazz records and I read about all the big American bands. I'm not an expert but I enjoy music.'

'Oh, yes, so do I,' Sarah said enthusiastically. 'Daddy bought a record player. He likes classical music, but when he is out I play my records. I like Guy Mitchell and Doris Day – blues and rhythm too.'

'I listen as much as I can,' Connor said. 'Mostly on the radio. I would like a portable one to take to work when we get them here.'

'What do you do?' Sarah asked.

Connor hesitated, then said, 'My people are farmers,' because he thought she might change her mind if he simply said he worked on the land.

'Oh ... my Dad is a builder.' Sarah looked shy. 'You won't be cross if I step on your shoes?'

'You won't. Just have fun and enjoy yourself.'

Sarah thought that she'd never enjoyed herself so much. The first dance was a bit frightening, because she was afraid of making a fool of herself, but by the time she'd danced two more she was feeling confident.

'I am having fun,' she told Connor as their third dance ended. 'I ought to go back to my friends for a while, but I should like to dance with you again later, if that is all right?'

'Why not?' he asked. 'Would you mind if I brought a friend over to join you? He can dance if he wants – and I'll ask your friends to dance too, if you like?'

'You're really good,' Sarah said. 'I think that would be nice – if you wouldn't mind?'

'Wouldn't say if I did,' Connor told her. He was about to walk away when one of the band members came to the microphone.

'We have a request for anyone who fancies singing on stage with us. We've been told that Connor Searles sometimes comes up and does a turn. Are you out there, Mr Searles?'

A ripple of applause went round the club and a few voices called out for Connor to go up. He hesitated for a moment, then looked apologetically at Sarah.

'I'd better go. I shan't be long.'

'Oh...'

Connor realized as he walked to the stage that she didn't even know his name. They had been laughing and enjoying themselves but hadn't bothered to exchange names.

He was greeted on stage by more clapping and some cheering. Connor grinned because he knew he could sing, equally as well as the lead singer in this band.

'Hi, Connor. I'm Terry,' the band member said. 'Do you know "Rock It For Me"?'

'Yeah, it was an Ella Fitzgerald song,' Connor said, feeling pleased because it was a song he knew by heart. 'I've done that one before at the club.'

'So I was told,' Terry said. 'All right – here we go, folks. "Rock It For Me" with your own heart throb Connor Searles and the Bad Boys.'

Connor stepped up to the microphone confi-

77

dently. He wished that Terry had suggested something more romantic so that he could sing directly to Sarah, but this was a good song and he knew the words and music by heart. He had a good ear and once he'd heard something a couple of times he could belt it out with the best of them.

Sarah and her friends had come down to the front, near the stage. Some of the crowd started dancing when the music began, but about twenty girls stood and just watched as Connor sang.

Connor put everything into his performance because he knew Sarah was watching. He'd considered it a bit of a laugh when he'd performed on stage here before, but this time he let himself go, even gyrating his hips as he'd seen a rhythm and blues singer do at the pictures once. He wondered if Sarah had any idea what the words meant. Rocking and rolling was a term for music but it was also a sly way of saying 'have sex with me'. A lot of the songs in the blues and black music in America were to do with sex, though most people didn't realize what the words meant. Sarah wouldn't because she was too innocent. She wouldn't realize that when he sang 'rock it for me, baby', he was saying 'let me make love to you'.

A storm of approval broke when he finished. The applause was prolonged and he had to do a repeat before the audience would let him go, but then he left the stage even though there were calls for another number. He walked over to where Sarah was standing with one of her friends. The one she called Phyllis was dancing.

'Could I get you two ladies a glass of orange?'

'Not for me,' Ann said. 'But thanks all the same. You were wonderful.'

'I wouldn't mind a lemonade,' Sarah said. 'I thought you were brilliant. You should be a singer, Connor. You would be famous.'

'I'm not that good,' he said and grinned. 'Besides, I couldn't do that for a living. I have a job. I'll get us some drinks...'

Tiddy was at the bar. He grinned as Connor came up to him.

'You were all right, mate. What is she like? Bet she don't go outside with you later.'

'I shan't ask. I like her. She isn't the sort you take outside for a quickie against the wall.'

'Getting serious, is it?' Tiddy leered at him. 'Wait until she finds out there's no money. You've got no chance. I'm after Jenny Briggs tonight.' He patted his back pocket. 'I came prepared. I ain't going to get caught out. I ain't ready to get married just yet.'

'No, well, you please yourself, but I'd rather wait for the right girl.'

He bought two glasses of lemonade and a beer for Tiddy and then walked back to Sarah. Phyllis had brought her partner over and Ann had accepted an offer for the next dance.

'Shall we go over to the window and get some air?' Connor asked. Sarah looked startled and he grinned. 'I'm not asking you to go outside. I like you, Sarah. If I wanted something like that, I'd know who to ask...'

'Oh!' Her cheeks went pink. 'Thanks. I suppose you think I'm a bit old-fashioned?'

79

'As a matter of fact I prefer girls like you. I want a girl who thinks something of herself.' He hesitated. 'I don't suppose you would come to the flicks with me one day this week?'

'Oh ... I'm not sure ... Yes, all right, there is a film I want to see. You might not like it – it's Judy Garland.'

'I don't mind what I see if it is with you,' Connor said and Sarah went pink. 'Shall we say Friday? I'll meet you outside at a quarter to seven.'

'Yes, all right.' Sarah smiled shyly. 'It's the first time I've been to the pictures with a man. I usually go with my friends...' She blushed again. 'You must think I'm silly. I bet you take girls out all the time.'

'I've been out with one or two,' Connor admitted. 'But not many – and none of them were as pretty as you, Sarah.'

'Hey, Connor!' He turned his head as the band member came up to him. 'I wanted to ask you a favour...'

'I'm not coming up again tonight,' Connor said. 'I'm with someone.'

'We're doing a gig next Thursday night in Cambridge and our lead singer is going to be away on holiday. Would you stand in for him? We would pay you, of course – five pounds.'

'I'm not sure,' Connor frowned. 'I haven't done all your stuff. I might not be any good.'

'You could learn. You could practise with us this weekend if you like.'

'I'm not sure. No, I don't think so. I'm a bit busy.'

'If you change your mind, give me a buzz.' Terry thrust a crumpled-looking card into his hand. 'You've got a good voice and you could be a big asset to the band.'

Connor shoved the card into his pocket. 'Thanks. I'll think about it and let you know.'

Sarah looked up at him as Terry moved away. 'Why didn't you say yes? I think Rock 'n' Roll groups can earn a lot of money.'

'If they hit the big time,' Connor said. 'The Bad Boys are just a local group. I doubt if they get paid much. You heard what he offered.'

'Five pounds isn't bad for one night's work,' Sarah said. 'You never know where it would lead.'

Connor wasn't going to say so, but the money had been a big temptation. If he'd been on his own when Terry offered, he might just have accepted, but he wasn't sure he had the time. When Dan got back they would start harvesting and he would probably be asked to help out at neighbouring farms – especially during the potato harvest – and that wouldn't leave him much time for anything else.

'Shall we dance again?' he asked. 'I could walk you home later if you like – unless you want to go with your friends?'

'I'd like it if you took me home. I have to be back by half past ten – is that too early for you?'

'No, it's fine,' Connor said. 'I have to get up early myself so I usually leave around that time.'

It wasn't quite the truth, but he would have left whenever she said, just for the pleasure of walking her home.

Connor walked Sarah to her front door, kissed her on the cheek and reminded her of their date the following Friday. He had wanted to kiss her properly, but he knew she would be nervous of kissing him for the first time and he wanted to get to know her better.

He was smiling, well pleased with the world when he strolled back to the yard behind the club where he had left his van. Tiddy was standing by it, kicking at the ground and looking fed up.

'You're back, then. I thought you would be ages.'

'I just walked Sarah home. I told you, I'm not interested in anything else for the moment. How did you get on?'

'Bloody Brian Bates beat me to it,' Tiddy said gloomily. 'Come on, let's go. I've had enough.'

'Connor – just a moment!'

Connor hesitated as he was about to get into the driving seat. He saw Terry striding across the yard towards him.

'I'm glad I caught you. Look, I know I didn't offer you much earlier. What if we gave you ten pounds for the night? It is important and I know you could do it. I'll come over and go through the songs with you – on Sunday if you like?'

'Yes, all right,' Connor agreed, surprised at himself. 'If I can learn your stuff in time, I'll do the gig – but I can't promise anything else.'

'Thanks, mate,' Terry grinned. 'You've saved my life. That gig in Cambridge is the best thing we've been offered since we started. Phil is as sick as a pig at missing it – but he's going to

Spain with his girlfriend and her parents and he can't get out of it.'

'If I were him, I wouldn't want to,' Connor said. 'Bloody hell! That's the trip of a lifetime!' Most people went to Bournemouth, Devon or Blackpool for their holidays, if they were lucky.

'Yeah, well, it would be for most of us,' Terry agreed. 'But once we hit the big time the world is our oyster – and the Bad Boys are going places, believe me. We've got another six gigs lined up already, and a performance at a seaside show.'

'Well, I hope I don't let you down. I'll meet you outside the shop in Stretton High Street on Sunday at three. We'll go somewhere quiet and practise together...'

'Sure thing,' Terry said. 'Your gear looks great. You won't need anything different for the gig.'

'Right.' Connor nodded and got into the car.

Tiddy looked at him as he started the engine. 'What was all that about, then?'

'They want me to do a gig next week because their lead singer will be away.'

'You never agreed?' Tiddy stared at him. 'I know they like you down the club but it will be different at a real gig.'

'Singing is singing,' Connor said. 'It is just for a laugh. I'm only going to do it the once.'

He sensed that his friend was jealous. Tiddy hadn't liked it because Sarah had danced with him all evening and then let him walk her home. He had encouraged Connor to go on stage at the club, but now he was talking him down – perhaps because he sensed that Connor might be growing away from him.

'What will Dan say? He won't think much to it if you're out every night at a gig.'

'No, he wouldn't,' Connor agreed. 'But it won't happen. I told you, it is just the once.'

He was thoughtful as he drove them back to Stretton and dropped Tiddy in the High Street before heading off down the road that led to the fen and home. Ten pounds was almost as much as he earned in three weeks with Dan. He would have to see how things worked out, because that sort of money didn't grow on trees. He had no idea how much the rest of the band was earning, but as far as he was concerned it was riches!

He grinned as he let himself into the house. It would probably be just the once, but if he got the chance, he wouldn't mind doing a few more gigs. If he was serious about Sarah, he had to find a way of earning more money, because she would expect him to take her out. And if it came to marriage – which wouldn't be for several years – he would need a bit in the bank.

He had never thought of using his voice to earn him money. It hadn't occurred to him that his love of jazz and Rock 'n' Roll could be a way of earning a few extra quid. Even if the Bad Boys didn't need him more than once, there were other bands. Dan might not like him taking time off but they could talk about that if it happened...

Sarah walked in to find the house quiet. Her mother usually watched the television when she was on her own, but there was no sound and no sign of her either. Remembering that her mother had seemed a little odd before she went out, Sarah ran upstairs to her mother's bedroom. The door was slightly ajar. She tapped the door softly.

'Mum ... are you all right?'

There was no answer so she pushed it open and went in. Her mother was lying sprawled on top of the bed. She was obviously sleeping and as Sarah moved carefully towards her, she snored loudly and flung out an arm.

'Are you feeling ill, Mum?'

Sarah bent over. She noticed the small brown bottle on the chest beside the bed and picked it up, frowning as she saw that the prescription was for sleeping tablets. She hadn't known her mother took them. Perhaps she'd had a terrible migraine?

'I'm sorry, Mum.' Sarah bent and kissed her on the forehead. She could smell something but wasn't sure what it was, though it smelled a bit like whisky. She noticed the glass on the dressing table and picked it up, sniffing at the strong smell. Surely it wasn't a good idea to drink whisky at the same time as taking tablets? She went back to the bed feeling anxious.

'Mum...' Sarah shook her shoulder. 'Mum – are you all right?'

Her mother moaned and her eyelids flickered. Sarah shook her again and she opened her eyes.

'Sarah – what is the matter?'

'I was worried. You didn't take those tablets with whisky, did you?'

'Of course I didn't,' her mother said. 'I'm not that stupid, Sarah. I had the drink and went off without them. I wish you hadn't woken me. I shall have one of my headaches now.'

'I'm sorry. I was worried.'

'Silly girl! Go to bed, Sarah. I need to rest.'

'Yes. Sorry, Mum.'

Sarah went to her own room. She forgot about the incident with her mother as she undressed, smiling as she brushed her hair and thought about the dances she'd had with Connor Searles. He was different from all the other men she knew – exciting. She had wanted him to kiss her properly, but he'd just given her a peck on the cheek. He'd treated her with respect, and she believed he really liked her.

Getting into bed, she thought about their date for the following Friday. She could hardly wait for the days to pass.

'Are you in debt?' Frances asked, her eyes on her brother's face. 'Why didn't you tell me before?'

Dan lowered his gaze, his neck flushed with embarrassment. Frances had been pleased to see them, and generous, but he felt a distance between them, and it was almost like talking to a stranger at times. He didn't know his eldest sister as well as he ought. He thought that perhaps she'd never forgiven him for not believing her when Sam Danby had been bullying her just after the war.

'I hate asking for a loan, Fran. I wish I didn't have to do it now – but I need fifteen hundred, or two thousand if you could manage it.'

'That is a lot of money.' Frances frowned. 'I

don't understand why you need it all of a sudden. I thought you had almost finished paying off the bankruptcy?'

'Yes, I have, but things have been difficult and I need stuff for the farm – and I want to buy some cars to do up. I should like to take on more repair work for other people. I get asked to repair tractors and engines all the time, but for that I need equipment.'

'Are you talking about the garage you want?' Frances smiled. 'You should have asked before, Dan. I would have helped you to start in business for yourself ages ago. I approve of someone trying to get on in life.'

'I will pay it back,' he said, his shirt collar unaccountably tight. 'I don't want you to give it to me.'

'I can make it a loan if that's what you want,' Frances said. 'I don't want any interest and you can pay me when you like.'

'You're a brick,' Daniel said, feeling a little sick inside. He could imagine what Frances would say if she knew that half of the money would be going to pay Maura for keeping her mouth shut. 'I hate to ask, but I do need it quite soon.'

'I'll write you a cheque. You can pay it into the bank when you get home. Does Alice know you're going to start the garage?'

'I haven't told her. It won't be a garage with a forecourt just yet, but I have plenty of room for cars in the yard and I can leave most of the land work to Connor and the lad now. His name is Joe and he is a bit slow but he works hard and we don't pay him much.'

'That's a bit mean. You should pay poor Joe a proper wage – especially since you will be earning more now.'

'Yes, you are right. I don't know why I didn't think of this sooner. It's a waste for me to be on the land when I could earn more as a mechanic.'

'You didn't want to ask for a loan.'

'You won't tell Alice about this?'

'Not if you prefer to keep it between us,' Frances said. 'I've enjoyed having you all to stay. You must come again soon – and bring the rest of the family.'

'You would find the whole brood rather a lot,' Daniel said and laughed. He had dreaded asking Frances for the loan, but there was no other way of paying Maura off – and by asking for a bit more he had a chance to start making some money: the more he made, the sooner he could pay back the loan.

'I love to see my family. Emily doesn't come down enough – and Connor hasn't been for years. Tell him I would like to see him when he has the time.'

'I'll tell him, but he is his own master. You probably still think of him as a boy, but he is a man now. I suppose he will be thinking of getting married one of these days.'

'I'm only surprised he hasn't got a girl already.'

'They all run after him, but I don't think he has thought about it seriously.' Dan frowned. 'He is the only one of us who hasn't got anything. I should like to give him the fields on Stretton

Road one day, but I can't afford it until I can get my garage up and running.'

'Well, I think you should have a good start now,' Frances sat down at her desk and wrote swiftly. 'Just sign there – it is just to say that I lent you two thousand pounds. I'll write you a cheque and we're done.'

Daniel was a little surprised that his sister had put the agreement into writing, but he signed it immediately. Frances would keep her word and he could pay it back a bit at a time.

'You're so generous,' he said. 'Thanks a lot, Fran – this is really important to me.'

'Don't worry about paying it back until you're ready,' Frances said and slipped the agreement into her desk. 'I would have given it to you if you'd asked, but I know you're more comfortable this way. All I ask is that you visit me sometimes.'

'Of course we will. I know Alice has enjoyed herself and the sea air was good for her.'

'She does look better than when she came,' Frances said. 'I took her to have her hair cut and it suits her. She should keep it like that – and you should give her money for clothes, Dan. She hasn't got much that's really nice in her wardrobe. I offered to buy her a new dress from a good shop, but she wouldn't let me.'

'No, I don't suppose she would.'

Daniel felt a bit guilty. It would have offended Alice's pride to take such a gift from Frances. She had insisted that he bought his sister a nice present for having them to stay. He could just imagine what Alice would say if she knew that he had borrowed two thousand pounds from his sister. She hated taking charity and only the knowledge that she really needed a break from the children had persuaded her to come this time.

'Well, you spoil her a bit once you've got the business up and running,' Frances said. 'You wouldn't want to lose Alice...'

'She would never leave me,' Daniel said too quickly, and frowned as Frances raised her brows. 'I try, Frances. Maybe I have let things slip a little where Alice is concerned – but she knows I love her and the kids. We're all right together.'

'I thought Marcus loved me when we got married, but he changed so much during the war. You had a rough time too, but don't forget that Alice loves you.'

'I know, but in a way I was lucky. I didn't see much real fighting – just some guerrilla stuff and then the inside of a prisoner of war camp.'

'You make light of it but I know it must be there inside you,' Frances said. 'You are stronger than Marcus. I just want you and Alice to be happy.'

Daniel caught an odd look in her eyes. 'Is something wrong, Fran? I know you had a bad time after Marcus died. I wish I'd known what that devil was up to sooner. I would have made him leave you alone.'

'Most days I can forget it,' Frances said, but for a moment an odd, haunted look was in her eyes. 'I'm all right, Dan – when I'm not I'll tell you.'

'You know you can count on me if you need me.'

'Yes, I know. You and Emily have been good to me. Connor was too young to know what was going on – and Clay didn't care.'

'Clay only thinks of himself.'

'Do you ever see him?'

'No – and I don't wish to.' Daniel was angry. 'He has caused too much trouble for our family.'

'He is selfish,' Frances agreed. 'He wrote and asked me if he could bring his family for a holiday here. I haven't answered him yet.'

'If I were you, I should say no,' Daniel warned. 'If he comes, he will want something from you...' He broke off, his cheeks hot, because he had also asked her for money. 'I know I asked for a loan, but Clay...' He shook his head. 'You must do as you think best, Fran. I don't have the right to interfere.'

'I'm not sure how I feel. I don't have much time for Clay after what he did to Margaret – but I feel sorry for Dorothy.'

'We all feel sorry for her. I don't know why she stays with him.'

'Maybe because she doesn't have anything else to look forward to,' Frances said, such a bleak look in her eyes that Daniel was shocked. 'Someone there when you put the light out is better than nothing at all – even if he is a cheat and a liar.'

'Oh, Fran.' Daniel put his arms about her, giving her a hug. 'We shall come sooner next time. I'm sorry you lost Marcus.'

'It's Charlie I miss the most.' Frances blinked

away the tears that hovered. 'I didn't understand how lucky I was, Dan. You have everything that matters – Alice, a home and your children. Promise me you won't lose them by being careless?'

'No, of course I shan't. Are you sure there is nothing wrong, Fran? I would help if I could.'

'I know,' she said and turned away to look out at the sea. 'It's nothing – just that you are leaving and I shall miss you.'

'I'll get Alice to write and we'll visit soon.'

'Yes, please. You'd better go or Alice will come looking.'

Daniel nodded. 'Thanks for the money. I shan't forget.'

'Have a good journey.'

Daniel hesitated. He had a feeling deep down that something was wrong, but he didn't know what to say. If Frances wanted to tell him, she would – and Alice would be waiting.

Frances waited at the window until she saw them all get into the car. She lifted her hand to wave as Daniel drove away. Then she went to the desk and took out the paper Daniel had signed, tearing it into little pieces and tossing it into the wastepaper basket. Her will was divided between Emily and Daniel, with a few thousand to Connor, but it was best to be on the safe side. She wouldn't want Daniel to have to repay the loan if she died. As far as she was concerned it was a gift.

Frances sat down in the chair beside the empty fireplace. Already she could feel one of her black moods coming on. The doctors had told her that her cancer was one of the slow ones. They were going to give her some treatment but they couldn't operate because the tumour was too close to her brain – which meant that towards the end she might not know what she was doing.

It had all been explained to her carefully. Her symptoms were not too bad as yet, but the headaches would get worse and so would the feeling of tiredness and the dark moods that made her feel so desperate at times. At least she understood them now. She wasn't mad, but in time she might lose bits of her memory and people might think she had gone strange if they didn't know about the tumour.

Frances knew that Emily would insist she went to live at Vanbrough if she told her, so she had kept it from all her family. Perhaps towards the end she would go to Emily, but not yet. She wanted to hang on to her independence for as long as she could.

Four

Sarah hesitated outside the kitchen door as she heard raised voices. Were her parents having an argument? They seldom quarrelled as far as she knew. She would have thought they got on better than most. She knew that Janice's mother sometimes nagged her father and that he went off down the pub afterwards, but she had always thought her parents had the perfect marriage.

'I'm telling you, I shan't stand for much more of this!'

'You agreed to it, Millie. We keep going for Sarah's sake...'

'My name is Millicent! And I didn't agree to—'

Sarah opened the door and went in. She saw the look that passed between her parents as they became aware of her and sensed something. What were they keeping from her?'

'Is something wrong, Mum?'

'No, of course not,' her mother said. 'I was just complaining because your father is going away again this weekend.'

'It is a business trip,' Mr Jenkins said. 'I know I'm away a lot, but I want to keep expanding the business – at least until you get married, Sarah. I shall be giving you a good present, maybe a house of your own, and I'm putting money by for that.'

Sarah looked from one to the other. Their expressions gave nothing away, but she was sure they were hiding something from her.

'You are all right, aren't you?' she asked. 'Janice told me that her parents may split up – that isn't going to happen to you?'

'Certainly not!' Mrs Jenkins said. 'I do not believe in divorce. My mother would have had a fit if she thought I was getting a divorce. No, Sarah! You can put that right out of your mind. Everything is just as it ought to be.'

Sarah caught the look in her father's eyes and wondered. She had a feeling that he wanted to say something different but instead he just picked up his suitcase and left.

'Are you sure you're all right, Mum?' Sarah asked as the door closed behind him.

'Quite sure, my love,' her mother replied. 'Go to work, Sarah. You mustn't be late or you might get the sack.'

Sarah kissed her and left the house. She was thoughtful as she walked to work, stopping to look in the window of another new draper's shop that had opened at the top of the High Street. They were displaying a beautiful blouse in a colour called London Tan and she thought how well it would suit her, but she wouldn't get a discount here and it was too expensive. She thought that perhaps she ought to save some of her wages, instead of spending it all on clothes. She might want to get married one day and so far she had nothing in her bottom drawer.

A little further down the street, she stopped outside the ironmongers; they had a sale on and were selling a nice set of custard dishes at half price. Perhaps she should buy something like that this week. Or maybe she would just save the money instead, because if she did get married one day she would want a lovely white dress...

Connor was waiting when Terry pulled up on his shiny motorbike. It was a Harley-Davidson and something that Connor had lusted after from afar. He had never been as close to one before and his excitement showed as soon as he saw it.

'This is great! I wanted a motorbike but Dan said I would be better off with the Austin.'

'Have you got a car of your own? I'm asking because it would make things easier for getting to gigs. We all pile into one van but it would be better if we had more transport.'

'I thought it was only the once? Yeah, I have a car but I lent it to my brother to take his wife on holiday. I'm using his van at the moment.'

'I've been talking to the other guys. We might have a space for you, Connor. Some of them are a bit fed up with Phil, because he is letting us down and this isn't the first time.'

'I wouldn't want to take someone else's place,' Connor said, feeling uneasy. 'How would he feel about it?'

'We might go with an extra singer – do you play an instrument?'

'No, I've never tried.'

'It doesn't matter. I could teach you to strum a few chords on the guitar, just so that you can look the part. Hop on and we'll go somewhere off the beaten track to practise.'

'Really?' Connor grinned as he climbed on the pillion. 'This is great.'

'I don't wear a helmet,' Terry said. 'Hold on to me when we corner until you get the hang of it.'

Connor knew that Daniel and Alice were back when he drove into the yard that evening. Daniel had parked his car and the kitchen door was open. He parked the van and saw his brother on his way out to fetch more suitcases.

'I'll give you a hand,' he said, picking up the last three and striding towards Dan as he stood at the kitchen door. 'Did you have a good time?'

'Yes, we enjoyed it,' Daniel smiled. 'You were right, Connor. It did Alice the world of good to have a break – and it helped me to think things through. I'm going to keep Joe on and in time I might get another man in to help out. I'm going to be doing more repair work, for other people as well as my own restoration stuff.'

'That's great, Dan,' Connor said. 'But you'll need more equipment and that costs money.'

'I've got a bit spare,' Daniel replied, not quite meeting his eyes. 'Enough to make a start if I work from the yard. I can't start a garage with petrol pumps just yet, but maybe in a couple of years or so.'

'Well, that's great, Dan,' Connor said. 'I've got some news of my own. I've been asked to join a band. It will only be a few gigs here and there, in the evenings so I can do a day's work before I go. The extra money will come in handy. They are paying me ten pounds a time.'

'Ten pounds! That is a lot of money,' Dan said. He frowned. 'I know you don't get much from me but I haven't been able to afford it.'

'I get my board and lodging. But I shan't always want to live with you and Alice, Dan. I've got to think about the future and start putting some money by.'

'That sounds as if there might be a young lady somewhere?'

'There might,' Connor agreed. 'I've only just met her, Dan, but it has made me think.'

'Yes ... well, it had to happen,' Daniel said. 'As soon as I'm earning more I'll put your wage up. And you might get an acre from the allotment board if you put your name down. You could have your own crop then, and that would bring in a lump sum at the end of the year.'

'They turned me down last time I asked. I'm not sure I want the bother of it, Dan. I may be able to earn more from singing...'

'I suppose you might.' Dan looked doubtful. 'Don't get your hopes too high; it may not work out as you hope.'

'I'm keeping an open mind,' Connor said as he went into the kitchen. Alice was busy laying the table with plates and a pile of fresh bread she had buttered. 'It's good to have you home, Alice. You look very well.'

'Thank you. I've enjoyed myself, but it is good to be home. Mary is keeping the children until tomorrow so I thought we would have ham and tomatoes this evening. We bought some fresh ham from the butcher on our way home and the tomatoes are out of Mr Fletcher's greenhouse. They smell lovely – much better than you can buy in town.'

'I've been living on toast, eggs and bacon – and fish and chips,' Connor told her with a grin. He picked up a thick slice of bread and bit into it with enjoyment. 'Best thing I've eaten all week.'

'I knew what you would do,' Alice scolded laughingly. 'I told Dan it would be all grease and stodge. You can start eating your greens now, young man!'

'Yes, Mum!' Connor saluted. 'I'm glad you're back – really back.'

Alice nodded. 'There's something on the dresser for you. Frances sent it. She says she would like you to visit when you can.'

Connor picked up the large square envelope. It felt thick and when he opened it, he discovered a wad of notes.

'Bloody hell! There must be fifty pounds here at least.' Connor stared at the money in astonishment. 'What made Frances send me this?' He was usually lucky to get a card and a pound note for his birthday from his eldest sister.

'She can afford it,' Alice said. 'She insisted on sending presents for the kids. I suppose she thought you would rather have the money.'

'Yes, I should.' Connor pocketed the cash. He grinned as he thought of various ways of spending his windfall. 'It was generous of her. I'll ring her later from the call box and thank her.'

'Yes, you should,' Alice said. 'I bought you a magazine about jazz. It isn't much, but I know you like them.'

'Thanks.' Connor plonked a kiss on her cheek. 'You know what I like. I've been offered a place in a band for a gig next week. I don't know if they will keep me on – but it will be fun and they're paying me ten pounds.'

'You will be rich,' Alice said and smiled. 'Sit down and eat your tea, Connor – it will be sixpence to talk to you soon!'

'Half a crown at least,' he retorted and grinned at her. Alice was looking so much better and she was wearing that flowery perfume again. He was glad that Dan had taken her away for a few days; she deserved it. 'You wait until my record is up there at number one.'

'It wouldn't surprise me at all,' Alice said. 'I've always thought you had a lovely voice.'

Emily stood up as she heard the sounds of voices in the hall, her heart beating faster than normal. She had no idea why she should be nervous about this meeting with Vane's cousin. He had always been perfectly friendly.

'It's all right, Mrs Bates. I'll just go in,' a man's voice said outside the door. 'Lady Vane is expecting me.'

Emily was by the window looking out when the door opened. She didn't turn immediately.

'It is a lovely view from here. Vane was very fond of this room.'

'Yes, he was – and so am I,' Emily said and turned with a smile on her lips. 'It is lovely to see you again, Alan. It has been too long.' She went forward, hesitated and then held out her hand.

'Too formal, Emily,' he said and leaned forward to kiss her on the cheek. 'How are you – and young Robert?'

'Robert is growing up. He started boarding school this term and we miss him, but he was home for the holidays and he will be here again at Christmas.'

'Does he like it? I hated boarding school personally, but I suppose it is good for the character.'

'Yes...' Emily frowned. 'Vane put his name down just after Robert was born. I refused to let him go until he turned eleven – but he seems to be having fun. They do a lot of sport and Robert is good at cricket and rugby.'

'Well, that's all right, then.' His dark eyes went over her. Emily noticed that his hair had streaks of grey at the temples. 'How is life treating you? I know you must be busy – but you keep well, and happy?'

'I am busy but I think it keeps me fit.' Emily smiled. 'As for being happy – I'm not sure what that means. I enjoy my life and I love living here. I don't have time to be miserable.'

'I suppose that is a kind of happiness,' Alan said. 'Yet you should make time for yourself, Emily – get away to the sunshine and relax. I'm surprised that you haven't married again.'

'There was someone once. I had to make a choice between Paul and keeping my promise to Vane...'

'Did you make the right choice?'

'Yes, I am sure I did,' Emily said. There was no hesitation in her now, because it was too long ago. 'I wasn't really in love with Paul. If I had been, I would have gone with him – wouldn't I?'

'I suppose you would. We all make choices and we have to live by them.'

'We shouldn't be so philosophical this early in the day. Shall we have tea here or out on the lawn since it is a lovely day? I'm not sure how long this settled period will last. We shall be into autumn soon, but for the moment it is still summer.'

'Oh, outside, I think,' Alan said, standing back so that she could precede him. 'I spent some happy times here as a child. My parents visited every year in the summer and at Christmas. I continued it until my wife died and then some-how...' He shrugged his shoulders. 'I hope you didn't mind my inviting myself to stay?'

'I was delighted,' Emily said honestly. 'We don't get as many visitors as I should like. When Amelia lived here she entertained lavishly and often, but I prefer to keep my dinner parties small and intimate – and my house guests are infrequent.'

'It was an impulse,' he said. 'I shall rest here. At home my phone never stops ringing. Even if I try not to think of work, someone will ring and ask questions.'

'I know exactly how you feel,' Emily said and laughed softly. 'Now you are here and I insist that you forget about work. Enjoy your stay with us. You must think of this as your home for as long as you wish.'

'You are very generous.'

Emily shook her head. 'If things had been

otherwise, this might have been your home.'

'Vane would never think of leaving it away from his grandson, and a good thing too,' Alan said. 'Besides, running a place like this takes up far too much time – time I don't have.'

Emily nodded and turned away to ring for tea. He might change his mind if he knew that Robert did not have one drop of Vane's blood in his body. For a long time she had wondered if Amelia would carry out her threat to tell him, but she obviously hadn't bothered. Of course, she couldn't prove it – no one could, because Simon was dead and so was Emily's lover. Vane's will had been cleverly worded and there was no way anyone could claim the estate – though the title was Alan's by right.

Would she have given all this up if her lover hadn't been killed trying to rescue someone from a burning building in London during the war? It was difficult to remember how she had felt then, but she had been ready to leave. When the news came of his death she'd been devastated. Vane had given her a reason to live again – but it might all have been so different. She could have been simply a housewife living in suburbia with half a dozen children and no money. She shook her head, because the picture seemed unreal: it was as if she had always belonged here. Vane had known that, of course. Alan was speaking again and she brought her mind back from its wandering.

'I think I might try my hand at a spot of painting in watercolours while I'm here. I've always dabbled and the doctor said I need a hobby of some kind.'

'That sounds lovely,' Emily said. 'Feel free to paint whatever and wherever you wish.'

'I thought I would have a go at an impression of the house – not too detailed, but from a distance.'

Emily smiled. She had been foolish to worry. Alan would be a comfortable guest. She thought she would enjoy his company.

'You came, then?' Terry looked pleased as Connor got out of the car and came to join him. 'You found the place all right?'

'Yeah. I had to ask but it wasn't too bad,' Connor said. 'Where are the others?'

'Inside, setting up. We're going to have a run-through of the number I taught you on Sunday with all of us together. The gig doesn't start for half an hour so we've got a chance to go through the routine before anyone gets here.'

'Good. I could do with the practice,' Connor said. 'How many do you think will turn up?'

'Maybe two hundred – more if we're lucky. We put a few posters up round the town, but you never know with these things. They can be crowded or nearly empty.'

'We always get about a hundred at the club, especially when there's a decent band,' Connor said. 'I've never performed for real before – it's just a bit of fun at the club.'

'It doesn't have to be any different here. Besides, you're good. You've got a decent voice and you move well – a little like Elvis Presley from a clip I saw on the newsreel. If you grew your sideburns you could look like him too.'

'He's had a couple out with Sun Records, I think. I haven't heard his records yet, but I saw something in a magazine.'

'He is a big hit,' Terry said. 'They think he will be bigger than Bill Haley and the Comets.'

'I must get his record if I can find it.'

'Come over to mine and practise with us in the week,' Terry said. 'It varies from week to week, but Tuesdays are usually good. I'll put Presley on the player so that you can hear him.'

'The others agreed that I could join, then?'

'Yeah, I told you they would,' Terry said. 'Come on, the sooner we start, the better you will feel.'

Connor nodded and followed him inside. The room was many times larger than the club he was used to, and the floor was shiny. It looked like a proper dance floor, and there was a huge ball hanging from the ceiling, which shed twinkling lights in various colours as it moved.

Connor was aware of a feeling of apprehension. He had expected it to be just a small gig and similar to the club, but this was different – so much bigger. He wondered if he could match up to Terry's expectations. If he'd known, he might not have agreed, but he was here and he couldn't let them down. He would just have to do his best. At least he was wearing the right gear.

Looking at the faces of the other group members as Terry told him their names, he got the feeling that most of them were nervous too.

'Jack plays guitar. Ray is the bass guitar. Sam

is on drums and I'm on guitar as well,' Terry said. 'We can all sing a bit and we'll back you up with the chorus, but you'll be the main lead. We'll rehearse the song I taught you on Sunday. It's one we wrote for ourselves and it's called "Rock Me All The Way, Baby".'

'Yeah,' Connor grinned, thinking about what those words *really* meant. 'We're gonna have good rockin' tonight...'

Terry laughed. 'You say that to the girls with that look on your face and you'll have them swooning.'

'I hope I shan't let you down.' Connor glanced at the clock. 'We'd better get started. I need all the practice I can get!'

Sarah left the youth club earlier than her friends. She'd played darts for a while and listened to some records, but when Phil started to say things she didn't like she decided to leave. Somehow he knew she was interested in Connor Searles and she thought he was jealous.

'You don't want to go out with that loser,' he told her. 'His brother has a smallholding in Stretton but they've got no money.'

'I don't care about that,' Sarah told him. 'Besides, we're just friends.'

She thought about it as she walked home alone. She liked Connor a lot, but she knew her parents wouldn't think much to her going out with a man who had no prospects. They would think she ought to date the son of a local businessman. She wouldn't tell them anything just yet, because she didn't want her mother saying she couldn't go out with Connor. She was old enough to date who she liked, but she couldn't marry without her parents' permission until she was twenty-one.

For the first time in her life, Sarah was really interested in seeing someone. Phil had called Connor a loser, but as far as she was concerned he was a winner. She thought he had a lovely voice and he was polite and really good-looking. She couldn't wait for her date with him the next evening, and she wondered what he was doing at that moment.

When she got in her mother was watching the television. Sarah went upstairs and turned on her radio, tuning into a country and western programme she liked. She curled up on her bed with a magazine, listening to the music and munching an apple.

Her father was out again. She wondered why he had to work so hard that he never stayed home with them in the evenings these days. It was past midnight when she heard his car outside and then the steady tread of his footsteps up the stairs.

Dan saw Maura standing near the pub as he pulled the van to a halt. He knew she was waiting for him. He had expected it to happen one of these nights and he had some cash hidden in the van just in case. He was going to try her with five hundred pounds for a start. It was a lot of money and she really had no proof that her son was his child.

He wound the window down. 'Get in. I don't

want to talk here under the lights. Someone would see us and I don't want Alice to hear anything. If she does, you can say goodbye to your money.'

Maura glared at him as she got into the car. 'Where have you been? This is the third night I've come looking. If you hadn't turned up this evening, I was going to come to your house.'

Dan drove off, turning down one of the lanes with few houses. 'Come near my family and you won't get a penny,' he said. 'I'm not even sure that I'm going to pay you. I've no proof that you have a son or that he is mine.'

'I brought some photographs,' Maura said. 'I am not a liar, however much you might wish I was, and I'm not going away. I need money to bring David up properly and if you don't pay me I'll make sure everyone knows about that night.'

Dan pulled into a lay-by. 'Damn you,' he muttered, his face dark with anger. 'For two pins I would break your neck. It was all your idea. I don't see why I should pay for a one-night stand.'

'It wasn't like that and you know it,' Maura said. 'I didn't mean to trap you. I was miserable and you were lonely. It just happened. I'm not asking for myself. I just want to give my son the things he deserves.'

'I'm not a rich man, Maura, no matter what you may think.'

'You can afford a thousand pounds.'

'I can't raise that much,' Daniel lied. 'The most I can do tonight is two hundred and fifty.'

'That isn't enough,' Maura said. 'I want at

least eight hundred.'

'I'll give you two hundred and fifty.'

'If I don't get what I want, your Alice will get one of these in the post.' Maura passed him three photographs.

Daniel took them reluctantly. He looked at the pictures of a young boy. His throat tightened because they could have been of the boy he had tucked into bed earlier that evening. No matter how much he disliked it, Maura was telling him the truth – he had fathered a child with her.

'It's bloody ridiculous,' he said bitterly and thrust the photographs back at her. 'One night – one sodding night!'

'You don't have to swear! You know he is yours, don't you?'

'He looks just like my son Danny.'

'He *is* your son. He is entitled to something from you.'

Daniel reached into the glove compartment and took out a package. 'There's five hundred pounds here.'

'I want a thousand.'

'Maybe in a few months. I don't have that kind of cash lying around. You can go to Alice if you like, but if you do, you won't get another penny.'

'I'll give you three months,' Maura snarled and snatched the money, thrusting it into her bag. 'I'll count it later and I want another five hundred or you will be sorry – now you can take me back to the bus stop.'

Daniel held back a sharp retort. He felt like pushing her out and telling her to walk, but it was dark and deep dykes bordered the road. He had brought her here and the least he could do was to take her back – but he wouldn't be paying her another penny if he could help it.

'Don't come near my house or you will be the one wishing you'd never been born,' he warned as he started the car. 'You wouldn't want your boy to be an orphan...'

'You wouldn't dare,' Maura said but a little nerve flicked in her throat. She had pushed him as far as she dared tonight. She would wait for a while before making more demands. Five hundred pounds was a lot of money. More than enough to get her started in the little hairdressing business she fancied. She could put a deposit of three hundred pounds down and the rest of her windfall would keep her going until she had the shop up and running – and perhaps she could get some more out of him in a few months' time.

It was almost half past one when Connor switched-ed the engine off and crept in at the kitchen door. He didn't bother switching the light on because the moon was full and he could see enough to find his way up to his room. Carrying his shoes in his hand, he took the stairs carefully, avoiding the ones that creaked and breathing a sigh of relief as he reached his own room and shut the door behind him.

At last he could put the light on. Connor glanc-ed at his image in the old wooden-framed mirror on the wash stand, wondering why he didn't look any different. He *felt* different. He felt like crowing at the top of his voice, because the feel-ing of euphoria hadn't yet left him. He couldn't believe that he had been such a success. He'd thought they might scrape by as a band, but he hadn't known all the words of every song and a couple of times he'd had to improvise. He wasn't sure what made him do it, but each time he couldn't remember words, he looked at a girl in the crowd and said, 'Rock me, baby' or 'Sweet rocking baby ... rocking mama.' For some reason, it had worked like a charm and by the end of the evening the girls were screaming every time he stepped up to the front of the stage. At the end they had crowded to the stage and asked him to sign their autograph books.

He had felt as if he were dreaming. When they left the gig and Terry gave him not ten but twenty pounds, he'd just stared at the money.

'Why the extra?' he asked.

'Because you earned it,' Terry said. 'We've all got the same, but the manager booked us again next month – providing you were the lead singer.'

Connor pocketed the money. He didn't resent the fact that Terry had tried to get him to work for less, because he would have been satisfied with the ten pounds he'd been promised, but he would make sure he got his share in future.

'I don't see why not,' he said. 'I'll join the band on one condition: Phil is in too. I don't want to take his place. We can share the lead spots. I'll do the raunchy stuff that suits me and he can do the ballads.'

'We'll hear what he has to say when he gets back,' Terry said. 'I'm glad you're up for it. You can come to regular practice every week and

111

then you will know the words. You did pretty good for a first time – and everyone forgets the words sometimes.'

'I'm going to buy a record player at the week-end,' Connor said. 'Should I get a guitar too?'

'I'll meet you in Ely at two on Saturday,' Terry said. 'I'll come with you to Miller's and see what they've got. You want something that looks good even if you're only going to play a few chords.'

'I'm going to teach myself,' Connor said. 'If you show me a couple of times, I'll pick up enough for what I need.'

'What will your brother say to you taking time off to practise?'

He won't care as long as I'm around when he needs me. 'I'll have to practise out in the barn, though, because I should keep the kids awake,' Connor told him and grinned. 'I don't think Alice would appreciate that if she'd just got them to sleep.'

'That is the trouble with living at home,' Terry agreed. 'We have to practise in the garage, but one day I'm going to have my own pad – once we start earning real money. I'd love a recording studio of my own.'

'That would cost thousands!'

'Yeah, I know. It's just a dream at the moment, but one day I'll get there. Gigs like this don't pay much, but some of them pay as much as a thousand pounds a night.'

'Twenty pounds is as much as I earn in six weeks as a labourer, though I can earn extra piece-work when the potato lifting starts.'

'Peanuts compared to what is out there,' Terry replied. 'I've got a feeling we're on our way, Connor. The girls loved you tonight. If you work on your act, you could be big. The big stars in America earn hundreds of thousands of dollars from their records – maybe even millions!'

'A million dollars – what does that look like?'

'Unbelievable,' Terry said. 'I promise you it is out there – all we have to do is reach high enough.'

Connor laughed, because he hadn't truly believed his new friend. Terry was excited now, but one swallow didn't make a summer – next time the girls might be harder to impress.

Thinking about girls reminded Connor that he was meeting Sarah the next evening. She would be waiting outside the Rex cinema for him in Ely and the thought of her made him feel hot inside. One of Sarah's smiles was worth all that screaming nonsense at the gig.

Daniel had heard his brother come in. He frowned as he peered at the bedside clock in the darkness; the hands were luminous and he could just make out the hour. Connor was late. He would need some calling in the morning if he was going to be up in time for the milking.

Daniel cursed under his breath, because he knew he wouldn't get off to sleep again for ages. If this was going to be a regular thing ... For a moment he felt irritated with Connor, but then he realized that he wasn't angry with his brother for staying out late. Connor was entitled to make something of himself if he could. What was really bothering Daniel was the fact that he'd given that money to Maura. He had given in to her blackmail – and he had an uncomfortable feeling that it wouldn't stop there. Once you let a blackmailer get their hooks into you, they didn't let go.

Daniel turned over on his side, his mind going over his problem. He hadn't had much choice, because he didn't want Alice to be hurt. It had only happened once and it was a long time ago. Maybe he was a fool. He should have just told her and got it over with. The extra five hundred pounds would have helped him through the next few months. He'd taken on some work for neighbouring farmers, but he knew it wouldn't pay much. He couldn't charge the full rates. If he did, he wouldn't have any customers. He would only be able to charge properly once he had a garage and was seen as a business. At the moment he was just Good Old Dan, who did favours for mates and charged a couple of quid for parts.

He pulled a wry face in the darkness. Was he a loser? Was that why nothing ever went the way he planned? Poor old Henry had been a loser, but Clay was a winner. He'd grabbed the best of the land and got away with it, because Henry had wanted him out of the family business after their father died. Yet Daniel didn't want to be like his brother. He couldn't make himself do people down and the thought of what Clay had done to their stepmother turned him sick to his stomach.

If you had to be ruthless to be a winner, then maybe he was a loser. He sighed again, willing

114

himself to sleep. He had a lot of work waiting and he needed to be fresh in the morning.

Damn Maura! She wouldn't get another penny out of him, whatever she did...

Alice lay listening to the sounds of Daniel's steady breathing. He seemed to have gone off at last. She supposed it was Connor coming in late that had woken him. She had felt Daniel turning restlessly in the bed beside her, but she hadn't said anything, because she was too tired to get up and make tea.

Sally was teething and she'd had trouble getting her to settle. Alice loved all her children dearly, but there was no doubting that they took over your life, took everything you had and then demanded more. Sometimes she wished they hadn't had so many – at least not so close together. They ought to have stopped at three, but then she wouldn't have Sally, and she adored her baby.

No, she wouldn't want to part with any of them, Alice decided. Sally would be through the difficult stages soon and then she would have more time to herself. It wouldn't be so bad if they lived in the village. Living on a farm made so much extra work because the men tramped in mud every time they came for a cup of tea, and there were always people coming and going in the yard. Dan always invited them in for a cup of tea and Alice usually provided cake or biscuits she had made herself. People told her what a wonderful cook she was, but sometimes she seemed to do nothing but cook and clean.

Alice smothered the sigh that rose to her lips. It must be nice to live the way Emily did in that lovely big house of hers. She had people to clean and cook for her and her only son was at boarding school ... Alice frowned as she wondered if Emily ever got lonely. She was always busy, of course – too busy too visit her family as much as she would like – but was that enough for her?

She must be mad thinking about things like that at this hour! In another three hours she would have to get up and start work again. Alice smiled and turned over, closing her eyes. She had enough problems of her own without thinking about Emily's.

She knew it was going to be a busy day, because Dan had told her to expect visitors.

Emily saw her guest sitting in the front garden. His easel was set with a large board and the quality paper he used for his watercolours. He had been working on the same painting for a few days now. As yet she hadn't seen it nor had she asked, because it seemed rude, but she was growing curious. She decided to walk down to him and remind him that they had some friends coming for dinner that evening.

Alan looked up as she approached and smiled. Emily's heart caught, because his smiles had seemed very intimate of late and she thought they were becoming good friends.

'I thought I should remind you we have people coming this evening.'

'I hadn't forgotten,' Alan said and drew his hand back, studying the picture. 'I'm not sure whether this looks right. Tell me what you think, Emily. It is supposed to give an impression of the house from a distance rather than pick out every detail.'

Emily went to stand behind him. She caught her breath as she looked and saw something so beautiful that she felt tears in her eyes.

'That is quite, quite lovely,' she said in hushed tones. 'I had no idea you could paint so well, Alan.'

'I've always dabbled a bit but never had the time to get serious about it, but I think I may now. I've decided that I enjoy doing nothing but pleasing myself, Emily. I believe I shall spend the rest of my life doing it – and I shall travel.'

Emily couldn't stop looking at the painting. It appealed to something inside her, and she knew that this was how she saw the house when she closed her eyes and thought about it – as if through a haze of sunlight that blended everything to a soft blur.

'Those colours are so muted they just make you feel that you are looking through a veil and give the house a mystery that is intriguing. Vanbrough has been painted many times, but I like this better than all those formal landscapes Vane acquired.'

'Then it will be my pleasure to give it to you when it is finished,' Alan said. He wiped his hands and began to gather his bits and pieces. 'Would you carry my box, Emily? I don't want to smudge this and bits of it are still wet.'

'Yes, of course. The weather has been so glorious for you, Alan. I am not sure how long it will last.'

'Not much longer. I am sure I can feel a chill in the air. I shall leave when my picture is finished. I have plans to make, places to visit.'

'So soon? I've got used to having you here – and I like it.'

'I have loved every minute, dearest Emily, but I think I should make the most of what time I have left to me. If I am spared, I shall return for Christmas – if you will have me?'

'You must know the answer,' Emily said. She gave him a companionable look as they walked to the house together. 'I am going to miss you very much.'

'I shall miss you too. I would ask you to travel with me, but that would not be fair. You cannot leave Vanbrough.'

'No, I can't. At least, only for short periods. Are you sure you feel well enough to travel, Alan?'

'I am feeling much better. It must be the peace and quiet I've had here,' he said. 'Don't look so sad, Emily. Christmas is only just over three months away now – and I've been here more than a month already.'

'Have you? It only seems like a few days,' Emily told him. 'Well, you must do as you please, of course, but I shall miss you.'

'I'll send you a postcard, probably several.' Alan smiled. 'And I shall come for Christmas if I can.'

'Come whenever you wish. This is as much your home as ours,' Emily told him.

'You have certainly made it feel like home.'

His eyes met hers. 'I probably shouldn't say this, Emily, but I've fallen in love with you. No, don't bother to answer, my dear. I am too old and too worn out to be of any use to a lovely woman like you. You still have many years ahead of you. What I wanted to say was that you mustn't waste them. I know you love this place, and you are keeping a promise to Vane – but if the chance for happiness comes along, take it with both hands.'

'Alan...' Tears caught at her throat. She was filled with emotion and hardly knew what to say. He didn't require an answer, but he deserved one. 'I am very fond of you...'

'Fond isn't enough, Emily. I had no right to say anything, but I wanted you to know – just in case we don't meet again.'

Emily blinked as the tears stung behind her eyes, but she didn't cry. 'Of course we shall meet again. You will come for Christmas. I shall not take no for an answer.'

Alan laughed. 'I shall certainly try – and now let us forget this foolishness. I don't want to spoil my last few days with you.'

Changing for dinner that evening, Emily thought about what Alan had told her. His natural affection had made her realize that she could not continue to deceive him. He ought to know the truth about Robert. Alan was Lord Vane and it was wrong that he shouldn't know it. Emily had kept the secret for too many years, but circumstances demanded that she tell him the truth now.

She went downstairs when she was ready, finding Alan alone in the library. He was looking at the books in the poetry section and he turned with a book in his hand as she entered.

'Are you aware that this is a first-edition Byron? I've noticed several rare volumes, Emily. If you are ever in need of more money, you might find the answer on these shelves.'

'I would hate to sell any of Vane's precious books,' Emily said with a rueful look. 'I didn't know he had some first editions, but I knew that some of them could be valuable. I've had some pictures valued – just things from the attic – and I think they will keep us going for a while.'

'This place is far too expensive to be viable these days,' Alan told her. 'It must be a constant headache for you.'

'Yes, it is...' She hesitated. 'Alan, there is something I must tell you, but first I want to ask what you would have done with Vanbrough if Vane had left it to you.'

'I should have sold it,' Alan replied frankly. 'Vane knew it. We argued more than once because I told him it was a liability. My advice was to pull the wings down and refurbish the main wing – make it into a sensible house that would be comfortable to live in. He told me once that he would rather leave it to the nation than see me get my hands on it...' Alan lifted his brows. 'Does that set your mind at rest, my dear? I would not have cared for the place as you do – even though I enjoy visiting.'

'Thank you. But there is something you ought to be told...'

'Only if you wish it.' Alan smiled oddly. 'You should know that Amelia came to me with a garbled tale of Robert not being Simon's son. I told her that I simply wasn't interested.'

'If what she told you was true, it would mean that *you* are Lord Vane and not Robert.'

Alan gave a soft, mocking laugh. 'Do you imagine that interests me, Emily? I suppose Vane knew what he was doing. The wording of his will was quite specific – the estate and money was left to your son. He did not use the word grandson, which was perhaps a little odd.'

'Amelia threatened to tell you, but you've never said anything and I thought she had just forgotten about it.'

'Why should I say anything? Vane had the right to leave his estate where he chose. If he had left it to me, I should have found it too much of a burden. I think you were the perfect choice of custodian, Emily – and when Robert is older he may choose whether to continue or to sell. He will need to earn a great deal of money elsewhere if he wishes to keep this place going.'

'It is his home. He loves it, as I do. I think he will try to keep going if he can.'

'Agriculture won't sustain the estate. Times have changed, my dear. You will find it increasingly difficult to manage as the years go by.'

'I promised Vane to keep it intact for as long as I could, but once Robert is old enough he can decide for himself.' Emily looked at him curiously. 'Aren't you the tiniest bit angry that you were cheated of the title?'

'Not in the slightest. It would not have suited me,' Alan said. He turned his head as he heard voices in the hall, and then offered his arm. 'I

121

believe our guests have arrived, Emily. Shall we join them?'

'Yes, of course.' She took his arm, looking at him with affection. 'You really are the nicest man I know, Alan. I do hope you will come to visit me often.'

'If I had more time, I should ask you to marry me,' Alan told her. 'It wouldn't be fair or right, but it is what I should like – to spend my last years with you.'

'Oh, Alan, I am so fond of you...' Emily sighed. 'I know you want to travel, and I cannot spare the time at the moment, but there is nothing to stop us being the best of friends.'

'I think I should like a little more than that,' Alan said. 'But I shall not press you for an answer. 'Perhaps at Christmas...'

Emily nodded but said nothing as they went into the hall to greet their guests.

'So you're a member of the Bad Boys now,' Sarah said and giggled as Connor grinned. He was so good-looking and so exciting! They had just left the Rex cinema in Market Street and were walking back to her house hand in hand. This was the third time Connor had taken her to the pictures, and she'd seen him twice at the club. She really felt as if she were his girlfriend now. 'Is it as much fun as it sounds?'

'Yes – and no,' Connor told her. 'I enjoy the gigs but the practising is difficult to fit in sometimes, because we're into the potato harvesting now and I have to work longer hours. Terry and the others are annoyed if I can't get there at the start.'

'Can't you explain to your brother that you need more time off?'

'It isn't just my brother,' Connor said. 'Some of the men from the village help out with our harvesting, so I have to return the favour. Besides, Dan works even longer hours than I do. After he brings the load back to the yard he starts work on his job as a mechanic.'

'I remember, you told me he restores cars.'

'Yes, but he also does repairs for other people. He has two tractors in the yard at the moment that he is working on – and a van. Dan is really good with engines. If he had his own garage, he would be at it full-time. He might earn some decent money then.'

'My father was complaining about his car the other day,' Sarah said thoughtfully. 'He said the man he usually goes to is thinking of giving up soon, and he was complaining because the other garage charges twice as much.'

'Dan charges too little,' Connor said. 'I've told him that he should ask more now he's doing it as a business, but he doesn't like to charge a lot when he's dealing with friends. If he had the garage, it would be different, because he would bill them, as other people do.'

'Well, he will have to be more professional when it comes to charging,' Sarah said. 'My father doesn't do favours for friends. If they want a building job done, they get a proper estimate same as everyone else.'

'Makes sense to me. Dan will never make a proper living until he starts doing the same. I'll have a word with him, see if I can talk some sense into him.'

Sarah hugged his arm. They were nearly at her house and he hadn't said anything about their next date. 'Will you be at the club next week?'

'No, we have a gig that night. Terry says it is important, but he says that every week. I'll meet you at the cinema if you like on Friday.'

'We should go to the Public Room next week,' Sarah said. 'They've got *Calamity Jane* on. I think it will be good. I like musicals – especially Doris Day.'

'Yeah, right,' Connor said. It wasn't a film he really wanted to see, but it was a chance to sit in the back row with his arm around Sarah. She had let him kiss her a couple of times that evening. She seemed to enjoy their dates, and he knew that he wanted to be with her, even though it was too soon to think of anything more just yet. They came to a halt outside her door. He leaned forward and kissed her on the lips. Sarah kissed him back and he took her in his arms, holding her close. The smell of her hair was so good! 'Sarah, I—'

'Sarah!' The front door opened and they moved hastily apart as Mrs Jenkins looked at them. 'Your father is home. You had better come in at once!'

'Sorry, Mum. This is Connor Searles. We went to the pictures and he walked me home.'

'Good evening, Mr Searles,' Mrs Jenkins said. 'Sarah must bring you to tea one Sunday. She has to come in now, because her father has been asking where she is.'

'I'll see you next week,' Sarah told him. 'Bye, Connor.'

'Bye, Sarah.'

Connor turned away as she disappeared into the house and the door shut behind her. Obviously, Sarah had told her mother who she was seeing but not her father. Connor wasn't sure how Mr Jenkins would feel about it when he knew. He was a successful builder and well respected; Connor was a labourer and his wages were too low for him to be thought of as a prospective husband for Sarah.

The extra money Connor had been earning had been put back into things he needed to keep up with the other members of the band – and to buy cinema tickets and chocolates for Sarah. He would try to save something next time he got paid, but he knew that it was going to be a long time before he could afford to look for his own house.

'Who were you with?' Sarah's father asked as she walked into the kitchen. 'I didn't know you were courting. Why haven't you said anything?'

'We've only been out a few times, but...'

Her father's gaze narrowed. 'Who is he? Does he have prospects?'

'His brother has land and he works for him – but he sings in a band too. We don't go out much, because he is always working.'

'I want to meet him. I want to see what kind of a man he is – and if he has any chance of giving you the sort of life you've been used to.'

Sarah stared at him, feeling sick. 'Is everything a question of money?' she asked. 'Supposing I said I was in love with him?'

'You said you hardly knew him,' her father said. 'How can you be in love if you don't know him?'

'Connor is nice,' Sarah said, a hint of defiance in her face. 'He is polite and he treats me right. I do know him, Dad, even if we haven't gone out much.'

'I've always thought you a sensible girl,' her mother said. 'I knew you were seeing someone, but I thought it might be that young man you told me about at the youth club.'

'Phil isn't as nice as you think. His father may be rich, but he ... I don't like him. I want to see Connor – and if he asks me, I'll get engaged to him.'

'Not unless he asks me, you won't,' her father said and frowned. 'I'm not against him, Sarah – and I wouldn't be against your getting married next year sometime. However, I want to know what prospects he has. If he doesn't earn much, he might like to come and work for me. If he is prepared to work hard, he could be a big help to me.'

'Do you mean it, Dad?' Sarah flew to hug him. She glanced at her mother and saw that she was frowning. 'I know it seems sudden, but Connor is the first man I've ever really liked.'

'Well, be a good, sensible girl and we'll see how things go.'

'I don't want Sarah to get married too soon,' Mrs Jenkins said. 'She will only be twenty next

126

year; there is plenty of time for her to meet the right sort of man...'

'Connor is right for me,' Sarah said. 'You don't know him – but I know he is the only one I want.'

Five

'I've got a rush on with this tractor,' Daniel said to Connor the following Wednesday morning. 'You'll have to milk the cows when you get back from riddling.'

'I can't do it, Dan. I told you I had a gig on this evening. It is important. If I do the milking, I shall be late.'

'You're always rushing off somewhere these days. It's all very well, Connor, but I can't run this place on my own. You will have to cancel this time.'

'I can't do that – it would let them down. Sorry, Dan. You'll have to manage for yourself.'

'Is that your last word?'

'Yes it is. I don't mind putting in an hour or two extra when I'm not going out, but the gig comes first. I earn good money from the band.'

'And I don't pay you enough, I suppose?'

'I didn't say that.'

'No, but it was implied.' Daniel glared at him. 'All right, clear off to your damned gig and leave me with the chores. I scarcely see Alice these days as it is.'

'That isn't my fault. You took on the extra work, Dan. I'll help where I can but I'm not always going to be around...'

Daniel stared after his brother as he strode off,

got into his car and set off down the drove. He was angry as he slammed into the van and followed, though a part of his annoyance was due to the fact that his brother was right. Connor earned far more singing with the band than he did on the land. It wasn't right to expect him to give up all his free time, but that was exactly what Daniel had to do if he was ever going to make enough to pay back the money he had borrowed from Frances.

Daniel had spent three hundred pounds on tools and machinery he needed for repairing cars and the tractors that stood in the yard. Another four hundred had gone on five cars he intended to restore when he had the chance. He had paid the bank five hundred pounds to settle his overdraft, and after a few bills were paid that left him less than two hundred pounds.

He tried not to think about Maura or the fact that he had a son he had never seen. If she came asking for more money, he would have to fob her off with something, but he couldn't afford to pay what she wanted. Alice was already curious about the money he had been spending. She had thrown one or two hints about Frances at him, and if she got curious enough to ask, she would tell him he ought to give the money back. There was no way he could do it, and that meant he had to make a success out of the car repairs. He needed Connor to do his share and more but it looked as if his brother had ideas of his own. Daniel didn't blame him, but if Connor was dashing off all the time, it was going to make things even harder for him.

Connor felt guilty as he left that evening. Daniel was still hard at work on one of the tractors he'd promised for the next day. If it wasn't for the gig, Connor would have finished the chores for him, but he'd promised his friends he would be on time. Terry had said that this gig was very important and he'd told them that there might be a bonus for them all if they were lucky.

Connor had started to save towards a present for Sarah. He had seen a pretty gold locket and chain in a local jeweller's shop and he wanted to buy it for her next week. He could put a deposit down and then pay weekly, but he didn't want to get into debt. If he earned twenty pounds again this evening, he would be able to buy the locket outright. After that he might start saving for a ring, because he was thinking of asking Sarah to get engaged at Christmas.

When he joined his friends outside the venue in Cambridge, he was surprised to see other bands unloading their gear.

'I didn't know anyone else was playing this evening,' he said with a frown. 'How much are they paying us, then, Terry?'

'Nothing,' Terry said. 'It's a competition. We are competing against other bands for the prize of ... five hundred pounds and the chance of a record deal!'

'Five hundred...' Connor stared at him. 'That is a fortune! I'm not sure about the record deal but I wouldn't mind a share of the prize.'

'It's a hundred quid each if we win,' Terry said. 'The record deal could be worth thousands if we

130

got lucky.'

'Wouldn't that mean going away?' Connor asked. 'We would have to turn professional, go into it full-time...'

'That is my dream,' Terry told him and clapped him on the shoulder. 'If we win, it will be down to you, Connor. I've never expected to win before, because Phil wasn't good enough – but you are.'

'Don't get your hopes too high,' Connor warned. 'I've just seen the Flying Dragons unloading; they are terrific and very popular. I doubt if we can win against them.'

'Don't sell yourself short,' Terry told him. 'Just do what you've been doing every week since we started and we'll stand a good chance. If it doesn't come off, we might get second prize and that's two hundred and fifty.'

'I'm up for it,' Sam said. 'But it's the record deal I'm interested in. If we get that, we shall all be rich!'

Connor slung his guitar over his shoulder and picked up a part of the drum kit to carry inside. He felt a bit annoyed with Terry, because if they didn't come first or at least second this evening, he wouldn't earn anything – and he could have gone riddling to earn an extra fifteen bob.

Backstage, it was crowded because there were six bands entered in the contest that evening. Glancing round, Connor took stock. He realized that he recognized most of the faces; they had all played at the club at least once and he knew their stuff pretty well. Four of the groups were mediocre, but the Flying Dragons were a semiprofessional band and he knew they were good.

Connor didn't think they had a hope of winning, but he reckoned they ought to be a good second. He cheered up a bit as Terry gave him the thumbs-up. Fifty pounds was a lot better than twenty. He would put on the best performance he could and hope they managed to come out with a prize.

Connor stepped forward when their name was called out. He had been practising the new number all week and hoped he wouldn't forget any of the words. It was the song Elvis Presley was pushing up the charts in America and it was beginning to be popular over here. Connor had started to let his sideburns grow and, having seen a clip about Elvis on the newsreel at the pictures, he had seen that the singer moved in much the same way as he'd done instinctively from the start. Terry had told him he looked a bit like the American. Connor didn't think he did, but they both had dark hair and they could both take a song and make it sound sexy.

He stepped up to the microphone, gave his hips a little wiggle and smiled. A girl screamed and one of them called his name. Connor smiled at her.

'"That's All Right Mama",' he said and his words were drowned by a chorus of screaming girls, all of them now calling his name. 'Hush, baby,' he murmured. 'Here we go...'

The band started up and Connor belted the number out just the way he'd heard it over and over again that week on his record player. He'd played it so many times that Alice had threatened to break the record if she heard it once more. He hoped it had paid off.

As the music died away there was silence and then a storm of applause and clapping as the girls started chanting his name.

'Connor ... Connor ... Connor ... Connor...' They clapped and stamped their feet.

'Thank you ... Thank you!' Connor said. 'We have one more song for you this evening and it is Big Joe Turner's "Shake, Rattle and Roll".'

Connor belted the number out and the fans went wild. The girls were screaming his name and they were jiving in front of the stage and down the aisles. One girl threw something on stage. Connor bent down to pick up the artificial rose, dropped a kiss on the petals and tossed it back to her.

'Shake me, baby,' he sang. 'Come on and rattle my bones...'

Once again he finished to wild applause. He grinned and blew kisses to the girls.

'Rock me, baby, hot rocking mama.'

The girls were still screaming as he turned and walked from the stage. As he turned towards the dressing room, one of the Flying Dragons came up to him.

'Nice try,' he drawled. 'It's a pity the rest of your lot aren't up to your standard – but if you want to join a good group, ask me after the show. I could always use another singer.'

'Thanks, but I'm happy where I am,' Connor said. 'Good luck.'

The man looked at him as if he suspected he

was mocking him, but Connor genuinely expected the Flying Dragons to win. Their lead guitar was magic and the singer was pretty good. Besides, Connor had never considered giving up his job to go on tour around the country, which was probably what they would have to do if they won. He could just imagine what Daniel would have to say about that!

He went back to the dressing room and drank some squash he had brought with him. It was warm and too sweet, but it was better than nothing and he was thirsty. After wiping off the sweat, he went back to the side of the stage and listened as the Flying Dragons were announced. Terry and the others were listening too, their gear stacked out of the way.

A burst of applause greeted the new group and then they started playing and singing. Their first number was a catchy tune that had made it into the charts in America and the applause was generous when they finished.

The lead singer was speaking. 'This is a number of our own – it's called "Flying with Dragons"...'

He was cheered and applauded; a couple of girls screamed, but when the music started Connor was disappointed. The beat was there but the words didn't make much sense and the music sounded odd to him. He waited for the girls to start cheering but they didn't, and when the number ended the applause was not enthusiastic.

'I reckon they've blown it,' Terry said behind him. 'That Elvis Presley number you did was terrific and the second was great. I think we've got it in the bag.'

'I don't know.' Connor stared at him uneasily. If they won by some fluke, Terry would expect him to sign the contract and that was going to be awkward. It would mean leaving Daniel in the lurch. He hadn't expected anything like this when he joined the band, just a few gigs that put some extra money in his pocket.

'Quiet ... They're announcing the winners,' Terry said and grabbed his arm. 'Listen.'

'We are pleased to announce that the judges are unanimous in their verdict,' the announcer said. 'In second place and the winner of two hundred and fifty pounds is ... the Flying Dragons.'

'I told you! It has to be us,' Terry hissed, his face tense with excitement.

Connor watched as the other band members went on stage and graciously accepted their prize, even though he saw some sour looks come his way. He felt Terry's grip tighten on his arm as the announcer spoke again.

'Our winners this year are ... the Bad Boys!'

'Yes!' Terry punched the air and shoved Connor in front of him. 'Come on, Tiger, let's go get 'em.'

Connor found himself pushed on stage first. This time the girls were screaming like crazy. As he walked forward, the other members of the group hanging back as he took centre stage, a shower of objects came flying on to the stage: flowers, scarves and what looked suspiciously like a pair of silk French knickers.

Connor bent down to scoop them up and held

them to his cheek, then threw them back into the crowd. One girl screamed loudly and grabbed for them. Another girl tried to grab them from her and a scuffle broke out.

Connor picked up other items and threw them into the little crowd and the incident was turned to laughter as the girls scrambled to get them.

'Sweet rocking mamas,' he said and blew kisses to the girls. 'I love ya all...'

'The winners, ladies and gentlemen!'

Behind him, their gear had been brought back to the stage and the music started up once more. Conner grinned as he took his position, letting his eyes sweep over the crowd and settling on one pretty girl.

'Sweet rocking baby,' he crooned. 'Love me tonight...'

They played three of their most popular numbers and were at last allowed to leave the stage after each of them had said a few words of appreciation.

Connor headed straight for the dressing room afterwards. He was so thirsty and all he wanted was to splash some cool water on his face. He was just drying off when the others came in. They were grinning like Cheshire cats, pushing each other and laughing.

'We did it!'

'Yeah – we're gonna be rich!'

'The contract has to be signed by next week,' Terry said. 'I've been looking through it. I think I ought to get my father to run an eye over it. He is a lawyer's clerk and he will know if they are trying to pull a fast one – there's a bit about agents' fees that I'm not sure of.'

'We don't need an agent,' Sam said. 'How much are they paying us up front?'

'Five thousand pounds.'

His words produced a shocked silence.

'Give me the pen and I'll sign now,' Sam said. 'I've never had that sort of money.'

'Hang on until my father has a look,' Terry warned. 'It sounds good but they want fifty per cent of all future fees for setting it up. I'm not sure that it is a good deal for us. If our records take off, we could be earning hundreds of thousands of pounds...'

'Sounds good to me,' Ray said. 'I'll sign if the rest of you do.'

Jack and Sam murmured agreement.

'But they will be taking half our money,' Terry said. 'I think it ought to be more like twenty-five per cent, but I'll know after Dad reads it through. We've got a week to sign – what do you think, Connor?'

'I'm not sure I can sign,' Connor said. 'I have a job...'

'You can't throw away the chance of a lifetime,' Terry said, staring at him in dismay. 'Even as the contract stands, we will earn far more money than you've ever dreamed of, Connor. If things go well for us, we could be rich beyond our wildest dreams.'

'It sounds all right, but I'm not sure. I wouldn't sign until your father has read it, Terry – and even then I'll have to think about it.'

'They don't want us without you,' Terry said. 'Don't let us down, Connor. It's our big chance.'

'Let your father read it and I'll tell you when we practise,' Connor said. 'I shall have to talk to my brother. If I leave, he will need to take on a new man in the yard.'

'If the records take off, you can pay him out of pocket change,' Terry said. 'Don't be a fool, Connor. This could mean a whole new life for all of us. We shall go places – maybe America.' His expression was pleading. 'Don't let us down ... please.'

Connor hesitated. 'If your father can negotiate a better contract for us, I'm in, but I don't see why anyone should take a fifty-per-cent cut of our earnings.'

'Yeah! Now you're talking,' Terry said and grinned at him. 'I knew you wouldn't let us down.'

Connor turned away. He had a sick feeling at the pit of his stomach. He would be a fool to turn down this chance of a lifetime, but it meant leaving his home and family – and Sarah.

It was late when he let himself into the house. He tried to be as quiet as he could but he wanted a drink of water to take upstairs. Singing on stage could be thirsty work, and he was hungry. He hunted in the cool pantry and found some of Alice's apple pie. He had cut himself a chunk and was eating it when Daniel came into the kitchen.

'What time do you call this?' he demanded. 'You've woken Sally and it took Alice ages to get her off.'

'Sorry.' Connor finished the piece of pie.

'We're later tonight because we won a competition. I got a hundred pounds as my share of the prize.'

'Good grief!' Daniel looked thunderstruck. 'That's great for you, Connor. I'm very pleased – but this coming in late can't go on.'

'I shouldn't worry about it, Dan,' Connor said, angry because his brother had taken his good news and tossed it aside. 'I shan't be living here much longer.'

'What do you mean? Where are you going to live?'

Connor walked past him without speaking. He was too angry to say another word, because if he did he might say more than he meant.

Connor thought about his decision all week. Daniel hadn't said any more about their argument and he had kept out of his brother's way as much as possible. He was going to have to make a decision and it wouldn't be easy. Dan had been there for him after the war when the family had been splitting apart. He had hated living with Frances. She was on at him the whole time. He knew now that she had been going through a hard time, but as a young, rebellious youth he hadn't liked the way that she questioned his every move. He had got on well with Dan and Alice until he joined the band, but the late nights did wake the kids, and even if he hadn't been offered the contract, he would have had to think about getting his own place.

Connor half wished that they could just go on as they had been. He was earning enough to give him a good start, but if he went along with the band, he would be earning far more. His winnings that evening would buy a better gold locket than the one he'd been thinking of buying Sarah – and a deposit towards the ring he wanted for her. If he signed the contract, he could buy a really good one. It would mean he would be away for long periods – would Sarah accept that and still be his girl?

Connor had told her about the win when they went to the pictures that week, but he hadn't said anything about the contract. He had to make his own mind up about that – but if Terry came through with a better contract, he didn't really have much choice. He couldn't let the others down.

He wasn't really surprised when Terry turned up at the farm a few days later. He knew at once that his friend was excited and his heart began to thump like crazy.

'So what did they say?'

'I didn't need to push them. When I told them you wouldn't sign unless they reduced the fees and put up the advance they came through with a new offer. Apparently, they want you, Connor. An agent saw you that night and he has offered to take us if we don't go with the contest organizers. He rang me this morning. You won't believe what he offered us.'

'Try me. I thought that offer was good. I just wasn't sure about the fifty per cent.'

'They've offered thirty per cent now – and you get ten thousand on signing and we get five thousand pounds each!'

Connor felt as if someone had knocked the breath out of his body. Terry had to be joking.

'You're pulling my leg. That is thirty thousand pounds altogether...' Connor felt so stunned he hardly knew what to say. 'It doesn't seem fair on the rest of you that I get so much more.'

'Don't worry about that, Con,' Terry told him. 'We all know you're the star. Last year we didn't even get second prize. Besides, they are all getting five times what they expected.'

Connor looked at him uneasily. It was such a fabulous offer that he couldn't refuse. His friends would be left in limbo if he walked away now and that wasn't fair to them. He was between a rock and a hard place, because he had to let someone down whatever he did.

'You're walking out on me just like that?' Daniel stared at him, his expression somewhere between shock and anger. 'You know I can't manage the farm and my repair work without you. Joe is all right but he needs direction. If one of us is with him, he works hard, but if you leave him on his own, he'll stand around and do nothing half the day.'

'You will have to employ someone else to take my place,' Connor told him. 'I'm sorry, Dan, but this is a real chance for me to make something of my life. They are paying me ten thousand pounds just to sign and we could earn many times that if the records start to sell as well as they seem to think they may.'

'Ten thousand! I don't believe you.' Dan looked stunned. 'Do you have any idea of what you can do with that sort of money?'

'Yes, of course I do. I'm going to open an account at the bank as soon as I get the cheque. I have to pay thirty per cent agent's fees but that still leaves a lot of money.' He hesitated, then, 'I know I'm letting you down, but I could help with the wages of a new man until you're on your feet...'

'No!' Daniel glared at him. 'Keep your damned money. I don't want charity. If you've been offered that much, you have to go. I can't stop you, but I hope you know what you're doing, Connor. From what I see in the papers some of these stars get into trouble. Stay away from drugs and don't drink too much.'

'I've got too much sense for that,' Connor said. 'I'm going to ask Sarah to get engaged now that I can afford a decent ring. We can't get married yet, because I'm going to be on the road with the group. We've been told we shall be playing at various theatres and ballrooms up and down the country for a lot more money than we used to get for a gig – and we start recording our first record next week.'

'Recording...' Daniel shook his head. 'This all sounds too good to be true to me, Connor. I hope you've checked the small print of this contract.'

'Terry's father did that for us. We're putting out a couple of singles in the next two months. If they get into the charts, we shall record an album and we might even get on the TV. There's a programme for new groups like us.'

'Well, good luck. I hope it works out well for you.'

'I'm sorry I'm letting you down. You and Alice have been good to me, Dan.'

'You've done your share and for little enough,' his brother said. 'I'm not sure how I shall manage once you've gone. Even if I can find someone to take your place, he won't do all the extra hours you did – unless I pay double rates and I can't afford that.'

'I know it won't be easy. If money would help...'

'No, I told you once. I don't want your money. It makes things difficult but I'll struggle through. I always have.'

'Yes, I know.' Connor was silent. He felt guilty for leaving his brother in the lurch, but he would be mad to turn down the money he'd been offered and the prospect of a bright future. 'Well, if you change your mind, I'll be back every so often, because I shall want to see Sarah.'

'Will she want to see you? Most girls want someone to take them out and buy them presents. If you aren't around, she may start looking for someone else.'

'I know.' Connor looked thoughtful. He had almost turned his friends down because he was afraid of Sarah's reaction, but he couldn't let this chance go. It was too important. 'I was going to wait for a while before I asked if she would get engaged, but I have to ask now, because otherwise I may lose her.'

'You're going away on tour with the band?' Sarah stared at him in dismay. 'But when shall I see you?'

'I'll get back every few weeks. It isn't what I'd planned or wanted, Sarah, but I have to take this chance while I can. Even if the records don't sell, I shall have a few thousand in the bank and I'll be able to buy us a nice house. And I got you this...'

Connor took the leather ring box from his pocket and held it out. Sarah eyed it hesitantly.

'You've already given me that lovely gold locket. I don't need presents, Con...'

'This is an engagement ring. I know it is a bit soon. I had planned to wait until nearer Christmas – but if I don't ask you now, you will think I don't care and look for someone else.'

'I wouldn't do that – as long as I know you care.' Sarah looked up at him, her eyes wide. 'Are you saying you love me?'

'Yes.' Connor bent his head. He took her lips in a sweet kiss that made her moan softly and lean into him. He felt himself harden, knowing that she must feel the bulge of his erection burning against her. She didn't flinch or move away, just stayed pressed against him, her lips slightly parted. 'Sarah, I want you so much, but I'm not going to ask you to do anything yet. It wouldn't be fair until I see how things are going. Once we've got our feet firmly on the road to the success, I can marry you and you can come on tour with me.'

'Dad wouldn't let me get married yet anyway,' Sarah said. She hesitated and then looked up at him. 'He has been saying he wants to meet you. I think you should come in and tell him what you've told me. He will expect you to ask for his consent before we get engaged.'

'Are you saying yes?'

Sarah smiled, her mouth soft and inviting. 'You know I love you, Con. I think I have from the moment you asked me to dance. But you have to speak to my father before I can wear your ring. I know he will be at home, because he told me.'

'I'll come in now if that is all right,' Connor said. 'I shan't get over again until Sunday afternoon. We'll go for a ride in the car then if you like? Maybe have a drink or something.'

'Yes, please.' Sarah looked upset. 'I am going to miss you so much! I was hoping we would see more of each other soon.'

'You must go out with your friends,' he said and touched her face. 'I shan't expect you to sit at home all the time – but don't let anyone bring you home. Remember you're my girl.'

'I shan't go with anyone else,' she vowed. 'You must promise not to go chasing girls. I know they will be all over you. You've already got a reputation and no one believes me when I say I'm your girl.'

'Well, you can show them your ring,' Connor told her, kissing her once more. 'Let's go inside and talk to your father...'

Sarah put her hand in his. 'I'm sure he will say yes when he knows that you have a real future ahead of you, Connor.'

Daniel worked until it was too dark to see what he was doing and then went into the house. Alice was sitting with a pile of mending, but she got up as soon as he came in and started to make a pot of tea.

'You will kill yourself if you keep working so hard,' she said. 'I know you've always dreamed of having a garage, Dan, but this isn't the way to do it.'

'I promised the tractor for tomorrow,' Daniel said. 'Besides, Connor won't be here to help out after Sunday. He is meeting his friends on Monday and they are going somewhere up north to a club. He says they will be playing at three different clubs and then they start work on their first record.'

'It is like something out of a film. It has all happened so fast – Connor must think he is dreaming.'

'I just hope it lasts for a while,' Daniel said, 'and that he doesn't spend all the money on daft things. If the records don't sell, he may be back looking for work on the land sooner than he imagines.'

'I am sure that won't happen. I always thought he had a lovely voice. I used to hear him singing in the yard or the bathroom. He is as good as some of those songs he plays on his record player.'

'He isn't bad,' Daniel said grudgingly. 'I just hope he doesn't get into trouble, Alice.'

'You're thinking he was a bit wild when he was young. He was unhappy, Dan. His father died and the family seemed to fall apart. Emily went away; you were in the army and he had to live with Frances – and she wasn't fit to look after him because she had troubles of her own.'

'Yes, I know,' Daniel agreed. 'He knuckled down to work once he came to live with us. I suppose I'm still thinking he is a boy but he isn't – and he was bound to leave us sooner or later. I can't afford to pay him a decent wage.'

'You will find it difficult to pay anyone more than you gave Connor. Does that mean you will have to put your repair and restoration business on hold for a while?'

'Yes, I think it does. I'll manage to do what I've got booked in if I work evenings, but after that ... well, the cars I intended to rebuild will have to wait.'

'You couldn't borrow some money?'

'I don't want to go to the bank.' Daniel sighed. 'The interest they charge is crippling. It has taken me this long to clear my name. I don't want to end up with the bank foreclosing on us.'

'Frances wouldn't lend you some money?'

'No.' Daniel turned his back to her as he washed the grease from his hands. 'I can't ask her, Alice. I shall manage somehow.'

How the hell he would ever repay her what he already owed, Daniel didn't know. He was owed about a hundred pounds for work he'd done for neighbouring farmers. He knew they would settle eventually but some of them would hang it out until the last minute, because they weren't in a much better state than he was himself.

If he could take the time to repair and rebuild the cars he'd bought cheaply, he would stand to make a good profit, but he had the cows to milk and the work in the fields was constant. Maybe once all the root crops were stored he could find a bit of time, but by then the evenings would be drawing in. Besides, it meant he had to leave Alice sitting alone hour after hour, and any woman would get fed up with that after a while.

He regretted giving that five hundred pounds to Maura. If he still had that in his pocket, he could have afforded to take on a full-time labourer to help with the work. As it was, he could only take on someone for a few hours a week. Joe was a good-hearted lad, but you couldn't leave him to do the milking alone – and that meant Daniel would be tied to the yard in a way he hadn't been since Connor left school.

He wished his brother had never got in with that band, but that was being selfish. He couldn't expect Connor to go on working for a pittance all his life, but at the moment he could see no way out of this mess.

Sarah was surprised that her father seemed to take to Connor. She had expected that he might ask a lot of questions, but she'd thought he might be rude. Instead, he had listened with interest as Connor told him about the record deal. He seemed impressed and he'd agreed that the engagement could go ahead, though he said she was too young to marry until the following summer.

'That suits me fine, sir. It will give me time to see where I'm going and to save something for the future. I want Sarah to have a nice house and all the things she is used to.'

After Connor had gone, Sarah went back to the kitchen. She sensed tension between her mother and father.

'Is something wrong? You did like him, didn't you, Dad?'

'He seems a sensible young man to me. His family used to be well off, but the war was difficult for a lot of people. The farm lost money and the bank foreclosed on them. That can happen to anyone. If Connor is willing to wait until next year – and he can afford to buy that house he promised – then I see no reason why we shouldn't have the wedding in June.'

'Thanks, Dad.' Sarah threw him a smile of gratitude. June was nine months away, but it was better than waiting until she was twenty-one.

'I think it is much too soon. But I suppose if you still want to marry him next year, I can't stop you...'

'I *shall* want to marry him,' Sarah said confidently. 'I love him.'

'That is all very well,' her mother said. 'But how are you going to be when he's away for weeks at a time? You won't know where he is or what he is doing.'

'Connor says he will telephone me – and he'll get back as often as he can.'

'Fine promises – as long as he keeps them.'

Sarah was thoughtful as she went upstairs to her room. She wished her mother hadn't put doubts in her mind. It was going to be awful knowing Connor was far away from her, singing to lots of screaming girls. She knew what went on at the gigs, because Janice had been to one of them and she'd delighted in telling her of the way he seemed to sing to one particular girl each time.

Sarah understood that her friends were jealous. She was the one with a good solid background, a better job and now a famous boyfriend – because she didn't doubt it would happen. She had seen how much people enjoyed Connor's singing at the club. She liked to listen to him too. She wished he didn't have to go away to do it, but she knew he was working for a better future for them.

All she could do was believe that he loved her and make the most of the time when he came home on a flying visit...

Emily sat with Alice's letter in her hand. The news about Connor was wonderful. It made Emily smile to think that her youngest brother might be on the road to fame and fortune. It was true that Connor had a good voice, but she had never expected to hear him singing on the radio or see his name up in lights. Apparently, he was going to be on the radio quite soon – and his first record was due for release this week.

He came home for a few hours at the weekend, Alice had written. *But he wasn't in the house more than a few minutes. He brought presents for us all and then went off to Ely to see his fiancée. He is engaged to a lovely girl – at least I've been told she is, but, of course, we haven't met her as yet. I'm not sure how she feels about all this, but Connor seems very happy – and he has changed so much. He is so confident and he looks as if he owns the world.*

I've had a letter from Frances asking us to stay at Christmas, but there is no possibility of our getting away. Dan is managing with that youth I told you of before and a man who comes in part-time to give him a hand with the milking. Thank goodness the potatoes are up. It cost more to get them up than usual, but Connor used to work so hard. We shall miss him terribly, but I think it is wonderful that he has this chance.

Emily read between the lines. She guessed that her sister-in-law was worried about Dan and the way things were going. She wished that they could come to her for Christmas, but she knew it was out of the question, and Frances had refused all her invitations to come and stay. Emily would have to make time to pop down there before Christmas. She would take a brace of pheasants from the estate and some gifts – and she would have to try to visit Alice and Dan too, even though she had guests coming for a few days after Boxing Day. If Alan came, they would be alone for Christmas Day itself. She had only received one postcard from France since he left and she had begun to wonder if he was feeling worse. Her hand hovered over the phone seconds before it rang.

'Emily.'

'Yes, Alan.' Emily laughed as she heard his voice. 'I was just thinking of telephoning to see if you were coming for Christmas?'

'I am ringing to confirm that I shall be there tomorrow – tea-time at the latest.'

'Oh, that is lovely,' Emily said. 'I am so glad.

We can plan the tree and the Christmas Eve party together.'

'I should enjoy that, my dear.'

'Are you feeling any better?'

'Yes, I am much better.' Alan replied. 'I think the complete rest has done the trick, Emily. I dare say I shall live for a few years yet.'

'I am so pleased.' Tears wet her cheeks. 'I am longing to see you!'

'You sound as if you mean that?'

'I do. Of course I do.'

'Good. Expect me tomorrow.'

Emily smiled as she replaced the receiver. Her trip to Frances would have to be postponed. She could visit Alice in the New Year, because she knew she was always welcome in their home. Frances might be put out if she didn't visit, but she had been invited to stay and it was her own fault if she chose to stay at the hotel.

Emily's heart was racing. She had thought about Alan so much in the months since he was last here and now she could hardly wait for him to arrive.

Six

Connor opened his eyes and glanced around the hotel bedroom. The floor was littered with his clothes; he'd dropped them as he took them off. The wonder was that he hadn't gone to bed fully dressed, he'd been so drunk. They'd been invited to a big party at a posh hotel. The man giving the party was by reputation a playboy millionaire and he had invited them to spend Christmas on his yacht, cruising the Mediterranean islands.

Most of the group had been disappointed that they couldn't go because they had several bookings at theatres all over the country. Connor had been able to refuse with an easy heart, because he wanted to go home on Christmas Eve and spend the next day with Sarah and her parents. He had been invited to spend the night and would have dinner with them on the day. After that, he might just have time to visit Alice and the children before heading back to Liverpool. They were booked into a popular venue for Boxing Night and then had two days to rehearse before it was back to the recording studio to start on their album.

Their lives were mayhem sometimes as they packed their things and moved from one booking to another. Connor thought he had never worked so hard in his life, but they were being paid at least five hundred pounds each time they did a live show, and he sometimes got double what the others were paid.

Connor still felt guilty about the difference and he had insisted that they were paid in equal shares from the sales of their records. Their first release, which had been a song written specially for them by an American composer, had gone to number eleven in the charts. Terry was disappointed that it hadn't reached the top, but the second had been released for Christmas and had a seasonal lyric. It was already at number three and they were hoping that it would go all the way this time, but they were up against some big names. Connor was amazed at how well they were doing, but he knew that Terry had his eye on the big time. A lot of young groups enjoyed a brief moment of fame and then disappeared. Terry wanted the Bad Boys to make it all the way to the top.

Dressing in his favourite black drainpipes, Connor found a girl's silk bra under a pile of his own clothing. He stared at it in bewilderment, because he was certain he'd been on his own when he came to bed. He knew that several girls had been hanging around him at the party, though he'd done his best to avoid getting into a clinch with them, because he wanted to keep his word to Sarah.

It was getting harder and harder to stop his name being linked with girls who sang on stage with them. The manager said it was good business to link female stars to them, because of the publicity. One girl called Tina had draped herself over him when they left a theatre in London, kissing his neck and rolling her eyes when she was asked if they were courting.

Connor had untangled her and walked away, refusing to answer questions, and the next day the papers were full of innuendo about a secret affair. Connor had phoned Sarah's home that night and told her it was a publicity stunt. He promised there was nothing in the story and Sarah had said it was all right, but she'd also sounded upset. He had bought her a diamond pendant for Christmas and he was praying that she would believe him when he told her that none of the girls he'd met on tour measured up to her.

He groaned as he rang down to room service for coffee. The time it took to get through was longer than it should be, even though this was one of the best hotels they had stayed in so far. His head was hammering. He must have been mad to drink so much, but there had been loads of booze and everyone kept giving him drinks. He knew that there had been drugs circulating at the party, but he wasn't interested in trying them.

Connor suspected that Sam and Ray might have snorted some kind of powder. He wasn't sure what it was but he had heard them mention heroin and cocaine. Terry stayed well clear, as did Jack and Connor – though even Terry had been pretty drunk when the taxi brought them back to the hotel.

Connor dumped the bra in the wastebasket.

One of the girls at the party must have shoved it in his pocket. It wouldn't be the first time. There were some fans that followed the band from one town to another and most of them were girls.

'Alan! It is so good to see you!' Emily cried as she hurried down the stairs to meet him. 'Let me look at you – yes, you look so much better. You must have done just what the doctor ordered.'

'Yes, I think I did,' Alan said. 'I've been painting, sitting in the sun, reading and drinking good wine. I should have done it years ago, Emily. I worked all hours for God knows how many years, and it was hard to switch off at first, but I am so pleased I did.'

'You make me slightly envious,' Emily said and leaned forward to kiss his cheek. Alan turned his head and their lips met. She was surprised, but she didn't pull away. The kiss was warm and sweet and it made her yearn for things she had forgotten. 'That was nice ... we should do it again later, Alan. Come into the parlour and have some tea. You must be frozen. It has turned very cold this past couple of days and you've just come from France.'

'I wish you could have been there with me. It was perfect but for the fact that the English Channel lay between us.'

'Oh, Alan...' Emily reached for his hand. 'I have become so very fond of you, my dearest. I think I may have fallen in love with you.'

'But do you love me enough to leave this house and come away with me?'

'Please don't ask me that question yet. I want

to enjoy having you here for Christmas, dearest Alan – and then we can talk about the future...'

Daniel saw Maura coming towards him as he walked from the cattle market into the adjoining street. He had hoped she would leave the area once she had the five hundred pounds, but it looked as if she had hung around. If she was hoping for more, she would be out of luck. He had given Alice money to buy presents for her and the children, and he had only a few pounds left from the money Frances had loaned him. Unless he could find time to finish one of the cars he was struggling to restore in the little time he had to spare from the land, he would be in trouble soon. At the moment he hadn't a hope in hell of paying his sister back.

He was tempted to get into his van and drive off, but he knew that Maura would come and find him in Stretton if he did that, and he would rather have this out here in Ely.

'What do you want?' he asked brusquely. 'I'm broke so there's no point in you asking for more.'

'You might have bought a present for your son.'

'Why? I don't know him. I've only your word that he is even mine.'

'You've seen the photos. You know he's yours right enough.'

'I thought you were leaving once you got your money.'

'I never said that.' Maura scowled. 'I've open-ed my own hairdressing shop in Market Street and I'm doing all right. I still want that other five hundred, but I'll wait a bit longer – providing you buy David a present and bring it round.'

Daniel put a hand in his pocket and brought out three pounds. 'This is all I've got. You had better buy him something. I have no idea what he likes. I'm not coming there; it would be pointless to start something I have no intention of continuing.'

'You would know what he likes if you'd visited,' Maura said. 'He is only a lad and he needs a father.'

'Well, find him one, then,' Daniel grated angrily. 'But don't expect me to take an interest. I've got my own family.'

He walked past her, got into his van and started the engine. She jumped out of the way as he reversed. He knew that he was risking trouble by refusing her what she asked, but he wasn't going to give her more money. His problems were mounting all the time and at the moment he couldn't see a way out of them. Some of his potatoes had got the blight and he'd had to dump them. Coupled with the fact that one of the cows had an infected teat and couldn't be milked, that was enough to cut his income by nearly a hundred pounds. Unless things started to pick up he would end up going to the bank for more money, because he couldn't ask Frances for another loan.

He would have to find time to work on the sports car he had almost finished. He knew it would sell once he could get it running sweetly. He might get two hundred and fifty pounds for it if he was lucky, and that would pay some outstanding feed bills and buy the manure he needed for next year's crops.

Daniel sighed as he drove home. The endless grind to try and make ends meet was wearing him down. He thought about Connor, who had sent a card to say he would pop in on Christmas Eve, and found that he envied his brother the freedom to come and go. He wasn't sure that he would enjoy Connor's life, but it must be better than being tied to a job he had come to hate. If he could take a risk, he would sell the fields and concentrate on his cars, but with four children to feed it was too much of a gamble. More and more people were buying cars these days, but there were still a lot of people who didn't own one. If he gave up the farm too soon, he might be jumping out of the frying pan into the fire – and yet it was wearing him out doing both jobs, and Alice had started to complain that she never saw him.

Alice stood outside the small hairdressing shop in Ely. She had asked her sister-in-law to make her an appointment to have her hair cut. Mary had her hair permed or Marcel-waved by a man at the shop in the High Street, but Alice's hair had a natural curl and she didn't want a man to do hers. Mary had told her about this new shop, and she'd booked an appointment for her. Alice had noticed that the ends had been splitting recently and because it was too long it had become greasy again.

Putting her doubts to the back of her mind,

Alice opened the door and went in. A young girl came towards her and took her coat.

'Mrs Searles? I am Shirley. I am going to cut and set your hair for you.'

'Oh ... thank you. I think my sister-in-law came in to see you?'

'Yes. She asked me if I could fit you in and I had time today.'

Alice nodded, still a little nervous. She was asked to sit in front of a basin and a gown was slipped over her dress, a towel around her shoulders. She held another small towel to her face as she bent over the basin to have her hair shampooed.

'Shall I put a beer rinse on for you, Mrs Searles? It will help with the grease.'

'Yes, please,' Alice said through the towel. 'It has been a bit of a mess recently...'

She straightened up as the girl brought her back and rough-dried her hair with the towel. It felt wet as it was put back round her neck. Her hair was combed straight and then the girl asked how much she wanted taken off.

'I think about two or three inches,' Alice said. 'I can look after my hair easily when it has been trimmed, but it is ages since I went to a hairdresser.'

'You should come at least every three months. But it will feel so much better once it is done. You have really nice hair, Mrs Searles.'

'Thank you.' Alice smiled. She saw a woman who looked to be in her early thirties come in and sit behind the reception desk. The telephone rang and she answered, giving the name of the shop and then chatting as she booked an appointment for a regular customer.

Shirley gave Alice a layer cut and then parted her hair to one side; she finger-waved it and pinned it down to just above Alice's ears and then began to curl the hair into circles, clipping it with flat silver-coloured clips. When she had finished curling the hair at the back, she put a brown net over Alice's head, tied it at the back and lowered a hood dryer over her head.

'You can adjust it if it gets too hot,' Shirley said. 'Would you like a cup of tea?'

'No, thank you. I'll just look through the magazines.'

Alice flicked through the women's magazines that Shirley brought her. She seldom bought one herself because it just seemed a waste of money when they needed every penny for other things. This hairdo was an extravagance, because she could have had just a cut and that would cost less, but Daniel had given her some money to spend for Christmas and this was her personal treat.

The door of the shop opened and someone came in. Looking in the mirror, Alice saw a young lad and her heart caught. For one moment she thought it was her own son Danny, but his hair was slightly darker. He went up to the desk and talked to the woman, and she gave him some money from the till.

He must be the woman's son. Alice watched in the mirror as she talked to the boy and then followed him through to the back of the shop.

Shirley came to take Alice out of the dryer a

few minutes later. Alice kept her voice calm as she asked who the lad was, though her mouth felt dry and her heart was hammering like crazy.

'He is Maura's son,' Shirley said. 'Nice looking boy, isn't he? She is on her own now since her marriage broke up. It isn't easy bringing up a child alone. I give her credit for taking on a business like this, because it was a bit of a gamble. We're doing very well so far, but it must be a worry for her. She had a bit of a windfall and she put all her money into the shop.'

'Yes, it must be a worry with a young lad and no husband,' Alice said. She looked in the mirror, hardly seeing her own reflection because she felt so odd. When Shirley held the mirror for her to see the back, she nodded and said it was lovely. She thought it looked too set and stiff, but she could brush it out a bit more when she got home, and it would go how she liked it when she washed it herself. 'Thank you very much – how much do I owe you?'

'Seven shillings and sixpence,' Shirley said, 'because it was a full cut. If you had it trimmed regularly, it would be five and six.'

Alice gave her a shilling tip and left. She had been in a hurry to leave the shop, but now she wandered aimlessly along the street towards the bus stop. She had thought she might buy a pair of shoes from the shop in the High Street, but she didn't feel like it now. She felt cold and shivery, a little bit sick. The lad had looked about the same age as her own son, or maybe a little older, but the resemblance was so strong that she was sure in her own mind that they both had the same father.

The boy had looked very much like her husband must have when he was that age. Alice had a sepia photograph of Daniel as a boy, and the lad she'd just seen could have stepped straight out of the picture frame.

The truth suddenly jumped out at her – the owner of the hairdressing shop had a son by her husband! Alice wanted to scream but instead she found a wooden bench and sat down. Her hands were shaking as she tried to make sense of what she had seen. Had Daniel had an affair with that woman before he started courting Alice – or was it still going on?

Daniel didn't have time to carry on with other women now. Alice reminded herself that he worked all hours to try and make a decent living for them. He hardly ever went to the pub these days. It wasn't still going on. It couldn't be!

Alice took a grip on her thoughts. She had been so shocked to see the boy, because he could have been her own Danny. She felt sick and angry, because Daniel should have told her long ago, but she knew she had to find a way to live with the knowledge.

She needed to do some more shopping. She still had presents to buy for the children and she wasn't going to spoil their Christmas just because of what she had discovered. She was so angry with Dan, but she wouldn't say anything until after Christmas – although she didn't think she could bear him to touch her.

Daniel was working on a car when Alice walked

through the yard. He waved to her and called that he would be in for a cup of tea in a few minutes. Mary was sitting at the kitchen table. She had the kettle boiling and the cake tin on the table.

'Your hair looks smart,' she said. 'You look a proper picture, love.'

'Thank you,' Alice said. She put her parcels on the dresser and touched her hair. 'It feels a bit tight at the moment but it will be better when I've brushed it. Has Sally been good?'

'Yes, as always.' Mary sighed. 'I sometimes wish mine weren't all grown-up – even the youngest two are growing away from me. John is talking of getting married next year. It makes you feel old when your children get married, Alice. Of course, you've got a long way to go yet.'

'Yes, though Connor may get married soon. He isn't my son, but sometimes he feels like one. I think he is serious about marrying that girl from Ely.'

'I heard him and that group of his on the radio last night,' Mary said. 'They are saying his new record could be the number one for Christmas. He must be making a lot of money.'

'Yes, I imagine he is,' Alice said. She sat down at the table as her sister-in-law poured a cup of tea. Daniel came in from the yard but she didn't turn her head. She wasn't sure she could look at him, especially with Mary there.

'I thought there would be a cup of tea on the go,' Daniel said. 'Your hair looks nice, love – though I like it best when it grows a bit. I shall

164

have to help with the milking when I've had this tea. Joe can't manage to get the cows in the stalls on his own.'

'You should get a full-time herdsman,' Mary said. 'Or get rid of them and put all your fields down to arable. The price of milk is hardly worth having these days, so they tell me.'

'We don't do so bad,' Daniel said. 'It is an idea, though. If I got rid of the cows and pigs, it would make life easier.'

'Oh, pigs are all right,' Mary said. 'Feed them and they are no bother, that's what Henry always said, though it was mostly me doing the feeding, but cows are always needing the vet or injuring themselves – and the milking has to be done every day.'

'You've got a point, Mary,' Daniel said. 'It was all right when Connor was here. I could leave him to get on with things, but it's hard to get a man who will work for what I can pay him. There are better wages doing piecework or in the jam factory.'

'All the men and a lot of women are working in that new radio and TV factory in Cambridge,' Mary said as she sipped her tea. 'They pay decent wages. I've thought about trying it myself.'

'You wouldn't want a full-time job,' Alice said. She looked at her sister-in-law because she couldn't bear to look at her husband.

'No, not really,' Mary said. 'I might get a job in the jam factory, though. They take part-time workers there. I wouldn't mind working somewhere that pays more money.'

'Are you finding it hard to manage?' Alice asked but Mary shook her head.

'My eldest pays me a bit of rent and Janet starts work next year. She will pay four shillings for her keep. No, I can manage, Alice – but it gets a bit lonely at times.'

'You help out with the church, with flowers and fêtes and so on...' Alice was concerned; Mary didn't often mention her feelings. She'd taken it for granted that her sister-in-law was content with her life. 'Why don't you go and live with Frances? She did offer you a job.'

'I didn't want to move the children. Frances wrote and asked me for Christmas, but I turned her down. We shall have a house full as usual.'

'She asked us, too. We couldn't spare the time to go down. It is awkward, because she was so generous to us when we went down earlier this year. I have asked her here and I know Emily is always asking her to stay, too, but it seems she doesn't want to budge from the hotel.'

'Well, I suppose it is her life,' Mary said. 'I think I shall visit when Christmas is over, though. I like Frances and she had a rough time.'

'Yes, she did,' Alice agreed. 'I might come with you and bring Sally. Dan can manage here by himself for a while.'

Alice didn't look at her husband as she spoke. She knew he would find it difficult on his own, because he would have to look after the three eldest children. She had always said it wouldn't be fair to leave him, but at the moment she was angry and she felt like punishing him.

'Frances would like that,' Mary said. 'I saw

Dorothy yesterday and she said Clay was taking her down for a few days in the spring. I was surprised, because I thought Frances had refused to speak to him.'

'Maybe she thinks it is time to forgive him. It was a long time ago...'

She knew that Daniel would never forgive his brother, but perhaps Frances was more forgiving.

Frances massaged her temples. She had a throbbing headache. She had been feeling better for the best part of a week, but now her headache had returned and she felt as if her head would burst.

The doctors had told her that there had been little change in the tumour. It hadn't grown by any noticeable amount since her last visit to the hospital. She still had a few years left to her, they said; she was one of the lucky ones. A lot of people with brain tumours were dead within a year; hers was the manageable kind. They couldn't cure it for her and an operation was out of the question, because she might end up a cabbage, but they had given her medicines to help with the pain.

It would get worse in time, of course. Frances wasn't sure she could stand it if it became much worse than it felt now – but she still had spells when she felt fine. If she looked at herself in the mirror, she couldn't see any difference.

Emily had refused to come for Christmas because she had too much going on at Vanbrough. Frances had considered going to visit her for a few days, but she had Vane's cousin staying. Perhaps she would go later in the year.

Clay had rung her earlier that morning, wishing her a happy Christmas. He was ringing her more often these days. Daniel hardly ever got round to phoning, but then he didn't have a phone in the house. She knew that he had to go into the village to call her from the phone box. Sometimes it was already in use and he might have to wait ages. She had thought he might have one installed with the money she had given him, but it appeared he didn't think it important. If he'd had a phone, Frances could have rung him. She'd sent presents and cards, and Alice had sent a card and a present to her, of course, but Frances would have appreciated a phone call from her favourite brother.

She knew that Daniel worked all hours and she considered telling him that he had no need to worry about the loan. She didn't want the money back anyway. If he had rung her himself, she would have told him, but her letters went to Alice, and Daniel wouldn't want her to know he had borrowed money from his sister.

Frances sighed. She wasn't lonely, because there were always guests and staff, and there would be celebrations in the hotel. She had ordered a tree and the girls would decorate it soon. It wasn't quite the same as a family Christmas, though. She sometimes thought wistfully about the Christmases she'd known as a girl when her father was alive and her brothers and sister were still at home.

Frances thought that if Emily hadn't sounded a

little evasive when she rang her, she would have gone up to Vanbrough for the celebrations. It might be her last chance to spend Christmas with her sister...

No, of course it wouldn't! The doctors had been hopeful that she could go on for some years – if the tumour didn't start growing or the pain didn't get too bad.

What did it matter? Frances felt the black mood descend on her. What did she have to contribute to a family Christmas? She had no children and she had forgotten how to be happy. It was better that she stayed here alone. She would only ruin things for Emily if she went there.

Emily stirred and her hand moved across the bed. She touched a warm body and was instantly awake. Her lips formed a smile as she turned to look at Alan. He was still sleeping, his face looking much younger in repose. She resisted the temptation to stroke his cheek. Better to let him sleep, because, despite being so much better, he still tired easily.

They had made love every night since he came back to her. At first she had been nervous because it was so long since she had experienced physical passion, but Alan had made it easy for her.

'You are so beautiful, Emily,' he said as he took her in his arms the first time. 'I've wanted to make love to you for so long – almost since the day I saw you as a young wife and wished it was me standing beside you.'

'Alan,' she murmured against his lips as they

kissed. Her body was thrilling to his touch, all inhibition fled as they came together in a passionate embrace. 'I never knew you felt like that!'

'Of course you didn't,' he said, almost indignant. 'What kind of a man would I be if I had made a pass at Simon's bride? I might have wished I had seen you first, but I knew you wouldn't look at me.'

'I wish it had been you,' Emily told him softly. 'Simon never loved me. He couldn't love a woman; it wasn't in his nature.'

'My poor darling. What a terrible time you must have had. No one could blame you for taking a lover.'

'Terry was a fireman – and he loved me very much.'

'But you lost him and you've been alone all this time – but you have me now.'

Emily had found so much pleasure in Alan's arms. It wasn't the same as it had been with Terry. She had been head over heels in love with her fireman – the man she ought to have married – but it was much better than it had ever been with Simon. Alan was a considerate and passionate lover. He took his time, bringing her to a beautiful climax before giving in to his own. Emily was grateful for what he had given her. She hadn't even been aware of her need until she felt the release of pent-up emotions flood her. She was a passionate woman and she had lived too long alone. She knew that she needed the company, the touch of a man, and Alan was such a dear. She loved him even if she perhaps wasn't in love with him.

Alan opened his eyes as she leaned over him. He looked up at her, reaching out to touch her cheek. 'I love you,' he said. 'You have made me so happy, Emily. I never expected to feel this way again.'

'Nor I,' she whispered and bent her head so that their lips were in touching distance. Her soft hair fell forward over her face as she kissed him. 'This has been a wonderful few days, Alan.'

'Must it be only a few days?' he asked in a husky voice. 'We could go anywhere, Emily. You don't have to stay in this great mausoleum, darling. You've kept your word to Vane – but he had no right to ask it of you.'

'Don't talk – love me!' Emily pressed her naked body against him. He smelled of her, her perfume all over him. She nibbled at his ear, her body arching with pleasure as he began to caress her back. 'We'll talk later...'

Leaving Vanbrough was too difficult a subject to discuss in bed. For now all she wanted was to lose herself in his arms.

'I wasn't sure you would come.' Sarah's eyes filled with accusation when she opened the door to Connor. 'It must be a month since you were last here.'

'We've been busy,' Connor replied. He reached out for her, kissing her neck. 'I told you when I phoned. We had three singles to get out and we've been working on songs for the album, as well as haring all over the country to gigs and theatres. We've had three local radio interviews and one on the TV – did you see it?'

'It came on when I was at work. Mum saw it. She said there was some girl who kept making eyes at you and giggling.'

'She was just one of the presenters. I hardly noticed her, but I could hardly tell her to stop on television, could I?'

'No, I don't suppose so, but you could have telephoned me more.'

'I was on the road every day. We do the shows and then go back to the hotel. Mostly I just crash out on the bed as soon as I've eaten.'

'You've still had time for parties and night-clubs,' Sarah said, sounding sulky. 'I've seen pictures of you and there was an article in the paper three days ago. It said that you were engaged to that singer...'

'You know that isn't true!' Connor said. 'The publicity people are always putting rubbish out. We are trying to get noticed, Sarah. Our record sales are going up but we didn't make number one, even though everyone said we would. We stuck at number two for a while and then drop-ped to five or six. It isn't enough for the record company. They are looking for number one hits and if we don't give them what they want, we shall be out – that's why we have to take all the work we can get. If we do enough gigs, we should build a good fan base even if the records don't quite make it.'

'I don't see why it matters. You've earned enough to buy us a house – and my father would give you a job with his firm, Connor. If you worked for him, you could be here all the time and we could get married.'

'I don't want to work for your father,' Connor said. 'It wouldn't be a good idea, Sarah. I shan't do this for ever – just a couple of years or so. Most groups don't last much longer unless they make it big. We've done well for an unknown band – but we need that number one hit.'

'You must have earned a lot of money.'

'Yes, I have,' Connor admitted. 'Far more than I ever expected, and I've saved most of it, Sarah. When I pack it in we shall have a nice home. You might like a little car for yourself. Why don't you learn to drive? You could get out a bit more then – and it will come in handy when we have a family. I'll pay for the lessons. In another couple of years, I might go into business for myself. Besides, you're only nineteen – too young to get married yet. Your father said June.'

'I'll be twenty by then. When you asked me to get engaged I didn't think you were going to be away so much...'

'I know it can't be much fun for you. But I haven't asked you to stay home, have I? I want you to have some fun, Sarah.'

'How long do we have to wait? Couldn't we get married soon and then I could travel with you?'

'You wouldn't like it. We have to stay at some awful hotels sometimes. Please be patient for a while – your father wanted us to wait and by June I'll know if the records are going to make it...'

Connor knew that he couldn't marry until his career was established. The record company had told them it was important that he stay single and apparently available.

'The girls flock around you because they hope you will notice them,' Connor had been told. 'Just keep your distance but let them think they have a chance. When you have a string of number one hits you can do what you like, but there is a lot of competition out there, boys. You're popular now but you could go down like a stone if the fans take against you.'

'I'm engaged to a local girl,' he'd told their manager.

'Well, just keep it to yourself. You're on the brink, Connor, but you haven't made it big yet. One step out of line and you never will. The Bad Boys will just be also-rans.'

Connor had held his tongue in check, because he knew the others were relying on him. Sometimes when they were staying in some dump, where the plumbing kept him awake half the night, he wondered if this was what he really wanted from life. Sam, Terry, Jack and Ray seemed as if they enjoyed every moment of being on the road, but Connor couldn't help feeling that there was a hefty price to pay for their dash to fame.

'Let's not argue,' he said now. 'I've been looking forward to seeing you for weeks, Sarah. I've only got tonight and tomorrow – let's make the most of it while we can.'

He bent his head and kissed her. Sarah leaned into him, her lips soft and willing beneath his. He felt her body melt into him and the fire raged inside him. He wanted her so badly!

'It's just that it hurts when I read those things...'

'They are nonsense. Remember that I love you, darling,' Connor said, his arms tightening about her. His lips moved at her throat; he bit her gently, feeling as if he were putting his mark on her. 'I think of you all the time when I'm away and I dream of the time when you will be my wife. Please believe me, Sarah. I don't want the girls that follow us around. Some of the others take their chances, but I don't. You're the only one for me. It's as hard on me as it is on you, darling.'

'I want to believe you,' Sarah said and clung to him. 'I wish we could – you know, do it – but if anything happened, my father would kill me.'

'I could be careful,' Connor said, tempted almost beyond bearing. 'But maybe it's best we wait – at least for a while. In a few months things could be different. We might be able to marry sooner than we hoped...'

Two days later, Connor started the long drive to Liverpool. He would have to travel through the night to get to the theatre in time to set up and practise with the group. He had stayed longer than he ought with Sarah, because she'd cried and clung to him, begging him not to go.

Connor had felt awful. He hated leaving her when it was so obvious that she wasn't happy about the way things were going, but he didn't see what else he could do for the moment. Even if they didn't have the big hits the record company wanted, he was earning a lot of money from the personal appearances. It wouldn't be long before he had a nice nest egg put away. He knew the others were spending their money as fast as they earned it – easy come, easy go – but Connor couldn't believe that this would go on for ever. He wanted to make sure he had something worthwhile when the bubble burst.

He knew that in America the stars of Rock 'n' Roll were earning far more than they did, but you needed to get a record in the top ten charts over there to make that sort of money. Some of the best groups probably earned twenty or thirty thousand a night – perhaps more for all he knew. Maybe they should start asking for more instead of grabbing with both hands every time they were made an offer. He sometimes thought it would be better to get more for one good venue than race all over the place taking all they could get.

He yawned, feeling tired and wishing he were in a warm bed instead of on the road. People saw your name in the papers and imagined it was all glamour and that you earned fabulous amounts, but so far he had found it to be damned hard work! He couldn't grumble at the money, though. He already had more of it than he would have dreamed possible at the start, but if their records went platinum, he would be really rich. He had known what it was like to go out with a shilling in his pocket and the need to be secure was driving him on, even though in his heart he wanted to turn round and drive straight back to Sarah.

* * *

Sarah wept for an hour after Connor had gone. She hated it when he left her. She knew her mother was waiting for it all to go wrong, and her friends pitied her. They had been green with envy when they saw the big cross-over diamond ring Connor had given her when they got engaged, but now she saw pity in their eyes when they looked at her.

They all thought that Connor was just stringing her along. She had seen articles about him in the paper, and some of the pictures seemed to suggest that he was with one of the girls who sang on stage with the group at times.

Connor swore that he loved her, though, and most of the time she believed him. It was just that June seemed a long time away and sometimes she wondered if he would simply dump her before their wedding day even arrived.

'Sarah,' her mother called as she knocked at the door. 'I've made some cocoa, love. Do you want me to bring it up, or will you come down and get it?'

Sarah wiped her eyes. 'I'll be down in a minute,' she said.

'Don't cry, love. It isn't worth it. No man is worth crying for, believe me.'

'I'm not crying, Mum. I'll be down in a minute.'

Sarah went to the bathroom and washed her face. Connor was worth waiting for, even if it did hurt...

'What is wrong, Alice?' Daniel asked. The children were in bed and they had the big, warm kitchen to themselves. 'You've been quiet all week – not like yourself at all. What have I done?'

'Why should you think you've done anything?' Alice said. 'I'm just tired. Cooking for six isn't easy, you know.'

'I know, and you cooked mince pies and cakes to give away,' Daniel said. 'But you've always done that and it never bothered you before.'

'Well, maybe I've had enough of being a dutiful little housewife,' Alice said with a note of bitterness in her voice. 'I'm going to bed. I'm tired.'

'And when I come you will pretend to be asleep – or you'll say you're not in the mood. What have I done? I know you are upset, but I don't know why.'

'You should know.' She refused to look at him. 'I don't like secrets, Dan – and you've kept this one a long time. Tell me, when did you go with her – before or after we started going out? Her son looks almost the same age as Danny.'

'You've seen him?' Daniel's face went white. He didn't try to deny it. 'Damn her! When did she come here? I told her I would break her neck if she came telling lies to you.' He jumped up and walked over to the window, his back stiff. 'I didn't know about the boy. It was just one night, during an air raid in Liverpool. I was visiting Emily when she was stationed there with the Fire Service.'

'So it was after we started going out,' Alice said bitterly. 'Was it because I wouldn't let you for a start?'

178

'No, of course it wasn't,' Daniel said. He swung round to face her, his eyes dark with anger. 'She was drunk so I tried to get her home but the air raid started and we took shelter in a hotel. There was just one room left. I was going to sit in the chair but she asked me to get into bed with her and she started to cry.' He ran his fingers through his dark hair. 'It just happened. It didn't mean anything. I've never known why I did it. I wasn't interested in her. I only knew her as Emily's friend. They both worked for the Fire Service. Her boyfriend had been badly injured...' Daniel swore under his breath. 'The first time I saw her again was when I met her a few weeks ago in Ely. I swear I hadn't seen her or heard from her since that night. She demanded money for the boy and showed me some photographs. He looks like Danny, so I have to accept that he is mine in the circumstances.'

'I've seen him. It was her hairdressing shop I went to just before Christmas. The boy came in and I knew he was yours almost immediately. I asked Shirley, my hairdresser, who he was. I felt sick. I couldn't wait to get out of there.'

'So that's why you've been quiet since...' He walked towards her, reaching out to grip her shoulders as she would have moved away. 'Damn it, Alice. I didn't know she had a child. I haven't seen her since that night, not until she approached me.'

'And since then?'

'A couple of times. She wanted money. She was going to send you the pictures.'

'What did you give her?'

'Five hundred pounds. She wanted much more but it was all I could spare.'

'Where did you get it?' Alice threw him an angry look. 'From Frances, I suppose. She lent you some money – I wondered where it came from and now I'm sure. That is how you paid off the bank and bought those cars...'

'Yes, she did. I needed it, Alice. I had to give Maura something and I wanted to pay off the bank; there were other debts too.'

'How could you do that – borrow from Frances? It's why you took me there, isn't it – so that you could borrow from your sister?'

'It wasn't just for the money. You were tired. You needed a holiday. Don't look at me like that, Alice. I'm not a criminal!'

'I want that money paid back as soon as possible,' Alice said. 'It is humiliating to know that we owe Frances. How much was it?'

'Two thousand pounds.'

'What! How are we ever going to repay that?' Alice moved away as he held out his hand to her. 'Don't touch me! I'm not sure if I can ever forgive you – but it certainly won't happen until you pay Frances what you owe her.'

'I've been thinking about what Mary said the other day. If I sold the stock and put the fields to arable, I would have more time to do my repairs – and then I could save some money.'

'It will take half our lives to pay it back – and all that time we have to scrimp and save. Well, I'm sick to death of it, Dan! I'll never trust you again.'

'Don't be like this, Alice. I know what

happened was wrong, but it is all over.'

'I can't go back to that shop. What happens if our friends see that boy and put two and two together? It is so humiliating! Mary goes to that shop now. If she sees the boy, she's bound to wonder. I'm so angry with you, Dan.' She shot him a furious look. 'I'm going to bed. You can sleep in Connor's room for the time being.'

'Alice...' Dan sighed as she left the room. There was no point in going after her, because she wouldn't change her mind. He wasn't sure that things would ever be right between them again.

Seven

Sarah looked round the rails of good quality dresses and suits. It was her job to take them out one by one and brush away any dust that might have settled on them overnight. She quite enjoyed working in the classy dress shop in Ely High Street, and she was lucky because she got a twenty-five per cent discount on anything she wanted for herself. Her friends envied her because she could afford better clothes than they could; she had noticed that several of the girls she had known at school had started giving her odd looks when she met them at the club or the cafes they all frequented.

Phyllis said it was because they knew she was engaged to Connor Searles. It hadn't mattered when he was just one of the lads at the jazz club, but now he was on the radio and his records had been in the charts it was different. Phyllis and Ann were still her friends, but Janice hardly spoke to her these days, and a lot of the others sent some very unfriendly looks her way. Sarah knew that Connor was saving hard so that he could buy a nice house and things like that, but she couldn't help wishing that he would go back to being just the good-looking boy she had fallen in love with at the start. She longed to walk into the club with him and let everybody see it was her he wanted and not the girls he had his photograph taken with.

'Is something wrong, Miss Jenkins?' Sarah's employer came through from the back room. 'I want those rails straightened this morning if you don't mind – and I am thinking of having a sale.'

'Everyone is having a sale,' Sarah said as she started on the dresses. 'We sold such a lot at Christmas that some of the rails are a bit thin until the new stock comes in.'

'Well, the new lines will start coming at the end of January. To make room for them, we shall select anything that has a mark or was unpopular, and I think we'll start our sale on Saturday – so that means we shall be busy for a few days. If we are lucky, we can make a clearance before the new stuff arrives.'

'Yes, Mrs Hines. Do you want me to put out anything that has been marked? I noticed yesterday that one of the good dresses has a lipstick mark. It is too good for the sale really, but the mark will need to be got off at the dry cleaner's, I should think.'

'People are so careless! Yes, put that and anything else you find on this rail here – I'll take these suits to the back room, because they are fairly new in. We will make this the sale rail, Sarah. Put anything you find that you think needs to be discounted and I'll have a look myself later and decide on the price.'

'Yes, Mrs Hines.'

Sarah smiled as she began her task of tidying the rails. Some of these dresses were never going to sell for their full price, but she knew that Phyllis had her eye on a smart suit. She noticed that one of the better ones had a little thread pulled. It could easily be pulled back, but she would put it on the sale rail. If Mrs Hines reduced that, she would put it aside for her friend first thing on Saturday morning.

She smiled as she worked, thinking of Connor's passionate kisses when he'd driven her to a secluded spot the night he left. They had come closer to going all the way than ever before; she knew he had found it difficult to pull away at the last. A part of her wished that she had let him make love to her, but she was apprehensive – and not just because it would be her first time. Connor was becoming famous. She knew that a lot of girls followed the band from venue to venue, and she was afraid that the glamour and excitement of being a star would seduce him. He might fall in love with one of those beautiful girls he sometimes performed with on stage.

And yet Connor swore that he loved her. She believed him when they were together, but when he was away the doubt set in. You read about the things famous bands did in the papers and when she saw Connor's picture it made her feel that he was so far away – and not just in miles. She was just an ordinary girl. How could she be sure he wouldn't find someone else?

'Have you seen that little blonde who keeps screaming every time you blow a kiss?' Terry said to Connor as they came off stage that night. 'She can't be more than fifteen but she dresses as if she were older – tight sweaters that cling ... boy do they cling!'

'I can't say I've noticed particularly.' Connor yawned. 'I'm whacked. Thank goodness we've got a couple of weeks at the recording studio to look forward to.'

'I like being on the road,' Terry said. 'Aren't you coming this evening? We've been invited to a party – there will be plenty of booze and grass.'

'I don't touch that stuff.'

'You don't know what you're missing.'

'Thanks, but I'm not interested. I need some sleep.'

'Suit yourself, but remember this won't last for ever. If our next record bombs, we'll be dropped. The rest of us are going to make the most of the chances we've got.'

'Good luck to you.' Connor grinned. 'Go and get laid – I've got someone waiting for me at home.'

'She need never know,' Terry said. 'I've got a girl at home – well, sort of – but that doesn't stop me having fun. I don't want to get married for ages. There are too many sexy girls around. I want to sleep with as many of them as possible.'

Connor laughed. 'Casanova rides again? Good luck, mate. I would join you, but I happen to be in love.'

Terry shrugged and went off. Connor combed his hair. He was growing his sideburns and he thought they suited him. Sarah liked them and she was the one that mattered.

He slung his leather jacket over his shoulder.

He had bought it recently from a junk shop and it was a genuine RAF issue from the last war. He'd only paid a few bob for it, but the others had coveted it as soon as they saw it. He was wearing black drainpipes, a black roll-neck sweater and brothel creeper suede shoes as he left the theatre by the back door. He was walking to where he'd parked his car when the shadow came towards him out of the gloom.

Connor was wary, because they had been attacked a couple of times by youths, but as the shadow moved into the light of the lamppost he saw it was a young girl. She was wearing denim pedal pushers with red high heels and a tight red sweater; her blonde hair was caught up in a ponytail. He thought she looked very young and slightly vulnerable ... nervous.

'What are you doing here on your own?' he asked. 'Do you know it is nearly midnight?'

'I wanted to see you,' she said in a rush. 'I follow you wherever you go. I love you!'

'No you don't,' Connor said, amused. 'You love the man you see on stage, but that isn't me, young lady. I think you should go home to your parents. It isn't safe for a girl like you to wander about at this time of night.'

'I only had enough money for the fare here,' she said. 'I do love you. I've bought your records and I have your picture on my bedroom wall. Please, just talk to me for a minute. I've been waiting for hours.'

'It's cold out here.' Connor looked at her pinched face; she was shaking with cold. 'This is silly. I'll get you a coffee – there's an all-night

186

stand just down the road – and then I'll give you the bus fare to get home.'

'I want to be with you!' She rushed at him, throwing her arms about his neck. 'I'll do anything you want – anything. I could come with you wherever you go. I love you more than anything in the world.'

Connor carefully untangled her arms from about his neck. He smiled at her, because he was conscious that his suggestive movements and the way he talked to girls in the audience had brought this on. It wasn't the first time a girl had thrown herself at him, but it usually happened when the other guys were around or on stage.

'I'm honoured that you like me so much,' he said. 'But I have a girlfriend. I don't know your name...'

'Lisa. It's Lisa...' Tears welled up in her eyes. 'You sing to me every time. The way you look at me ... you talk just to me. I know you do.'

'I'm sorry, Lisa, but I've never noticed you before this evening. I sing to all the girls like that, because it is good for the band's image, but I'm in love with a girl from my hometown.'

Lisa stared at him, her eyes darkening. 'It isn't fair. I spend all my money following you. I'm in love with you and you *have* been singing to me. I know you have.'

'No, Lisa, that isn't true. I sing for all the girls. Come on, I'll buy you that coffee and then I'll give you the money to get home. Where do you live?'

'No!' Lisa stared at him wildly. 'It's all a lie. You're not what you pretend to be! I hate you!'

Connor stared after her as she turned and fled into the shadows. 'Don't be silly, Lisa. Let me help you to get home.'

There was no answer. Connor debated whether he should go after her. If she really had no money, it was dangerous for her to be on the streets of a big city like Liverpool alone at night. Anything could happen to her.

She was probably lying. She had built a fantasy in her mind about Connor, and the story about having no money was probably just a part of all that nonsense. She had hoped he would take her back to his hotel – which any of the other band members might very well have done. Connor knew that his friends regularly slept with girls who came to the shows; they couldn't understand why he didn't grab the chances that came his way.

Lisa couldn't have been more than fifteen, Connor thought as he got into his car and drove back to the hotel. He had more sense than to go with an underage child, even if he'd fancied her. She was well developed for her age, but she wore too much make-up and he preferred the kind of clothes Sarah wore.

He was still thinking of Lisa as he went up to his room. She was so young to be away from home. He wondered if her parents had any idea where she had gone. A tiny prick of guilt kept him awake for a while, but he was tired and finally he slept.

Alice looked at the letter that had come from Frances that morning. She had written to say that she would like them to visit soon. It was written in a friendly tone, but in the light of what Daniel had done it felt almost like a summons.

Alice had enjoyed her stay the previous summer. She would have liked to go down again, but she felt embarrassed. It was humiliating to know that Daniel had borrowed from his wealthy sister. Alice hadn't minded that they were always short of money. She'd understood that things were difficult because of the bankruptcy. They had managed to keep the few fields they had because Daniel had put them in her name. He had cleared himself now, but she felt that the stigma still hung over them – and now he owed all that money to Frances.

He had given five hundred pounds to that woman in the hairdressing shop! Alice wasn't sure what made her angrier – the fact that he had a bastard son or that he had borrowed so much money from Frances.

She had been so shocked and hurt when she saw the boy who looked like her own son, but if Daniel was telling her the truth, it had happened only once and a long time ago. That didn't make it better, because she hated the thought that he had been with another woman after they got together. Yet she knew that the same thing had happened to so many women during the war; their men were away fighting and there were always other women around. She was fairly certain that there hadn't been anyone else for Daniel, though he had worked with the Resistance in Greece until the Germans took him prisoner.

She wouldn't let herself think about that, Alice decided. She wouldn't have minded so much about what happened with that woman if she hadn't brought her son to Ely. Alice would hate it if Mary or one of her friends put two and two together and felt sorry for her.

Alice had begun to regret shutting Daniel out of their bedroom. She missed having him beside her at night, and not just because it was so cold now that the weather had turned icy. The old house let in draughts and it was always cold in winter, even with fires in the kitchen and bedrooms. She didn't keep a fire going overnight in the bedrooms, because it might be dangerous while they were sleeping, even though she kept the guards in place. Instead she piled more and more blankets on the bed. Her pride wouldn't let her back down – at least for a while yet. She was still angry with him and she had no intention of visiting Frances until they could pay at least some of what they owed her.

Daniel had started to take his milking herd to the market. He was gradually selling them off. He said he was going to plant more wheat and barley this year, though he was talking of applying for a larger allocation of sugar beet, but that was a matter of luck because everyone wanted to grow the lucrative crop.

Alice knew how much Daniel wanted to work on the cars. He really needed a garage forecourt to sell them, because not many people would bother to ride into the fen to look at a second-hand car. If he'd had any sense, she thought angrily, he would just have told her about his bastard son and kept the five hundred pounds to start up the garage.

Alice grudged that money. That woman didn't deserve it, because from what Daniel said she'd thrown herself at him – and she shouldn't expect him to pay for what had been an act of kindness.

In her heart of hearts, though, Alice admitted that it must be hard to be left alone with a growing son to bring up, but she wasn't going to feel sorry for that woman!

She had her own family to think of; they didn't exactly go without things, but it would have been nice to buy Danny a new bike instead of the second-hand one his father had done up for him. Not that Danny minded; he had been over the moon when Daniel gave it to him.

Oh damn! Alice wished she'd never seen the young boy in Ely. She couldn't help thinking about him and his mother. Why should she have that shop when Alice could have used the money for so many things? It just wasn't right.

Maura looked at herself in the mirror. She was still attractive but it didn't do her any good, because she had a child to look after and men just weren't interested in taking on other men's sons. Her first husband had sworn he didn't mind, but things had got worse and worse between them; then one night he'd simply walked out, leaving Maura to pay the bills. She had discovered they were behind with the rent and she'd had no chance of paying, so she'd packed some suitcases and moved on.

After that Maura had moved from place to

place for months, never staying long, finding work that was seldom sufficient to pay the bills. It was when she was feeling close to despair one night that she'd had the idea of blackmailing Daniel Searles.

He had given her five hundred pounds, which was enough to start up her small shop in Ely. Maura was a good hairdresser and she had been lucky to find Shirley, who was looking to change jobs and had a core of loyal customers who had come with her. Maura was making more money than she'd ever had in her life, but still she wasn't satisfied. She wasn't sure what she wanted, but she knew she needed more – a bit of fun in her life. A new man.

Maura still thought Daniel Searles one of the most attractive men she'd ever met, but she was under no illusions about his feelings for her. He wouldn't touch her with a barge pole. But she was sure there must be others who would if she gave them the chance.

Her son was sitting in the corner of their tiny sitting room reading comics. She got up and went over to him, ruffling his hair. He looked up at her, a hint of resignation in his eyes.

'You don't mind if I go out for a while, do you, love? You'll be all right on your own?'

'I'm all right,' he muttered and scowled at her. 'Don't come home drunk, Mum.'

'It was only once,' Maura said, though she knew it had happened more than once over the months they'd been moving around the country. 'I'll give you some money for sweets in the morning.'

David grunted but didn't say anything more. Maura shrugged and went to put on her coat. The pub was only just round the corner. She would have a couple of drinks, see if there were any likely men, and if she didn't strike lucky, she would come home.

She went out of the sitting room, down the stairs and out the back door. David would be all right. He was perfectly capable of looking after himself for a few hours.

Connor stood outside the recording studio. It had taken nearly four weeks of intensive work, but their first album was almost ready to be released. He had stayed on after the rest of the group had gone, because he'd become friendly with the guy who was in charge of the mixing. They had talked about various things that could be adjusted, and Connor had hopes that the album would be a success.

It was harder to get a hit album than a single – at least that was what they had been told. He would have felt happier if one of their previous singles had gone to number one, but the last release had only reached number five. The record company was making noises and Connor sensed that the album was their last chance to make it with Moon Records. If the album flopped, they would be looking for a new label.

'What are our chances?' Connor asked when the others had gone.

'I think two of your solos have a chance of being a hit,' Steve told him. 'I shall recommend that Moon puts one of them out as a single at the same time as the album and that should sell the album for you.'

'You don't think they were too sentimental?'

'I think the mix of ballads and rock is just right,' Steve said, looking thoughtful. 'Have you considered going as a solo artist, Con?'

'What makes you ask?'

'I don't think your backing group is good enough. If you want to get right to the top, you should make the break now. With a good group behind you, you could be mega.'

'I've never thought of it,' Connor said truthfully. 'Terry took me into the band. I would never have started in the business if it weren't for him. It would be a bit mean to let them down now.'

'It's just a suggestion. You will always work with the Bad Boys – if being on the road is what you want. However, if you want top billing at a theatre and a big recording career, you need to make the break – and you should think about a different label, one of the major companies. Moon Records are all right. They got lucky a couple of times, because they take untried bands and put them on contracts that mean they take most of the profits. Your aim should be to get on television, but I don't think your group has what it takes. I think you could do well yourself, as a solo artist.'

'How do I get out of our contract – if I ever wanted to go solo?'

'You need a good lawyer. I'll put you in touch with someone if you decide to make the break.'

'Thanks. I'll give it some thought.'

'I'm going to a party tomorrow evening,' Steve said. 'Some of the guests are people you should meet – the men behind the real successes. You should talk to some of them.'

'Right. Give me your number. I'm not sure where I'll be tomorrow, but if I can make it, I'll give you a buzz.'

Connor knew they weren't due to go back on the road for another week. He had been wondering if he should go home, but now he thought that it might be better to stay around. Steve knew this business inside out. Connor wasn't thinking of breaking up with the rest of the band, but it might be a good idea to look for another label. First of all they needed to improve the group. He thought they could do with someone on saxophone. Terry hadn't wanted to take anyone else in, but Connor knew Steve was right. The band was popular but to make it right to the top they needed something more.

He remembered the night they had won the competition that started all this – and the band that had come second. He would like to get together with some of them and see what kind of sound they could produce.

'We don't want anyone else.' Sam glared at Connor when they met the next morning as arranged. 'We're doing fine. I've never earned as much money in my life. Why spoil things?'

'I just think we might do better if we got a couple of extra members on board,' Connor said. 'We didn't make it to number one, Sam. I think we could do that if we got a saxophone player and maybe a keyboard.'

'We would have to split the money seven ways then,' Ray said. 'It's all right for you. You get more than we do.'

Connor heard the resentment and sighed inwardly. He had been afraid this might happen one day. 'Not on the records,' he reminded him. 'I didn't ask for more money for the gigs but it was the way things were when we signed.'

'We wouldn't have won the first competition without Con. We owe what we've got to him,' Terry said, frowning. 'I know what you're saying, but I need to think about this – it would change what we are.'

'We could go from being quite successful to being at the top!' Connor said. 'I don't know about you, but I don't want to spend my whole life on the road. A good record company would pay us enough to make that unnecessary – especially if our records took off.'

'We're doing all right. We're in the top ten,' Sam chimed in.

'In this country,' Terry said. 'We haven't been picked up by America – the really big money comes from over there.'

'I'm doing all right,' Sam said. 'I vote we stay as we are.'

'I've been invited to a party this evening,' Connor said. 'I've been told there are people I should talk to about moving on to another label. I'll let you know what they say.'

'I'm sticking where I am,' Sam said. 'You're getting too big for your boots, Connor Searles. Just because the girls scream and throw their knickers at you, it doesn't mean you can tell the rest of us what to do.'

'I'm not trying to tell you what to do. I just think we could do better.'

'Well, I'm happy with what we're doing,' Sam said and got up. He went out, followed by Ray a moment later. Jack lingered for a moment looking undecided and then followed the others.

'Sorry about this, Con. They are stupid to resent you, because we wouldn't have got this far without you. You're the star. I know it and I accept it, but the others...' He shrugged his shoulders. 'Are you thinking of moving on – going solo?'

'I've been advised I should,' Connor told him frankly. 'But I would rather improve what we have, Terry. We're good friends but I'm not sure how long I want to spend going from one hotel to another, never having quality time to spend at home. I want to buy a house and get married.'

'You would still need to do personal appearances if your records hit number one.'

'A few – on radio and maybe TV and good theatres. We've been grabbing everything they offer us just for the money. Some of those places are sleazy dives, Terry. I want something better for the band.'

'I know you're right,' Terry said. 'You talk to a few people tonight and see what you come up with, Con. I'll talk the guys round. If you can swing it, we'll do it your way.'

Connor dressed carefully for the party that evening in black drainpipes and a maroon jacket with a velvet collar; he wore an open-necked white shirt and white socks. At the last minute he slipped the gold signet ring Sarah had given him for Christmas on to the third finger of his left hand. Whatever happened in the future, he was going to ask her to marry him soon. Tomorrow morning he was going home for a few days.

The party was being held in an exclusive hotel in London's West End. A group of girls had gathered outside and started yelling and screaming as soon as Connor got out of his car and handed his keys to the valet. Photographers took his picture as he went inside. He was directed to the entertainment suite, where he found a crowd already drinking and talking. Music was playing in the adjoining room and after taking one of the drinks circulating on trays, he went through to listen.

'These guys are going places,' he heard Steve's voice say. Connor looked round at him, nodding his agreement. 'Can you hear that guy on saxophone? It's what your group needs.'

'Yes, you're right,' Connor agreed. 'I've always known something was missing. I've suggested it to the lads, but they aren't too keen.'

'Use it as your excuse to get out. Come and meet a friend of mine. He has just set up a new label. He is looking for bands to promote. I think you might be just what he is after.'

'Would he want the others?'

'Maybe just you. He might want to pick a backing group for you – professional musicians,' Steve said. 'Just meet him and talk to him for now. You don't have to decide anything in a hurry...'

Connor nodded. As he followed Steve back into the crush he caught sight of a young girl dancing. Her blonde ponytail struck a chord in his mind but he couldn't think why for a moment, and then it came to him that she looked very like Lisa, the young girl who had approached him in the shadows outside the venue in Liverpool.

What was she doing at a party like this? He wondered for a moment but then decided that he must be mistaken. Besides, it didn't make any difference. He hadn't been interested in her that night and he wasn't now.

'Rosco – this is Connor Searles,' Steve was saying. 'He is the singer I was telling you about this morning.'

'Rosco Jansen. Nice to meet you, Connor. I've heard you on the radio. You have a good sound, but you need stronger backing. I could put you in touch with some decent musicians if you were interested?'

Connor shook hands. 'You're American, aren't you? I think I've heard of your label.'

'We're pretty big over there,' Rosco said and grinned. 'I'm looking for some English artists to promote here and in the States. I was hoping to get a skiffle artist I'd heard of called Lonnie Donegan, but he was already tied up. But there are a few names I'm still interested in, and you're one of them.'

'What about my group?'

'Forget them, Connor. You need professionals. You've done great so far, but unless you get help you will sink and disappear into the blue. It happens to a lot of promising talent.'

'I signed a contract with Moon Records. I'm not sure I could get out of it just like that...'

'I am sure we know someone who would help you,' Rosco said. He reached into his jacket and took out a card. 'Come and see me when you've made up your mind to ditch the losers and we'll talk. You are a winner, Connor, but only if you make the right choices.'

'Thanks.' Connor put the card into his hip pocket. Rosco had seen someone else he needed to talk to and was already moving away.

'Enjoy yourself,' Steve said. 'Rosco isn't the only one interested. I'll find you when I need you.'

Connor nodded. He drifted back to the room where the dancing and music was going on. A different band was up on the stage. He recognized the singer from the Flying Dragons and moved closer to the stage. They were still good, he thought, but they needed another singer because they weren't quite strong enough in their vocals. Suddenly, the singer, Paul, glanced down and saw him. He lifted a hand in salute.

'Folks, we have Connor Searles with us – come up and give us a song, Connor!'

Connor shook his head but Paul jumped down and grabbed his arm, pulling him back with him. A round of warm applause greeted them.

'What are you going to give us, Connor?'

'"Rock Me Sweet Mama"?' Connor asked. 'You know that one?'

'Of course we know it,' Paul said. He turned to

his group and gave the signal and they started to play.

Connor loved the sound they were making. He started to sing and Paul joined in the chorus. Their voices blended perfectly. They grinned at each other, because they both knew it was magic. Something had happened and the room had come alive as everyone moved towards the stage. Some people were dancing, but others stood entranced by the new sound.

When the song finished there was a storm of applause and people yelled out for more. Connor and Paul put their heads together and came up with another number they both knew well. They took it in turns to sing the verses this time and the magic was stronger than ever. The applause was thunderous but Connor wouldn't be persuaded to do another number.

'Call me,' Paul said. 'I think we should talk, Con.'

'Yes, I think we should,' Connor said. He walked away from the stage and then felt a hand on his arm. He looked down and saw Lisa. She looked prettier that evening and she was dressed in expensive clothes that told him she came from a family that should know better than to let her roam around Liverpool alone at night.

'What are you doing here?'

'My father brought me,' Lisa said. 'He is a producer and he could help you to get better theatres for your shows.'

'Why should he do that, Lisa?'

'You did remember me!' Her face lit up. 'I knew you cared about me. I shouldn't have run off that night when you offered to help me.'

'Did you get home all right?'

'I had plenty of money,' she said and dimpled at him. 'I hoped you would take me to your hotel if I told you I was broke.'

'How old are you, Lisa – fifteen?'

'I'm eighteen.'

'Don't lie to me. If I'd taken you back with me that night, I could have been locked up for years.'

'I wouldn't have told,' she said, and took hold of his arm. 'I've got a room here for the night. Why don't we go upstairs? I'll be anything you want me to be...'

'Lisa, you deserve a good spanking!'

Lisa giggled. 'That sounds fun. Would you like to spank me, Connor?'

'No, but I think your father should,' he said. 'Go and play with someone your own age, Lisa.'

'I want to play with you,' she said. 'If you don't oblige me, Connor, you might be sorry.'

'I should be sorrier if I did.'

Lisa reached up and kissed his cheek. 'Spoilsport! I'll catch you later.'

'Not if I see you first,' Connor said, but he was laughing.

Steve came up to him. 'Stay away from Lisa Meadows, Con. Believe me, she is trouble. Her father sent her to boarding school because they couldn't control her, but she ran away and went missing for months. She turned up a few days ago and said she wasn't going to school any more. She sings a bit and she wants a job with a band.'

'By the look of her she's jailbait,' Connor said. 'She came on to me one night in Liverpool when I was leaving the theatre. Told me she had no money to get home. I said I would give her the fare but made it clear I wasn't interested in anything else she was offering and then she ran off. She was trying it on again this evening.'

'Be careful of her,' Steve warned. 'Girls like that can land you in a lot of bother. Forget the silly idiot; I've found someone else who is interested in you.'

Connor went along with him, but he was already getting ideas of his own. He thought he knew exactly what he wanted to do...

'You should come to the dance at the church hall this weekend,' Phyllis told Sarah when they met for a coffee that evening. She lit a pink Sobranie cigarette and puffed at it inexpertly, patting her neat pageboy bob with her left hand. Her fingernails were crimson and she was wearing a tight pencil skirt and a skinny jumper. 'You stay at home far too much these days.'

'It's all right for you,' Sarah replied. She hadn't changed out of the smart suit she wore for work and felt a little uncomfortable in the café, which was frequented by teenagers. 'You can flirt as much as you like, but I'm engaged. Not many men ask you for a dance when they know you're courting. I either have to dance with you or stand and watch.'

'Take your ring off for the night. I think you're daft to stay home and listen to music on your own. I bet Connor doesn't just sit around in his hotel room on his own at nights.'

Sarah nibbled at her bottom lip. Phyllis was voicing her private fears and she was distressed enough as it was, because her thoughts were tortured with pictures of Connor going out with glamorous girls.

'I don't want to get involved with anyone else.'

'You don't have to. Just come out and have some fun. Connor shouldn't expect you to stay home all the time.'

'He doesn't. He just said not to walk home with other guys.'

'Well, then, there you are. We'll go together and walk home together – it can't do anyone any harm, can it?'

'I suppose not,' Sarah sighed. She was bored with staying home. Phyllis was right. It was about time she went out and had some fun again.

Connor left the party at ten that evening. He had given his keys to a valet so that he could park the car in the hotel's secure section. He'd seen by the look in the man's eyes that he didn't think much of the baby Austin Connor drove. All the guys he knew in the business had bought big flashy vehicles as soon as they could afford it, but he clung to the car Daniel had given him; it was reliable and he usually managed to go places in it without being noticed.

The valet gave him an odd look as he collected his keys. Connor wondered about it, but put it down to the unspoken resentment he came across in men of all ages. They looked at him and wondered why he should be making records and mixing with the great and glorious. He wasn't famous enough to be universally admired, but he was doing too well to be accepted as one of the lads.

He had noticed it the last time he went home. He had called at Tiddy Jones' house to drop off a small Christmas gift, but the atmosphere had been chilly. The barely hidden resentment in Tiddy's eyes had made him realize that he could never go back to what he'd been before he'd signed that record contract. He had to go forward – maybe it would be as well to move on from the Bad Boys. Unless he could persuade them that it would be a good thing to find some new members...

Connor loved the sound the Flying Dragons had. He wanted something like that – richer, with more feeling than he got from the Bad Boys.

Lost in his thoughts, it didn't occur to Connor that he could smell perfume until he had been driving for some minutes. He sniffed the air and then frowned, because he recognized that smell – it was the perfume Lisa had been wearing at the party.

'Where are you?' he said. 'You might as well sit up. I can smell your perfume.'

He heard a giggle and then movement as Lisa got up from her crouching position and sat on the back seat.

'How the hell did you get the valet to let you in?'

'I was nice to him,' Lisa said and smirked at

him in the driving mirror. 'Besides, he knows my father and he wants to work in the theatre – he thinks he can sing, but he can't. Not like you, anyway.'

'Some people don't like the way I sing.'

'Most do – they just think the Bad Boys are rubbish.'

'You are talking about my friends.' Connor frowned at her. 'What did you think you were doing? I'm not taking you home with me. He pulled over to the side of the road and brought the front seat forward. 'Get out, Lisa. You can catch the bus or take a taxi home.'

'I want to spend the night with you.'

'I don't want to spend it with you. Maybe in three years I'll think about it.'

Lisa leaned forward, flung her arms about his neck, then sank her teeth into him and bit hard. Connor thrust his arm out to push her away; he put a hand to his neck and touched the bite.

'You vixen!'

He got out of the car, went round to the passenger side and grabbed her arm, yanking her forward so that she fell on her knees.

'You're hurting me!'

'I'm sorry, but I've had enough of this,' Connor said. 'Just get out of my car and stay away from me. I'm not interested in you, Lisa, and I never shall be!'

Lisa scrambled out of the car. She stared at him, a mixture of anger and frustration in her eyes. 'No one speaks to me like this! You will be sorry!'

'Go home and grow up,' Connor said and got

back into the car. He drove off, glancing in his mirror as she still stood there. For a moment he felt uneasy, because she was wearing only thin clothes and it was cold out. Then he hardened his heart. She was a silly girl and it was time she learned her lesson. She was lucky she had played her trick on him and not some of the other guys in the business, because she might have got more than she had bargained for.

Eight

Maura fumbled with her door key, dropping it and nearly falling over as she bent to retrieve it. She swore as her head went round and round, but managed to grab the key. She held her right hand with her left as she struggled to open the door, eventually accomplishing it. The door clicked shut behind her as she shed her jacket, letting it fall to the ground where she stood just inside the door. Stumbling, she got as far as the small sitting room and collapsed into the nearest easy chair before she passed out.

She was too drunk to be aware that the door from the hall leading to the bedroom had opened or that her son stood there staring at her. She was snoring as he walked over to her, his face white and set, eyes dark with something between anger and misery. His hand reached towards her and then dropped. He shook his head and turned away, going back the way he had come.

Maura snored loudly, her mouth open, garish red lipstick smeared over her cheek, the smell of cheap perfume and cigarette smoke clinging to her. She had no idea that in his room a small boy had curled up into a ball, arms wrapped around his body as he tried to block out her image and stop himself crying.

Alice got up, because she found it impossible to sleep. She hated lying alone in this big bed she'd shared with Daniel since they married; she was cold and lonely and life didn't seem worth living. Knowing she wasn't going to get back to sleep, she got up and went downstairs to the kitchen. It was warmer here because Daniel had banked the range up high so that it would keep going overnight. It provided hot water as well as a means of cooking, and it was easier to keep it burning day and night than to get it going again.

Filling a kettle, Alice put it on the range. She wasn't sure what to do about the way things were between her and Daniel. Her anger had cooled, and although the hurt was still there it had become muted because she was beginning to realize that she had been unfair. If she believed her husband, then what had occurred with that woman was a mistake – something he'd regretted as soon as it had happened. Alice recalled that when they'd been told Daniel was missing during the war, she had sometimes wondered about the future – and if she'd been that way inclined, she could have found someone to comfort her. She had refused all offers and clung to the hope that Daniel was alive. Her luck had held and he'd come back to her. He was everything that she wanted in life. She loved him too much to throw it all away.

The door opened just as Alice was in the act of pouring boiling water into a large brown pot. She jumped and a little of the water splashed on her arm. She yelped and Dan came towards her, taking the kettle back to the range and coming back to look at the red mark on her arm.

'You overfilled the kettle again,' he said. 'Shall I rub some butter on the burn for you?'

'It was only a drop. You made me jump. Don't look like that, Dan. I'm not blaming you.'

'All I do is hurt you...'

He looked as miserable as she felt and suddenly Alice found that her sense of humour was back. 'Oh, Dan, what a pair we are.' She smiled. 'It wasn't your fault. I was thinking and I didn't hear you – and I'm sorry.'

'You haven't done anything wrong. This is all my fault. I've let you down. I can't even provide a decent living for you...'

'Now you're being daft!' She moved towards him, reaching out to put her arms about him. A sigh of relief broke from her as he caught her tight, his face buried against her neck as if he were trying to absorb the very essence of her. He wasn't going to shut her out as she'd feared he might. 'I'm sorry for making you sleep in Connor's room – and I'm sorry we quarrelled. We may not have much money, but you give me all the things I really need, Dan. We have a home and plenty of food and all the important stuff.'

'It isn't what I planned. I want to give you so much more!'

'You will one day. Now that you've decided to sell the cows you'll have more time to spend on your cars and one day you'll get the garage, love.'

'It all takes so long. I should never have given her that money...'

'I've been thinking about that,' Alice said. 'I'm glad you did give her something, Dan. Not for her sake, but for the boy. He is your son and I wouldn't want him to starve. At least you've given her a chance to get on and make something of her life.'

'You're too generous, Alice. She was married so she had her chance. She only thought of me when she ran out of luck.'

'Well, it doesn't matter. Let's just forget about it, Dan. I want us to be together again. This sleeping in different rooms doesn't work. I'm lonely without you. I want you back with me.'

'Are you sure? You can really forgive me?'

'I'm not saying it doesn't hurt,' Alice said. 'But it would hurt more if you weren't around. I love you, Dan, and I want us to be happy again. I don't care if we can't afford everything we'd like to have yet. One day we shall, because I know you will get there in the end. You're my Daniel and you'll make things right for us one day.'

Daniel took her in his arms, looking down at her face. 'I love you so much, Alice. I had forgotten how much until I thought I'd lost you.'

'Then what are we going to do about it?' she asked, a teasing light in her eyes as she raised her head.

'Do you really want tea?'

'I can think of something I want more...'

'Alice.' Daniel breathed and laughed. 'Did I ever tell you that you're a wanton hussy?'

'Many times.' She gurgled with laughter.

'Come on, then, you daft lump, what are you waiting for?'

'How did you get on last night?' Terry asked when the band met in the hotel lounge the next morning. 'Did you meet anyone important?'

'I was introduced to a couple of people who might be useful,' Connor said. 'One thing I did learn is that we need to make the group bigger. We shall never get that number one hit unless we take a big step forward. If we stay as we are, the records will eventually flop and then we'll be finished as far as the big money goes.'

'We'll still get plenty of gigs,' Sam said. 'My opinion hasn't changed. I think we should stay as we are.'

'I'm with Sam,' Ray said. 'What about you? Terry? Jack?'

'I'm with Connor. I think we need to move on,' Terry said and Jack nodded.

'I believe I know what we need.' Connor felt excited as he saw hesitation in the faces of the other two. 'We could bring in the Flying Dragons and then—'

'No way!' Sam said. 'There are five of them, damn it! We wouldn't get enough to make it worthwhile.'

'We could ask a lot more if we had the right sound...'

'But we're already in the charts and they haven't even got a record deal yet.'

'Because they need another singer. Paul is good but he isn't strong enough to lead the group. That's the reason we won that night,'

Connor said. 'Paul invited me on stage with them last night and it was magic...' He hesitated, then said, 'I'm thinking the future lies that way.'

'Are you saying that you'll go with them?' Sam asked, but fell quiet as two men in dark raincoats came towards them through the hotel lounge. 'Look up, bloody coppers.' He looked nervous, his eyes darting away as the men approached.

'Excuse me, gentlemen, but is one of you Mr Connor Searles?'

'Yes, I am,' Connor said and got to his feet. 'Is something wrong, Mr...?'

'Inspector Evans, sir,' the taller of the two said. 'And this is Detective Madely. Could we have a word with you in private, sir?'

'I don't have anything to hide,' Connor said and frowned. 'Do you mind telling me what this is about?'

'Do you know a girl called Lisa Meadows, sir?'

'I have met her twice – or three times if you count last night as twice,' Connor said, feeling cold at the nape of his neck. 'She was at the party and then she got the parking valet to let her into my car. I knew she was there because I smelled her perfume and I stopped the car and made her get out. She wanted me to take her to my hotel but I told her to go home.'

'So you do not deny that she was in your car last evening?'

'No – why should I?' Connor felt the ice sliver trickle down his spine. 'She was angry when I told her to grow up and go home. What has she

213

said to you?'

'Lisa Meadows was raped and beaten last night,' Inspector Evans said, looking grave. 'Her father called us this morning. He says that she has named you as her attacker.'

'Connor wouldn't do that!' Terry burst out. 'He never touches the girls. We get them coming on to us all the time but Con never goes with any of them. He is engaged.'

'Is that true, Mr Searles?'

'She attacked me in the car after I told her to get out. She bit my neck and I pulled her out of the car. She said I hurt her arm and I apologized, but told her to go home. I left her standing there...' Connor felt sick. 'If she was raped, it must have happened after I left her. She was just a kid. I should have taken her back to the party...'

'She is fifteen years old, which means any man who has sex with her – with or without her consent – would be arrested and quite possibly imprisoned.'

'I know that,' Connor said. 'I wasn't interested in her or any of the others. I am sorry if she was attacked – especially as I abandoned her in the middle of London – but it wasn't me.'

'We should like to make a search of your room and your car, Mr Searles – and if you wouldn't mind coming to the station, please. It would help us if you could make a full statement about what happened last night.'

'Do you want me to get a lawyer, Con?' Terry asked.

'I don't think that will be necessary yet,'

Inspector Evans said. 'We are not arresting Mr Searles. He is merely assisting us in our inquiries.'

Connor took his car keys and the key to his room and gave them to the Inspector. 'Help yourself. It wouldn't be the first time I've had girls put things in my pockets or my car – but I didn't rape her or beat her. I can't prove it, but I'm telling you the truth.'

'At the moment I am inclined to believe your story,' the Inspector said. 'But Miss Meadows was raped and she is blaming you – that doesn't mean she isn't lying, of course.'

'I'll be back and we'll finish this later,' Connor said to the others. 'Believe me, the girl is lying.'

He followed the inspector from the hotel. He was being treated politely so far, but he was under no illusions. If they found anything incriminating, they wouldn't hesitate to arrest him. He felt cold all over, because whatever the police did, it was what Sarah thought that mattered. If she believed him capable of rape, it would finish them.

'What is the matter with you?' Maura asked as she saw her son's face when he returned from school that evening. 'You look as if you've been fighting.' She took hold of his arm, tipping his face so that she could look at the cuts and bruising. 'Haven't you got more sense than to get into fights?'

'Leave me alone. It wasn't my fault.'

He tried to pull away but Maura held on to him. 'What happened? I'll complain to the

215

teachers.'

'As if they would listen to you...'

'What do you mean?' She shook him as he refused to answer. 'Tell me or you'll get nothing to eat tonight.'

'They called you a whore,' David said sullenly. 'They said you went drinking and picking up men at the pub every night...'

'Who said that – the teacher?'

'No. Billy Williams and his mates.' David flashed a look of resentment at her. 'I called him a liar and went for him and then they all set on me. The teacher blamed me for starting it and I lost my gold stars.'

'You shouldn't have got into a fight over it,' Maura said. 'You know it isn't true.'

'Isn't it?' David stared at her. 'You were drunk again when you came in last night. Your lipstick was all over your face and your nylons had a hole at the top of your leg. You looked just what they said you were.'

Maura struck him hard across the face. 'Damn you! How dare you talk to me like that?'

'You promised you wouldn't do it,' he said and held his hand to his face. 'You tell lies and you don't care about me. I hate you!' He rushed from the room, slamming the door of his bedroom and locking it behind him.

Maura pulled at the handle. 'Open this door, David! Let me in. I want to talk to you.'

'Go away. I hate you!'

'David ... I'm sorry. I shouldn't have hit you. Let me in and I'll bathe your face, put some cream on it for you.'

'Go away. I can do it myself.'

'I'm sorry,' Maura said again. 'I just get lonely and miserable. I won't do it again, I promise. Come out and we'll have fish and chips and go to the pictures. There's a John Wayne film you want to see on at the Rex. Please come out, love. I really am sorry. I promise I won't do it again...'

'I was about to come looking for you,' Terry said when Connor met him that evening in the hotel bar. 'You should have let me get that lawyer for you. They had no right to keep you so long.'

'I went for a drive and then walked by the river for a while,' Connor said. 'I gave the police a statement, they gave me a cup of tea and then I left. I was told to let them know if I was thinking of leaving London and they said they would be in touch if they needed anything more.'

'And that is it?' Terry asked. Connor nodded and Terry swore. 'Then how the hell did this happen?' He thrust an evening newspaper at him. 'Who went to the papers?'

Connor looked at the headlines and saw a picture of him walking into the police station with Inspector Evans.

'Connor Searles held on suspicion of the rape of a fifteen-year-old girl,' he read aloud. 'Damn them! How did they get this, Terry? Evans said that it wouldn't be made public unless I was charged!'

'I didn't say anything, but...' Terry looked angry. 'It might have been Sam. After you left ... well, he was bitter. He wants you out, says you've got too big for your boots. He was Phil's

217

mate and he wants Phil back in again. I tried to tell him that Moon Records will cancel the contract if you leave...'

'I think they will cancel it anyway once they see this,' Connor said, his eyes glistening with anger. 'You should announce the break-up of the group and distance yourself while you can, Terry. I imagine this is the end of my career as a singer.'

'Surely it doesn't have to be,' Terry said. 'I'll talk to the record company – and the papers.'

'If they believe what this rag has written, they won't listen,' Connor said. 'I'm quitting while I'm ahead, Terry. I shall tell the police they'll find me at home if they want me.'

'Don't quit,' Terry urged. 'Let Moon break the contract if they want to – you'll get some sort of a deal from them if you do that.' He looked gloomy. 'I suppose this means they won't release the album...'

'Probably,' Connor said and grimaced. 'I'll let them make the first move – but I still think it would be better for you if you distance yourself from me, Terry. I don't want to ruin things for the rest of you.'

'It's that rotten little bitch that's done it!' Terry looked furious. 'You should get a lawyer and go after her, Con. Make her admit she's lying.'

'If Sarah believes this rubbish, she will ditch me. I should go home and square things with her and my family if I can.'

'You'll probably find some people think you're guilty...'

'As long as Dan and Sarah know the truth, the

218

rest of them can go to hell.'

'I'm really sorry, Con. I wish I'd been with you last night.'

'She would have blamed us both then,' Connor said. 'I don't know what is going on in that mixed-up little head of hers, but she must be pretty miserable to do something like this.'

'Don't feel sorry for her. I could wring her neck!'

'Stay well clear of her,' Connor advised. 'The police found nothing in my room or my car that could incriminate me. At the moment it is just her word against mine.'

'What about blood tests, you know...?'

'I'm not sure if they found any semen on her. I suppose they might try to match it up but they didn't ask for anything like that from me. They were polite and seemed to believe my story, but that may be just to keep me from bolting. I was warned not to go abroad, but I can go home as long as I let them know. So that is where I'm going.'

'What about the gig next week?'

'Find yourself another lead singer, even if it is only temporary.'

'I don't think Phil can step into your shoes. I know Sam wants him in, but we'll go back to being what we were – just a local band that gets a few gigs and appearances at weddings if we're lucky.'

'I'm sorry. I've let you down, but I think it was heading that way even if this hadn't happened.'

'It's not your fault.' Terry swore loudly, anger getting the better of him. 'Maybe we'll get together again somehow.'

'Maybe.' Connor shrugged and walked away. All he wanted was to get home; he had to talk to Sarah before she saw the national papers.

Maura stared at her son's bed and went cold all over. It hadn't been slept in all night. She hadn't gone out, even though he wouldn't open his door to her. Instead she had taken half a bottle of whisky to bed and fallen into a deep sleep. She hadn't heard David go out and she had no idea how long he had been gone.

A shaft of fear went through her. Had David run away? Where could he go? He had no cousins or uncles to run to in this country and he couldn't have enough money to travel to his grandmother's house in Ireland, because he didn't do a paper round and she only gave him a shilling for sweets every now and then.

Maura had a wash in cold water to freshen herself up. Her mind was still fogged from the drink. She should never have had that half bottle of whisky. She had promised David she wouldn't, but after trying to persuade him to come out of his room she had given up and gone to bed. She wasn't sure why she drank so much, but she just felt so low and miserable these days. She wanted someone to love and care for her and there was no one – just her son. But she had driven a barrier between her and David and now he'd run away.

Maura wasn't sure whether she ought to go to the police or whether it would be better to wait for a few hours. David was probably just sulking. She would look stupid if she reported him missing too soon – and the police would want to know why she hadn't heard him leave. If she waited for a few hours, the smell of the whisky would have gone and she wouldn't have to explain.

She was a single mother, and if the police started asking too many questions, she might lose David altogether. He was probably just sulking, she reassured herself, because he couldn't have much money and he wouldn't have any idea of how to get to Ireland...

The morning had hardly got going. Dan was busy working on a small Austin car he had bought cheap. It had been left outside in all weathers and some of the bodywork had gone rusty and the engine had seized up. He had managed to get the engine running again fairly quickly, but he'd discovered some holes in the rear wing. He could fill them and paint over but that would mean he was selling someone a car that could cause problems. He hadn't realized that there was so much rust when he bought it and he was trying to decide whether to try and buy a new wing or simply pass it on as it was and reflect the defects in the price. He knew the axle was sound enough, because he'd just finished inspecting it.

He slid out from underneath the car to find he was being watched by a young lad. A feeling of shock and dismay went through him as he recognized the boy. There was no mistaking those features, even though his hair was darker and curlier than Danny's.

'Hello,' he said, sitting up and looking at the boy. 'How did you get here?'

'I came on the bus and then asked where you lived. I walked here.'

'Why did you come? Did your mother send you?'

'She doesn't know I know about you.'

'Oh ... what do you know?'

'She says you're my father. At least, that's what she says when she is drunk sometimes.'

'Does Maura get drunk?' Daniel stood up.

'It happens once or twice a week. She gets lonely.' David's eyes were on him. 'Didn't you want to marry her? She says you wouldn't and she had to marry Dad – I used to call him that until he left us, but she says you're my father. Are you?'

Daniel cursed Maura for her loose tongue and her bad habits. 'I didn't go out with your mother. How did you come along? Is that what you're asking? Well ... it was an air raid and she was ill. I had to look after her and it just happened. We hardly knew each other. I didn't know about you until a few months ago.'

'She told me that you gave her money for the shop and at Christmas. She just said you were my real father. She wouldn't tell me your name then, but when she was drunk she said it – and I looked in her things. She has your address written down.'

'Yes, I expect she has.' Daniel frowned. Where does your mother think you are now?'

'She doesn't care what I do. She hit me last

night for fighting with boys at school – but they were calling her names. Dirty, horrible names.'

'Yes, I see,' Daniel said. 'She shouldn't have hit you for that, lad. Fighting isn't a good idea, but sometimes you have to stand up and be counted.'

'She may be drunk and go with men sometimes, but they have no right to call her those names.'

'No, they don't, and I'm sure it isn't true. She may just be lonely.'

'She is lonely and unhappy since Dad left us.'

'So why did you come looking for me?'

'I want to go to Ireland. My grandmother lives there. She will let me live with her.'

'She might not want to take on a lad of your age.'

'She will – and my uncle will help me when I leave school. I can leave school soon in Ireland and work with them on the land. My uncle left school when he was fourteen.'

'What will your mother say about that?'

'I don't care what she says.'

'She loves you, David. If you leave her, she won't have much left, will she?'

'Why should you care? She means nothing to you – and nor do I.' David hunched his shoulders. 'I thought you might help, but I shouldn't have come.' As Dan remained silent, he turned and started to walk away.

'No, don't go,' Daniel said. 'I can't send you to Ireland unless your mother agrees, but if it is really what you want, I'll talk to her about it.'

David turned and looked at him, uncertainty in

his face. He looked vulnerable, young and frightened, and Daniel's heart went out to him. He might be the result of a mistake one much-regretted night, but he was a child – and he was his son. He hesitated and then saw Alice walking towards him across the yard. He was conscious of the sharp stink of oil on his clothes and the acrid stench of the pigpens. His wife had enough to put up with living here and now he was going to ask even more of her.

'This is David,' he said. 'He came looking for me because he was cross with his mum and he wants to go and live in Ireland. I said I'll talk to her for him.'

'You had better bring him into the kitchen.' Alice smiled at the boy. 'I've just made some seed cake and lemon curd tarts. Could you eat some before Dan takes you home?'

'I don't want to go home,' David said and a tear ran from the corner of his eye. He wiped his hand across his face, smearing dirt he'd picked up on his walk. 'Can I stay here until she says I can go to Ireland – please?'

'I don't know,' Daniel said. 'You really should go home.'

'It's a Saturday,' Alice said. 'David can stay with us. Danny and the others are playing in the drove somewhere, but they will be home soon. Perhaps they should meet their cousin David...'

'Perhaps they should,' Daniel said, nodding because as usual Alice had found a way to deal with the situation. 'Is that all right with you?' Alice nodded. He looked at his son. 'What about you, David – do you want to stay with Alice

224

while I talk to your mother?'

'Yes, please. I didn't have any tea or break-fast.'

'Then you might like a cheese sandwich as well as your cake,' Alice said and held out her hand. 'Shall we see what we can find?'

Connor knocked at the door of Sarah's home. It was mid-morning and he had begun to wonder if everyone was out, because several minutes passed before Mr Jenkins came to open the door. He was wearing a smart suit with a shirt and tie and looked annoyed.

'Oh, it's you,' he said and glanced down the street as he heard backfiring from a motorbike. 'You had better come in. I want to talk to you, young man, though I'm not sure Sarah will. I was due to leave here an hour ago, but I couldn't go with my daughter in such a state. She has been crying for ages.'

'She has seen the newspapers? I hoped I would get here first. I've driven all night...'

'You look like it,' Mr Jenkins remarked as he took him through to the kitchen. 'We'll talk here. I'll make a cup of tea. My wife isn't feeling too well and Sarah was awake half the night. You had better tell me your side of this, because I'm the only one in this house willing to give you a hearing, Connor.'

'I didn't touch her – at least I pulled her arm when I made her get out of my car and she said it hurt. I give you my word I didn't do what the papers are saying I did ... She is only fifteen.'

'Why was she in your car in the first place?'

225

'The parking attendant had the keys while I was at a party. I could smell her perfume after I'd been driving for a while. I stopped the car and made her get out. It wasn't the first time she'd come on to me. We get it from fans all the time – they call the girls groupies. They follow the bands from venue to venue. Most of them just try to put things in your pockets or throw things at you on stage. Lisa wanted me to take her to my hotel but I told her to get lost. She said I would be sorry and the next thing I know the police arrived. Apparently, she was raped and she blamed me – but I swear on everything I hold dear that it wasn't me.'

'Can you prove you left her and went to the hotel alone?'

'No. The others were out. I didn't see anyone until the morning. Unless someone saw me alone as I went to the lifts – the receptionist gave me the key, but whether she will say I was alone I don't know, because she was talking to her friend. I know what it looks like, but I didn't do this, Mr Jenkins. The police are keeping an open mind. I gave a voluntary statement. I haven't been arrested but I have been warned not to leave the country.'

'They know you're here?'

'Yes.' Connor ran frustrated fingers through his thick dark hair. 'I've told you the truth, sir. I wanted Sarah to know before the morning papers came out.'

'It was in the Cambridge evening paper. They must have phoned it through from London. I like to know what is going on so I take it regularly,

226

but Sarah picked it off the mat when it was delivered.' The kettle had started to whistle. He poured water into a china pot just as his wife entered the kitchen. She was dressed and wearing a floral apron over her dark green skirt and cardigan, but her face was pale and there were shadows under her eyes. 'It's none of it true, Millie. Connor has just told me his side of it and I believe him.'

'I'm not sure Sarah will. She is crying again and she won't come down. I'm sorry but she says she doesn't want to see you, Connor.'

'If she would just let me explain what happened.'

'I'll do that for you. Sarah is very young, Connor. We've tried to keep her innocent and perhaps we've sheltered her too much. She sees things as black and white – and at the moment she is too hurt to be sensible. Let me talk to her and you can come back tomorrow when she's had a chance to calm down.'

'I really want to see her. She needs to know that I love her. I want to get married soon.'

'We'll have to see what happens,' Millicent Jenkins said. 'Sarah needs time to think about what she really wants. Come back tomorrow as my husband says and she may see you then.'

Connor looked at her in frustration. Short of charging up the stairs and banging on Sarah's door there was little he could do but leave.

'Tell her I love her, please.'

Outside in the car, Connor stared moodily in front of him. He'd been given a fair hearing, but he sensed that Mrs Jenkins was against him, perhaps because she'd spent the night comforting Sarah. He was angry and frustrated, but there was little he could do if Sarah refused to see him. He didn't know where he was going from here, because all he'd thought about since the previous morning was talking to Sarah, hoping that she would listen and believe him.

He couldn't go back to London until he'd seen Sarah. Besides, he wasn't sure he wanted to sing with the band again – any band. He'd felt good up on stage, flirting with the girls, and he hadn't given a thought to the reputation that he was gaining. Now it all seemed tawdry and pointless.

He decided to go to Daniel's house, because there was nowhere else until this started to blow over.

Daniel went into the hairdressing shop. A girl was shampooing a customer and another lady had rollers in her hair. They stared at him with hostility, because this was a ladies' hairdressing salon and he was intruding. Maura was standing behind the reception desk. She glared at him as she saw him.

'What can I do for you, sir?'

'I think we need to talk – about David.'

Her eyes widened. She hesitated, looked angry and then twitched her head towards the back of the shop.

'You had better come through,' she said. 'I shall only be a few minutes, Shirley.'

Daniel followed her through into what was obviously the staff area with chairs and shelves stocked with towels, lotions and shampoos. It smelled of something strong, like ammonia. Maura turned to face him, a glitter of defiance in her eyes.

'Is he with you? How did he find you? Have you spoken to him – told him...?'

'You already did that when you were drunk, apparently,' Daniel said coldly. 'He found my address in your things and caught the bus to Stretton, then walked to my home. It is a long walk for a lad who isn't used to country ways.'

'Don't look at me like that,' Maura muttered and looked shamed. 'I don't drink all the time. Just when I get desperate.'

'I'm not here to judge you,' Daniel said. 'You were drunk the night I took you home – when all this started. It seems you haven't learned your lesson. What are you going to do about the boy? He wants to go to his grandmother in Ireland.'

'That would suit my mother,' Maura said bitterly. 'She is always writing to me, telling me to go home. If he went without me, she would be in her element.' She shook her head. 'I'm not having it. You should have brought him back with you.'

'He didn't want to come and I can't blame him. It isn't much of a life for him here. He is bullied at school and then you hit him for fighting. He was standing up for you, because they were calling you filthy names.'

'I didn't mean to hit him,' Maura said. 'I love him. He knows I care about him.'

'It didn't seem that way to me,' Daniel told her. 'I think you've got a lot of fences to mend with your son, Maura. Why don't you start by taking

229

him to Ireland for a holiday?'

'What is it to you?'

'You made it my business when you came looking for me,' Daniel said, his mouth tight with anger. 'I'm going to keep David with us for tonight and bring him back tomorrow when he has calmed down. I can't force you to do what is best for him and I can't force you to stop drinking – but he is my son and I won't see you drag him into the gutter. Alice knows about you and about David. I reckon she would take him in if I asked her.'

'You can't take him away from me!'

'I can if you make yourself an unfit mother! It isn't a threat, Maura, just a warning. He is with us and he's safe. I'll bring him home tomorrow and after that it is up to you.'

Maura stared at him without speaking. Daniel left her and went out through the shop. He was glad to get outside, because the atmosphere was steamy and smelled strongly of lotions and perfume. He walked down the street, deciding to call in at the newsagent's to buy some sweets for the kids and a box of chocolates for Alice. A board was outside the shop proclaiming some headlines. Stopping to read them, Daniel's blood ran cold. He forgot about the sweets as he turned towards his car.

Connor had been accused of raping a fifteen-year-old girl! It made him feel sick. Once upon a time he would have sworn it was a lie, but his brother had gone off and left him in the lurch. He wasn't sure what Connor was capable of these days.

Maura felt cold all over after Daniel left her. She had never dreamed David would go to his father. She had mentioned that she'd been given money for him from his real father, but she didn't know she'd talked about Daniel when she was drunk.

How many times had David watched her when she was too drunk to know what she was doing? She felt hot and cold by turns as she realized what he must have felt – what he'd seen!

He was being bullied at school because of her. Maura felt the vomit in her throat. She ran outside to the yard toilet and was violently sick. Walking back to the rest room she rinsed her mouth with water and took a look at herself in the mirror. She had dark circles under her eyes and her skin was getting puffy. If she wasn't careful, she would die before her time – and she would be alone. As soon as David was able he would leave her. He would go to his grandmother and uncle in Ireland.

Maura knew that her mother would lecture her on her morals and the likelihood that she would end in hell, but she would take David in and care for him, give him a better life than Maura could. Perhaps she should take Daniel's advice and give her son a holiday in Ireland. Shirley was capable of looking after the shop for a couple of weeks.

Maura knew she couldn't live in Ireland herself, because she would find it too confining. Her mother was a strict Catholic and she would be bullied into going to church and to confession

– but David could stay if he wanted. She would take him and then come back...

'Connor!' Alice pushed a cup of hot strong tea in front of him as he finished telling her why he was home. The kitchen was warm, familiar and comforting with its smells of baking and herbs. 'That is awful, love. You should sue them for telling lies about you in the papers!'

'Thanks, Alice.' Connor gave her a grateful smile. He thought how pretty she looked, and happy – much happier than she had been a few months earlier. 'That is just like you – no questions, no doubts, just tea and sympathy. Thanks for believing me.'

'Of course I believe you. I know you, Con. You wouldn't do something like that – besides, you love Sarah.'

'Yes, I do, and I wouldn't – but I'm not sure Sarah will believe me. I went there first thing, before I came here. Mr Jenkins gave me a fair hearing, but Sarah's mother is angry. She knows Sarah is upset and ... I think she wants Sarah to break it off with me.'

'No! She couldn't,' Alice said and looked upset for him. 'That is so unfair. I know this must be a shock for her, but it isn't your fault. If Sarah loves you, she should stand by you – show you she cares.'

'Perhaps she doesn't,' Connor said. He toyed with the handle of his cup. 'Sarah is still very young. I know she is as old as you were when you married Dan, but you were different. Sarah's parents have sheltered her from the harsh reality

232

of life. She hasn't had to face things the way you did...'

'We had a war to fight. I loved Dan so much but he had to leave me as soon as we were married and for a long time I believed he might have been killed. You grow up quickly when you're faced with things like that – and you understand what is important.'

'Yes, I know. Dan was lucky to find you. I know you've had hard times, Alice – but you're still in love, aren't you?'

'Yes, I am,' Alice said and smiled. 'Things weren't right between us for a while but we're over that, Connor. I'll let Dan tell you about it himself, but let's say I understand how your Sarah feels – and I know that she will see sense in time if she loves you.'

'I wish I were as certain. I have to see her tomorrow, Alice. Is it all right if I stay here for a few days? I need to think about what I'm going to do...'

'This is your home, Con. Dan has gone out for a while, but I dare say he will be back soon.'

'I doubt he will be as forgiving as you. He thinks I ran out on him and he warned me it would end in tears.'

'Well, he should be understanding. Things are all right for us now,' Alice said. 'He's working on a car in the yard and he has sold the milking herd, but we've kept the chickens and pigs for the moment.'

'And the geese,' Connor said with a grin. 'One of them ran at me when I came in.'

'They should be in a pen. I bet the boys let

them out,' Alice said. 'I'll have to catch them or they will make a mess everywhere.' She looked at Connor. 'Your clothes are too good or I would ask you to give me a hand.'

'I'll go up and put some old cords on. Then I'll come and give you a hand.'

Nine

Alan was sitting in the walled garden. It was early spring but in places where the wind could not reach the sun was warm enough if you wrapped up well, and the flowerbeds were already ablaze with colour. He had fingerless mittens on his hands, a battered old hat pulled low over his forehead and a scarf around his throat. The half-finished painting in front of him was coming along well, and he had a feeling of well-being, of contentment.

Living here with Emily was as close to Paradise as he was likely to get this side of the great divide. He would have liked her to marry him so that they could travel together a little, but he knew that if he pushed too hard, it might spoil what they had together.

Alan had dreamed of being Emily's lover and he was very grateful that she had given him this time. He knew that it would not last for long. Sometimes his heart behaved oddly and he was breathless for short periods. Once or twice in the night he had felt really ill, and he was thankful that although they were lovers they did not sleep together. His pride would not let him tell Emily that his doctor had warned him he was on the slippery slope. She would wrap him in cotton wool and she might not let him make love to her. He didn't want to be treated as an invalid. He wanted to make the most of this gift he had been given. One day he would have to leave her, because he was determined not to become a burden to her, but he believed he had a short time left to him. Perhaps a few weeks or months...

'Alan, time for tea!'

He heard Emily's voice calling him and got to his feet. He could see her standing on the terrace and he thought, as he often did, how lovely she was. It was hardly fair to her that she was stuck here, bound by that stupid promise to Vane. She was young and there was so much love in her. He wished that he was young and dashing and could carry her off with him to a land of sunshine where she could live the way she was intended. She was such a passionate woman; he knew she needed what they had together as much as he did, and in Alan's experience that was a rare and precious thing in a woman of her class.

He knew that she struggled to keep this place afloat and it made him angry. He wished that he could take the burden from her, but she would not have let him even if he'd been rich enough. When he was gone she would have something, but not to throw away on this place – no, it was for her, to set her free...

He got up and began to walk towards her. Sometimes he felt so weary, but not today, when the sun was shining and Emily was waiting for him.

* * *

Connor had just finished penning the last of the geese when he saw his brother drive into the yard in the van. Daniel got out and stood staring at him for a moment and then turned, walking into the house without a word or even a nod of his head. Connor frowned, because he guessed that Daniel had seen the papers – and his reaction was obvious. He believed that Connor was guilty.

Anger roiled inside him. He strode towards the kitchen just as the children came running across the yard. Danny flung himself at him, and Connor swept him off his feet. He greeted all his brother's children with smiles and promised them sweets when they got in the house. Then he saw the other boy, standing back a little from the others. His hair was darker than Danny's but in all other respects they could have been twins.

'You don't know our cousin David,' Danny said. 'Mum said he's a distant cousin but he looks like me, doesn't he?'

'Yes, he does,' Connor agreed. 'Hi, David. Nice to see you. Are you all coming in now? I think Alice has been baking again.'

'Mrs Searles bakes nice cakes,' David said. 'Are you my ... Mr Searles' brother Connor? I heard you singing on the wireless. I think you're good. I should like to buy your records, but I don't get much pocket money.'

'Thank you,' Connor said. His anger had cooled now. He couldn't say anything in front of the children and perhaps that was as well. 'I've got some copies of my new records for you, kids – you too if you like, David?'

He shut from his mind the worrying thought that perhaps the singles would not be released now. Daniel glanced at him as they walked into the kitchen as a group. His expression was a mixture of doubt, annoyance and uncertainty. Alice had told him Connor's side of things and he was mulling it over.

Connor decided to let it go. He didn't want to argue with his brother, especially in front of the kids. He left them sitting down to Alice's lemon barley and cake and went upstairs, changing into his usual gear. He took his gifts of records and sweets down to the kitchen, making sure that 'cousin' David got his share.

'I'm going for a walk,' he announced. 'I'll speak to you later, Dan. I have some thinking to do.'

He wandered along the drives for a while, enjoying the peace and the sound of a meadow lark that hovered overhead and sang his song. Connor's thoughts were chasing themselves in circles because he didn't know what he wanted to do for the future. He had been caught up in a whirlwind, and the brief time he'd spent rushing from one venue to the next had been lucrative. Despite the high fees for agents and the record company's share of the proceeds, Connor had over forty thousand pounds in the bank. It was nowhere near as much as he might have made if the records had gone to number one and got into America, but it was far more than he'd ever expected. Enough to buy a house and go into business.

He recalled seeing a sign in the village about a

property for sale. It was a large piece of land with commercial buildings on it and might make a garage. Maybe he would buy it and let Daniel set up the garage he'd always wanted; it would still leave him plenty to buy a house and start up in business for himself – if only he knew what he wanted to do with his life.

Connor had come to one conclusion and that was his time on the road had finished. He didn't want to go back to that kind of life. Recording contracts and theatre work were another matter, but he probably wouldn't get a chance to work as a singer again. He had no idea what else he could do, but he knew he didn't want to go back to the life he'd had before he became a singer.

He had to think of something different. In the meantime he was going to find a phone and ring Terry. Terry would know if the record company had been in touch...

'You don't have to see him tomorrow,' Mrs Jenkins told her daughter. 'Just because your father seems to think he is telling the truth, it doesn't mean you have to put up with this, Sarah. Even if there is no truth in this story, it isn't what you want – is it?'

'I don't like Connor being away all the time,' Sarah admitted. She had stopped crying after her father told her that he was convinced the story in the papers was a lie, but her nose was still red and her expression was miserable. 'People will think it is true even if it isn't – and the girls will look at me and laugh behind my back. They were jealous when they saw the presents he gave me, and his picture in the papers, but now they will think he doesn't really care about me.'

'Is that why you are upset?'

'Yes...' Sarah blushed. 'It isn't just that, Mum. But I don't like people staring at me and whispering behind my back. I do love Connor and I like going out with him, but he's always away. I feel stupid if I go out with my friends, because I know they are saying things...'

'That is what you get when you marry someone famous,' her mother said. 'If it upsets you, Sarah, perhaps you should break off your engagement. He will never want to stay at home and do a proper job like your father could give him.'

'Mum!' Sarah stared at her. She felt sick and tears were pricking her eyes again. She loved Connor and she wanted to believe him, of course she did, but perhaps her mother was right. She didn't think she could bear to face her friends knowing what they would say about Connor. 'I do care about him, but...' She shook her head and sighed. 'I'm not sure if I want to marry him now.'

'Supposing I take you away for a few weeks,' her mother suggested. 'Would you like to go and stay with me at a hotel in Bournemouth? You could write to Connor and tell him you need to think things over.'

'Yes.' Sarah caught at the lifeline her mother offered. 'I'll ask work if I can go on holiday – and I will see Connor, but I'll tell him I need some time to think things through.'

'Yes, I think that is fair,' Mrs Jenkins said and

smiled at her. 'Remember, I shall still think the best of you whatever you decide. You do not have to marry him, Sarah. You can give him his ring back and that will be the end of it.'

'You think there is some truth in it, don't you?' Connor asked. They had gone out to the yard together to look at some of Daniel's cars and talk. 'I saw the way you looked at me when you first came back from Ely.'

'I wasn't sure,' Daniel replied. 'Once upon a time I would have been certain it was a lie – but you've been mixing with people that get caught up in all kinds of things. You might have been drunk or—'

'On drugs?' Connor arched his brows. 'Come on, Dan. You should know I wouldn't touch that stuff. As for rape – I've never forgotten what Clay did to Margaret. If you think I would do something like that to a kid – that is what she is, Dan, a fifteen-year-old kid!'

'Sorry. I should have known you wouldn't. To tell you the truth, my head was mixed up. I had just been to see Maura Jacobs – David's mother – and I was angry. Seeing those headlines made me as mad as fire. I had been lecturing Maura about her behaviour and then I saw that you had been accused of rape...'

'You should be angry. I'm angry that they've printed those lies and that the other papers have followed suit without asking for my side of the story.'

'You've probably made it worse by running away. They will think it proof of guilt.'

'They can damned well think what they like! I phoned Terry. He says the company is pulling our contract – it may be too late to stop a couple of singles going out, but the album won't see the light of day.'

'I'm sorry,' Daniel said. 'That is rotten luck. You were doing so well.'

'I've got some money put by. Enough to see me set up in a business of some kind – when I decide what I want to do...' He hesitated. 'I've spoken to John Tench about that land in the village street, Daniel. He wants a thousand pounds for it. I reckon it would cost another thousand to set it up as a garage with a decent showroom. There are buildings already – of course, you would need to apply for planning permission for change of use, but Tench is on the local council and he says a garage is needed. He thinks you would get the permission for change of use easily.'

'Sounds a good opportunity, but I don't have two thousand pounds to spare,' Daniel said, smothering a sigh. 'I'm doing better since I got rid of the milking herd but the garage is still a long way off.'

'It doesn't have to be. I can afford to buy it and pay for whatever you need, Dan. I don't want anything from it, but if you want to pay me back one day, you can. As far as I am concerned, it is something back for all you've done for me. You and Alice gave me a home after Frances went off her head that time – and I've never paid a penny in rent.'

'You worked for your keep,' Daniel said. 'You

don't owe me anything, Con.'

'Well, the option to pay me back is there,' Connor said. 'Alice deserves it, Dan. Even if you don't want it for yourself, think of her. You could sell the land, move into a house in the village and have a better life for yourselves. Alice would make more friends, mix with other women more than she can stuck here in the fen. You could have a television too.' He grinned because he knew his brother had secretly hankered for one for a long time.

'Won't it leave you short?' Daniel was hesitating. Connor felt pleased, because he knew his brother was weakening.

'To be honest, I'm rolling in it, Dan. I haven't splashed my earnings on new cars, because the one you gave me suits me fine. I was saving for a house at first but the money kept coming in and I've been putting it by. It will set me up in a business when I'm ready. I don't know yet what I want to do – but I've finished with gigs and being on the road all the time.'

'You won't go back to recording?'

'I doubt I shall get the chance. The police can't prove anything, because I didn't touch her – except pull her out of the car – but mud sticks. I doubt if a record company would touch me now.'

'Sue her and the papers for defamation of character.'

'Don't think I haven't thought of it,' Connor said, eyes glittering. 'I'm going to speak to Sarah tomorrow, but after that I'm going back to London. I'll talk to someone I know about a lawyer. I want a retraction in the paper, but if Lisa refuses to admit she lied...'

'It isn't fair that you should lose so much. I'll take your money, Connor, because it is just what I need. I know I can make a success of the garage and one day I'll pay you back with interest, though it won't be for a while yet. I owe Frances some money and I want to pay her as soon as I can.'

'I'm in no hurry.' Connor gave his brother a sharp look. 'So just who is Cousin David?'

'Alice didn't tell you?'

'She said she would leave it to you.'

'He is my son. I met his mother, Maura, during an air raid in Liverpool during the war. She was drunk and I took her home. We had to take shelter in a hotel and she was crying ... She begged me to hold her and...' Daniel shook his head. 'I've never known why I did it. She was pretty enough, but I had Alice and I never intended it to happen. I've wished a thousand times it hadn't. I suppose that's why I wasn't sure what you'd done, Con. Things can just happen without your meaning it...'

'With a girl who is willing and old enough, perhaps. Rape is another thing, Dan. I'm not like Clay.'

'Clay.' Daniel looked angry. 'Did you know he's had the cheek to go creeping round Frances? Alice said Frances had told her she'd had another letter from him asking if he could visit – and she has told him he can.'

'Does she know that he raped Margaret? His own father's widow...' Con's mouth thinned in disgust. 'I should have thought she would tell him to take a running jump.'

'I think Emily may have told her. I know Frances wouldn't have anything to do with him for years, but perhaps she thinks it is time to forgive.'

'I'll never forget or forgive,' Connor said. 'Do you see anything of him?'

'We nod if we pass in the street. Maybe Frances is lonely. We've asked her to stay and I know Emily has too, but she won't come. She wants us to go there again, but I never seem to have time.'

'Frances and I ... well, she wasn't exactly a loving sister when I had to live with her during the war. I know she went through a lot at that time, but I've never felt the same about her. I suppose I should visit, but I'm more comfortable with Emily.'

'I know she was a bit hard on you, but you should consider visiting her, Connor.'

'I've thought about going to see Emily,' Connor said. 'Frances ... well, we don't get on as we ought. She probably believes every word the papers say about me.'

Frances put a hand to her temple. Her head was throbbing and she felt ill. The headlines in the paper about Connor had brought the past back to her. Clay had raped Margaret. Sam had tried to rape her and then he had her shut away in a mental institution, because she wasn't fit to be the mother of his grandson. Frances thought she would have died there if Emily hadn't somehow

245

found her and got her out.

Frances felt the despair of that time sweep over her. She glanced over her shoulder nervously. She never felt safe these days, even in her own suite at the hotel. Sometimes the dark depression that descended on her was so terrible that she was tempted to take her own life.

She was so lonely. So afraid! She wished that her family would visit her, but they all made excuses about being too busy. Emily was wrapped up in her new lover, and Daniel was always working. Alice wrote to her regularly, but letters were becoming harder to read and almost impossible to write. Her hand shook and the words got jumbled on the page so that she wasn't sure what she was saying. She didn't want to tell anyone that she was ill – she couldn't bear fuss over nothing – but she was lonely.

Clay had visited, though. Something had happened while Clay was here – something Frances regretted. She couldn't remember but she thought she might have signed something. She wasn't sure what, because her head was all over the place.

Frances knew that the kind of loneliness she felt came from within. It was a black well that would swallow her up one day. She would be sucked down into the darkness and that would be the end. Sometimes she wished that the end would come quickly, but then she was afraid. If she could be sure that it would be the end of pain – a quiet peace that would let her rest – then she would welcome death, but she sometimes saw visions of hell.

A little cry of fear left her lips. Were the demons that plucked at her flesh real or imagined? Sam had said she was mad, and perhaps she was – perhaps she would not die but live on in chains of madness...

No, she wasn't mad! Sam was playing tricks on her, taking his revenge from the grave. He couldn't do that, could he? Frances hadn't killed him, but she thought she knew who had. Rosalind, Sam's wife, had hinted at something. Frances hadn't told anybody. She'd been glad that he was dead – that he couldn't haunt her any more.

She looked towards the corner of the room. Sam was there. Staring at her from empty sockets where his eyes had once been. His flesh had turned to dripping sores and he raised his arm to point at her.

'Come and join me, Fran...'

'No!' Frances cowered away, covering her eyes with her hands. He wasn't really there. He was just one of the hallucinations she was having from time to time. The doctor had told her she might as her condition got worse, but it was happening so quickly. She had thought she would have more time. She must write to Emily. She wanted Emily. She was afraid she might have done something stupid. She wanted Emily to know before it was too late.

She got up and walked unsteadily towards her desk, but before she could get there her head started whirling. She gave a gasp and stretched her hands out in front of her as she fell...

Connor was thoughtful as he drove into Ely the

next morning. He had been rehearsing what he wanted to say to Sarah, but he wasn't sure she would believe him – or that she would even see him. He had let her down. Carried away by success, he had gone along with the others and the record company. He should have fixed a date for the wedding and married the girl he loved. Sarah could have come with him on the road until they found somewhere to live. If she had, this stupid business would never have happened.

He was feeling apprehensive as he knocked at the door. Mrs Jenkins opened it and told him to come in.

'Please wait in the sitting room, Connor,' she said in a flat, cold voice. 'Sarah will join you in a moment. I believe she has something to tell you.'

Connor didn't much like the sound of that, though he knew he was lucky Sarah would even see him. He waited until he heard the sound of her footsteps, turning as she opened the door and entered. She looked lovely, very beautiful and young.

'Sarah,' he said. 'It isn't true, please believe me. I wouldn't do anything like that! You must know I wouldn't...'

'Daddy told me he believes you. I was very hurt, Connor. I cried all night, because I hated reading those terrible things. It was awful.'

'None of them were true. I love you. I just want to get married and forget about singing.'

'No!' Sarah flushed as he looked at her. 'I mean, I'm not sure. Even if I believe you, it makes no difference. All the stories about you

248

and other girls I read in the papers. Some of it has to be true, Con. I don't want to live that way – never sure where you are or what you are doing...'

'It wouldn't be that way,' Connor said. 'I haven't made up my mind what I should do yet, but I want us to be together all the time. I'll buy us a nice house and start some kind of a business. Please don't say it is over, Sarah. I do love you...'

He moved towards her, but she jumped back as if she were afraid of him. Connor stood absolutely still. Did she think he would harm her?

'Listen to me,' she said. 'I'm going away for a long holiday with Mum. We're going to Bournemouth. While we're away I'll think about what you've said – and then I'll decide.'

Connor stared at her and suddenly he was angry. If she loved him, she wouldn't believe one word of those lies; she would want to get married straight away. She had liked having a boyfriend other girls wanted at the start, but now she was behaving like a silly child.

'Be careful you don't take too long to decide,' he said in a cold voice. 'Because I might change my mind.'

He walked past her to the door, carried by his anger.

'Connor – you don't mean that! You can't expect me to forgive you just like that!'

Connor turned to look at her. 'You have nothing to forgive,' he said. 'I had plenty of chances but like an idiot I stayed true to you. Grow up, Sarah. Start thinking like a woman instead of a child.'

He left her standing there and went out the front door, letting it slam behind him deliberately. He loved Sarah but he wasn't going to beg. If she loved him, she would know that he hadn't been playing around, no matter what the papers said.

He was a damned fool to care!

Connor had driven half the way home before pain took over from the anger. He loved Sarah and he was fairly certain he had just burned his boats. She would hate him now for sure – and her mother would tell her it was good riddance to bad rubbish.

'I'm really not surprised,' Sarah's mother said when she went into the parlour and found her daughter in tears. 'I've never thought he was the right one for you, dearest. I didn't want to put pressure on you, but you can find someone much nicer – much more our sort.'

'Oh, Mum,' Sarah said and blew her nose hard. 'I don't want someone like that – nice and dull. I want Connor. He makes me come alive and I love him.'

'Then why didn't you tell him so?'

Sarah shook her head. She ran from the room because she was going to cry again if she listened to her mother. Connor had always run after her, told her repeatedly that she was wonderful and that he loved her. It had shocked her when he told her he might not wait while she made up her mind – and then he'd said she should grow up!

Throwing herself on the bed, she wept until she couldn't cry any more. She got up and went into the bathroom, bathing her face with cold water. She looked such a mess and now she was angry again. How could Connor say such things to her – and after what he'd done too!

But what had he really done that was so wrong? Sarah knew the girls threw themselves at him; it had happened when they'd been out together and at the local dances before he started making records. He always grinned and answered them in a friendly way, but he hadn't shown any interest. He said it was a part of the job, and in her heart Sarah knew he hadn't raped that girl. Connor wouldn't do anything like that – even when he was angry with her he'd just walked away.

She sat on the edge of the bed and thought about things – about what she would do if she didn't marry Connor. She had a good job at the dress shop but she only really came alive when she was with Connor, in his arms, kissing him. Even if he had flirted with some of the girls, it didn't really matter, because he loved her – at least he *had* loved her.

Sarah didn't know what to do. She was going away with her mother for two weeks. She couldn't change that and she didn't want to, because she still needed time to think – away from her friends and people she knew.

Besides, she wasn't going to run after Connor like one of his groupies. He would come back. If he loved her, he would come back and ask her to forgive him. She refused to think about what she would do if he simply accepted that it was over between them...

'Yes, I spoke to Sarah,' Connor said when Alice asked him. 'She says she needs time to think about it – but I can't see what needs thinking about. Either she loves me or she doesn't. I think it is over between us, Alice.'

'Surely not? You're upset, Connor – angry. You need time to calm down and get used to the idea that Sarah isn't perfect.'

'What do you mean?'

'She is lovely and you love her – but we all have our faults,' Alice said. 'She is upset, Connor, and she has been a bit silly, but it doesn't mean she won't come to her senses when she's had a little time. Besides, she is young and you have to make allowances for that.'

'Maybe she is too much of a child to think about getting married,' Connor said. 'I think her mother wants her to break it off with me.'

'She won't if she loves you. She didn't say it was over – did she?'

Connor shook his head. 'No, just that she needed time to think things over. I told her not to take too long.'

'That was a bit harsh,' Alice said with a gentle smile. 'Why don't you go back and see her this evening?'

'No, I don't think so.' Connor looked stubborn. 'I'm going back to London to talk to some lawyers and then I think I'll visit Emily.'

'Are you sure you're not making a mistake?'

'I'm not certain of anything,' Connor told her.

'But I've no intention of begging. Sarah wants time to think, so I'll give it to her.'

He walked upstairs, still feeling raw with hurt pride. Sarah couldn't think much of him or she wouldn't need time when he asked her to marry him. He hadn't touched that girl and he was going to fight back, but anyone who knew him should know in their heart that he was innocent.

'Lady Vane? This is Tara Manners. I work for Mrs Danby...'

'Yes, I remember you,' Emily said, feeling a little shiver down her spine. 'Is something wrong? Frances is all right, isn't she?'

'She says she is,' Tara said. 'She had a faint or something yesterday and I called the doctor to her. He ordered her to bed, but she seems better this morning. She said it was just a little chill that turned to a fever, but I have a feeling there is something more serious.'

'Why? I don't understand.'

'She has seemed strange recently – not quite herself.'

'In what way?'

'Forgetful ... hesitant ... I'm not sure how to put it, but she isn't the same.'

'I see. Is Frances in the hotel?'

'She went out for a walk.'

'I shall telephone her later.'

'You won't say that I rang you?'

'No, I shan't mention you, Tara. Thank you for telephoning. I shall speak to my sister this evening.'

Emily replaced the receiver. She frowned as

she went to look for Alan. It was almost four months since she'd seen Frances, and that had been just a flying visit to deliver Christmas presents. It must be six weeks since she had spoken to her sister. She had been so wrapped up with Alan that she hadn't noticed the time slipping by. She wondered whether she ought to pop down to the hotel rather than just telephoning. She would have a word with Alan and see if he had any plans for the next week or so. He could come with her if he chose.

'Have you seen Mr Leicester?' she asked the housekeeper as they met in the hall.

'I believe he went to the garden on the west side, ma'am. He said he wanted to make the most of the fine weather.'

'I'll see if I can find him,' Emily said. 'We'll have tea in the small parlour in half an hour, please.'

'Yes, ma'am.'

Emily parted from her and went through several parlours at the front of the house until she came to what was known as the music room. It overlooked the west garden and there was a French window, which led down some stone steps into a sunken garden surrounded by a grey stone wall. As she opened the long windows and went out on to the terrace her eyes travelled over the beautiful scenery: tall trees, a lily pool and smooth lawns. It was quite a fine view of the house from the end of this garden, and sure enough Alan's easel had been set up in a vantage spot. However, he did not seem to be sitting there. Her gaze moved on to the lily pond and what she saw made her give a little cry of alarm. Alan appeared to be lying half in and half out of the pool. He must have gone to look at it and slipped or fainted.

Emily went quickly down the steps towards where his body lay. Fortunately, his face was not in the water or he might have drowned. She felt for a pulse – it was there, though very faint. She made a brief examination, but nothing appeared to be broken. He must have had a seizure or a blackout. Emily got to her feet. She spotted someone in the house and waved her arms, calling out for help.

A man came to the French windows. As he left the music room and started walking towards her, she saw that it was her brother Connor. Emily frowned because she had received a letter from Alice that morning. She had known that the stories in the newspapers must be lies, of course, but Alice's letter had confirmed it.

'I'm so glad to see you,' she said as he sprinted to join her. 'I was going to try and telephone you, but now you're here and we can talk – but first I need help. Alan seems to have had a blackout or something. I wonder if you can manage to carry him into the house so that the doctor can see him in his room?'

'I can manage that,' Connor said. 'But are you sure we should move him?'

'I don't think he has broken anything. We can't leave him here. The doctor might be ages before he gets here. Can you lift him alone or shall I get someone to help you?'

'I think I can carry him. I might be a singer

255

these days but I've carried dead weights enough on the farm.'

'He isn't dead!' Emily cried. 'I know you didn't mean it that way ... I'm in a panic. Please help him, Connor. He has been ill but I thought he was so much better...'

Connor bent and lifted the man. He was heavy but manageable, at least for a short distance. He hoisted Alan over his shoulder as he would a heavy sack of wheat and walked into the parlour. Emily followed behind, looking uncharacteristically nervous.

'Put him on the sofa and I'll get someone to help you take him to his room,' she said. 'Poor Alan. I am afraid he may be really ill this time.'

'He doesn't look too good,' Connor said. 'Chin up, Emily love – he isn't dead yet.'

Connor was in the music room looking through his sister's record collection when she came back downstairs after the doctor's visit. He saw she was looking upset and guessed the news could not be good.

'How is he?'

'Alive but still unconscious,' Emily replied. 'I think he must have known this was coming but he hadn't said anything about feeling unwell. I am so glad he is still here. He was talking about leaving for France next week.'

'Perhaps he didn't want it to happen here.'

'No, he would hate to think he was a trouble to me – but, of course, he never could be.' Emily caught back a sob. 'He told me he was ill when he asked if he could stay here last year, but he

256

was doing what his doctor told him. I thought ... he would have several years.'

'You love him, don't you?'

'I am certainly very fond of him,' Emily said. 'I tried not to let myself love, because I seem to lose every man I care about – lovers, I mean.' She shook her head, as if to clear her thoughts. 'What about you, Con? This rubbish in the papers is scandalous. You should sue them.'

'I've been in touch with a lawyer. I tried to speak to Lisa and her father but they wouldn't see me. My lawyer says it's best if I stay clear and leave it to him. He says he'll get someone to find out more about her and see what he can come up with.' He raked his hair back from his temples. 'Trouble is, Sarah seems to believe the stories – at least she is fed up reading them.'

'Has she broken off the engagement?'

'Not yet, but I think her mother is trying to persuade her.'

'I am so sorry, Con. This is rotten luck, especially when you were doing so well.'

'I'll get over it. I'd almost had enough of being on the road anyway. It isn't as glamorous as it sounds, Emily.'

'No, I don't imagine it is. Have you thought what you will do?'

'I'm still trying to work that one out,' Connor replied ruefully. 'I couldn't go back to working on the land. I wouldn't fit in any more – and I need to move on. I just have to think of something I could do that would interest me.'

'You know you are welcome to stay here until you come to a decision. I have more than enough room...' Emily sighed. 'I managed to get the repairs done at the dower house. They cost me an arm and a leg – all of the money I got from selling those pictures. Unfortunately, they didn't fetch as much as I hoped, though one did reach its reserve at auction, thanks to your suggestion. However, the house is ready for tenants to move into. I have it with an agent but so far no takers.'

'You're not having much luck either.' Connor was thoughtful. 'This is such a beautiful place, Emily. It seems a pity that more people can't see it...' He looked thoughtful and Emily gave him a little poke in his arm.

'What are you thinking now?'

'I've stayed in a lot of hotels these past months – some luxurious ones and some right dumps. Have you ever thought about the potential this house has, Emily?'

'You mean ... turn it into a hotel?' Emily stared at him. 'I couldn't do that, Con. It is Robert's heritage and God knows what Vane would have thought! Besides, I wouldn't have the faintest idea how to start.'

'You wouldn't need to open all of it – perhaps the East Wing? You would need more bathrooms and washbasins, toilets – but you could soon learn all you need about hotel management.'

'I don't have time,' Emily said with a shake of her head. 'Besides, I couldn't think of it ... No, it isn't possible. I'll manage somehow.'

'I think Vane would say it was a good idea,' Connor said. 'No, don't look like that, Emily. If he knew what a struggle it was for you to keep everything together, he would tell you that you should either sell or make it a business. You could open the estate to the public; let them pay to look round the gardens, and use one wing as accommodation for guests.'

'You make it sound so easy,' Emily said and sighed. 'Even if I thought Vane would have agreed, I'm not sure I could handle all the work it involves – and it would cost a lot of money to set up.'

'I have money. I could do a lot of the work myself – set up a little building company, but work exclusively on the estate, at least until it was up and running.'

'I couldn't ask you to invest your money here...'

'Why not? I would take a share of the profits when you start making money – and it would give me somewhere to live.'

'You're serious about this, aren't you?' Connor nodded. 'When did you come up with this idea?'

'Just now,' he said. 'I suppose the building work has been in my mind for a while. Sarah's father would have taken me on with him before the record deal came up, but I didn't want to leave Daniel in the lurch. As it happened I did that anyway, but I've made it up to him. He has the land and the money to start his garage. After I did that work on the dower house I thought about taking up restoration work one day – and I have the money to set up my own firm now.'

'You're making it sound tempting.' Emily looked at him thoughtfully. 'Don't think I'm not grateful for the offer, Con, but I need time to consider. I really do have my hands full running

the estate, but I suppose with you here I might...'
She shook her head. 'I mustn't rush into a decision like that, because the estate is only in my care. It will go to Robert when he is twenty-five.'

'That is still a long time in the future,' Connor reminded her. 'If you don't do something you will end up selling land or treasures from the house over and over, until you're left with a big house and nothing else.'

'I know you're right – but I still need to think this through.'

'It was just a suggestion,' Connor said and smiled. 'I'm not twisting your arm, Emily – but I think I know where my future lies even if you don't take my advice.'

'And what about Sarah?'

'I don't know. She says she needs time, so the only thing I can do is to give it to her.'

'Will you stay here?'

'If you will have me. Is there anything I can do to help you? You will want time to look after Alan while he is ill. I'm pretty good at maths so I could keep accounts or do any jobs that need seeing to in the house or on the estate.'

'I was going to inspect some cottages this week. I've been told they need work – one of them has a leaky roof and that will definitely have to be done. If you could sort out the estimates for me...'

'I would enjoy that,' Connor said. 'It will give me an idea of what builders charge for their work. I think I should do a bit of research before I start the business.'

'You're really thinking of settling in this area?'

'It's as good a place as any other. I have friends here – and I would be close to you. I can find a house of my own in time.'

'You could live here until you know what you want. In fact, I would be happy if you made it a permanent arrangement, Connor. There are plenty of outbuildings where you can set up your yard. Even if I don't go through with the idea of the hotel, I would love it if you made your home here.'

'Thanks, Emily.' Connor narrowed his gaze. 'It won't bother you if people read that stuff in the papers?'

'We'll get a retraction,' Emily told him and looked determined. 'One thing about being Lady Vane is that you know people with influence. I'll contact some of my friends and see if we can't get an apology from the paper that started all this.'

Ten

Sarah wandered disconsolately along the beach at Bournemouth. There were a few brave souls, most of them with dogs, battling against the stiff breeze that blew in from an angry sea. The water looked grey with an underlying brownish tinge and white crests, reflecting the unbroken cloud of the sky above. It was too early in the season for most people. Only one summer show was open; the others started the week after they returned home. There was a dance advertised for that Saturday night, but without friends Sarah was reluctant to spend her evening on the fringes waiting for someone to take pity on her.

She had been to all the cinemas, and she was bored sitting in the small hotel lounge listening to someone play the piano in the evenings. This holiday had been a mistake, she realized, feeling miserable as she stood staring out to sea. A dark head broke the surface of the water. She thought it must be a seal and felt excited, but there was no one to share the moment with her. Her mother hadn't wanted to brave the beach that morning. She had gone to have her hair done, making Sarah promise to meet her back at the hotel for lunch.

Overhead, gulls cried, the eerie sound they

made bringing Sarah to a deep awareness of her loneliness. Oh, what was the point of staying here? It hadn't helped her to resolve her doubts. All it had done was bring home the knowledge that she was still in love with Connor.

'Hi there.' The voice startled her. She swung round and saw a young man in baggy, worn trousers and long boots up to his thighs. He was wearing a thick roll-neck jumper and his dark hair was cut very short. He had a rugged sort of face, skin tanned and wind roughened, and she guessed that he was a fisherman. 'You look lost. Are you on your own?'

'I'm on holiday with my mother,' Sarah said. His manner was friendly, and in her loneliness she hesitated, lingering despite the warnings her mother was always giving her not to speak to strange men. 'There isn't much going on yet, is there?'

'The tourist stuff is only just starting. If you lived here, you would know about the clubs for locals. Do you like jive or Rock 'n' Roll?'

'Yes ... yes, I do,' Sarah said and her heart caught. She was about to say that her boyfriend was a singer, but she'd taken off her ring. 'Is there a club here, then?'

'Yes. We meet on Friday nights at the Old Oak – that's a pub the locals use. You probably don't know it. It isn't near the seafront. You would need to catch a bus – unless I picked you up?'

'That's this evening...' Sarah thought quickly. She didn't know him but the alternative was another dull evening at the hotel. 'I don't know you – what's your name?'

'It's Rod Seagrove. My father owns a fishing trawler and in the summer I take visitors round the coast in my own boat.'

'I'm Sarah,' she said and held out her hand, then dropped it and laughed in embarrassment, because it was too formal. 'I should like to come with you this evening, Rod – just as a friend. I'll pay my entrance fee – if the club is open to visitors?'

'They will let you in if you go with me. It costs five shillings for a one-night membership.' He hesitated, then asked, 'Where shall I pick you up?'

'Do you know the Sea View Hotel? It is just a small place up there.' Sarah pointed to the cliffs above them. She glanced at her wristwatch. 'I should be getting back for lunch. I'll leave the hotel and walk towards the bus stop at the bottom at seven.'

'All right. I'll see you there,' he said. 'It will be fun.'

Sarah nodded. Her heart was racing as she walked away. Already, she was beginning to wonder if she had done the right thing. She didn't know the young fisherman – and she was still engaged to Connor, even if she had taken off her ring.

'Do you think David is all right?' Alice asked Daniel when he came in for a cup of tea that afternoon. 'We haven't heard anything since he went home.'

'He didn't want to go, but I told him running away was no good because he would end up in trouble with the police. Maura seemed sober when I handed him over. She told me she was making arrangements to take him to Ireland for a holiday.'

Alice fiddled with the handle of her teacup. 'He seemed a nice lad. I hope she keeps her word, Dan. I wouldn't like to think of him having to cope with her getting drunk. He is only a child, for all he looks so serious.'

'You felt for him, didn't you?' She nodded and Daniel smiled. 'Do you want me to call in one day next week and see how he is? I think it is half-term holiday – or is that the following week?'

'The week after,' Alice said and shook her head because Daniel never knew what day it was, let alone when the school holidays were. 'I think you should go tomorrow. It is Saturday and he will be home from school. I'll get up early and bake a cake for him.'

'You really are bothered about that boy, aren't you?'

'He looks like Danny – and he's your son,' Alice said. 'I've got a bad feeling about things, Dan. I'm not sure why but...' She sighed. 'I suppose I'm just being silly, but he did come looking for help.'

'Yes, he did,' Daniel said. 'You're a good woman, Alice Searles, and your instincts are not often wrong. I'll go over tomorrow and see what is going on...'

Sarah put on one of her best dirndl skirts and a tight pink jumper with matching flat shoes. She wanted to fit in with the other girls at the club, ignoring the pretty dresses hanging in the wardrobe that she usually wore for an evening at the hotel. Her mother looked at her oddly as she went to her room.

'That is a pretty jumper,' Mrs Jenkins said. 'Are you ready for dinner, Sarah?'

'I'm not hungry, Mum,' Sarah said. 'I met someone today. I'm going to a Rock 'n' Roll club with her.' She crossed her fingers behind her back as she lied. 'I've got to go because I'm catching a bus and I'll meet her there.'

'I'm not sure you should, Sarah. I don't really like you going out with people you don't know. This is a big town and you might get lost...'

'Mum! I'm nineteen. I'm old enough to make my own decisions. Besides, I'm bored with sitting around in this hotel every night. I want some fun.'

'I thought there would be more on,' her mother admitted. 'I've been asked to join a whist-four this evening. I suppose you are old enough to know what you are doing – but be careful of the men you meet at this club. What is the girl's name?'

'Rose,' Sarah lied, crossing her fingers again. 'I've got to go, Mum. Have a good evening. I shan't be too late.'

'I want you back here by eleven at the latest,' her mother said. 'Are you sure you have enough money for bus fares? I should keep enough for a taxi if I were you, because you never know if you might need one.'

'Yes, I've got plenty,' Sarah said. 'I'll be home

on time.'

She kissed her mother's cheek and escaped. Sarah didn't enjoy lying to her mother, but it was ridiculous that she should have to tell her everything. A lot of her friends had already had sex with their boyfriends. The only reason Sarah hadn't was because Connor was away so much. Not that she had any intention of going that far this evening, but she might let Rod kiss her a few times. If she didn't have some fun soon, she would die of boredom!

Maura stared at the clock on the mantle. It was nearly nine and she was dying for a drink. She'd got rid of every bottle she had in the house after Daniel Searles' visit. Her intentions had been good. She'd really meant to keep off the booze until she took David to Ireland to stay with his grandmother, but the need inside her was becoming unbearable. It was like a gnawing ache, an itch that couldn't be scratched.

She couldn't bear it! She needed a drink. Just one little drink to take away the craving, the emptiness deep down inside her. There was nothing wrong with that, was there? All that fuss just because she'd had a couple too many once or twice. She would only have one. She just needed one small drink. Where was the crime in that?

She got up and walked softly through the hall to David's bedroom, glancing inside. Her son was fast asleep. He wouldn't miss her for half an hour. That was all she would be, just thirty minutes. Long enough to have a drink and talk to someone.

She went into her bedroom, changed her skirt and cardigan for something more glamorous, put on lipstick and perfume and smiled at her reflection. She still looked attractive when she was dressed up. She was too young to stay at home every night with a young boy. She needed the company of men – and she needed a drink.

Maura had already forgotten her intention to have one drink and then go home. It was a while since she'd been to the High Flyer pub. Would there be anyone new? Sometimes men from out of town came there to drink; they were members of a fishing club and they were usually out for a good time – playing away from home.

Her heart raced as she went into the bar and discovered that it was full of men. Her eyes went over them and she saw that most of them were strangers to her. She went up to the bar, waiting for her turn.

'Well, what have we here?' a deep voice asked from her right. 'I think things just got interesting, boys. Buy you a drink, pretty lady?'

'I'll have a whisky, if you don't mind,' Maura said. She appraised the man who had spoken. He was dressed in decent clothes and looked as if he had a few bob in his pocket – and the gleam in his eyes told her that he was looking for company. He wasn't really her type, too big and bulky, but she was past caring. She smiled, forgetting her son sleeping at home. 'My name is Maura – what should I call you?'

'Call me Pete,' he suggested and his hand moved to touch her backside, giving it a little squeeze. Maura didn't move away or glare at him. He was making it obvious that he wanted sex, but so did she, so that was just fine. 'I think we are going to have ourselves a good time...'

Sarah glanced at the clock on the wall. It was already nearly eleven o'clock. She'd been having so much fun she hadn't noticed the way the time was going. There was a small bar and Rod had bought her two glasses of gin and orange, which she had drunk straight down because she was thirsty. He had nuzzled her neck during one of the slower dancers, and she had let him, even though she didn't really fancy him. He looked different dressed in drainpipes and leather jacket, his hair slicked down with oil that smelled strongly of some heavy perfume. Connor always had the fresh smell of soap on his skin.

Rod was a good dancer and he'd introduced her to his friends. She had danced with several of the men at the start of the evening and chatted to the girls, but the last few dances had all been with Rod. Sarah had enjoyed herself, but she felt a little apprehensive as she told him that she had to leave soon.

'You don't need to go for ages yet,' he told her. 'Stay for another half-hour, Sarah. We're having a good time, aren't we?'

'Yes, it has been fun,' Sarah replied and smiled. 'I've enjoyed myself – but my mother will worry if I'm later than eleven. I could catch a bus if you tell me which one I need.'

'Don't be like that,' Rod said and looked annoyed. 'I'll take you back to your hotel, Sarah.

I brought you and I'll see you home. Just another couple of dances and we'll go.'

Sarah hesitated. A little voice in her head was saying she should go now. She thought Rod might have had a few beers too many and she didn't really want a snogging session in the car. Dancing with him had been fun, but she suspected that he would be looking for more than a couple of kisses. At the start of the evening she had been up for it, but now she had changed her mind. She didn't want anyone but Connor touching her and kissing her.

'All right, one more dance,' she told him. 'But first I have to go to the cloakroom...'

She kissed him on the cheek and walked away, disappearing into the cloakroom to fetch her coat and bag. She had money in her purse and some in her coat pocket too. If she couldn't find the right bus stop, she would look for a taxi.

She left the club, going down the stairs and through the pub. There was a lot of raucous laughter in the bar and it was very busy. She hadn't realized what a rough crowd it was when she'd arrived, but it had been early then and she'd been with Rod and his friends. Now she was alone and she felt suddenly vulnerable as a couple of men wolf-whistled her. She ignored them and went outside, aware now that it was dark, late and, worst of all, she had no idea where she was. She knew that Rod had driven for some twenty minutes or so before they reached the club, so she wasn't going to be able to walk home.

The door from the pub opened, spilling light

on to the pavement. Sarah started to move off but hearing a shout behind her she glanced over her shoulder and saw one of the men from inside. He lurched towards her, making a grab for her arm. Sarah gave a little scream, dropping her handbag as she fled down the street. The man didn't attempt to run after her, but Sarah was too nervous to look back or retrieve her bag.

She ran for some time, because she was frightened. She was alone in the streets of a strange part of town. She had only a pound or so in her pocket and she couldn't think straight. She wished she had stayed for that last dance with Rod. Even if he had tried it on, she didn't think he was the sort who would make her do anything she didn't want to. She had behaved like an idiot and this was all her fault.

She was crying now. She seemed to have been wandering for ever and she didn't know where to go. She hadn't seen a taxi since she left the pub, and she realized that it had been naïve to think they would be easily available at this hour. There were plenty of taxis at the sea front where the hotels and theatres were located, but here in the middle of this residential area there were none.

Perhaps she could find a phone box. There might be a number for taxis in there – or she could ring the hotel and ask them to contact one for her. If she only knew where she was...

Sarah saw the lights of a car approaching. It slowed to a halt and she gasped as she saw it was a police car. One of the policemen wound down his window and looked out at her.

'Are you all right, miss?'

'No,' Sarah almost sobbed with relief. 'I was attacked as I left a jive club and I dropped my bag – and I'm only here on holiday. I need to get to my hotel.'

'Where are you staying?' the officer asked. He leaned over and opened the rear door for her. 'Do you want to make a statement about the attack? Did the man steal your bag?'

'I dropped it as I ran away,' Sarah said, feeling foolish as she slid into the back seat. 'He grabbed my arm, that's all. I was frightened. I should have waited for Rod.'

'Had a row with the boyfriend?' The young police officer smiled at her. 'You should have asked the landlord to call you a taxi, love. There are some rum folk about at night. You're all right now. Where are you staying? We'll drop you off.'

'Thank you,' Sarah said. 'My name is Sarah. I'm so grateful...'

She felt so foolish as the police car sped through the streets and then she began to recognize her surroundings. The car stopped outside her hotel. She got out and thanked the officers again. The young one grinned at her. He handed her a small piece of paper.

'Here – ring this number tomorrow, Sarah. You never know, your bag might have turned up.'

'There was only a lipstick, hanky and some money in it,' Sarah said. 'I'll try phoning but it doesn't really matter – thanks so much for helping me.'

'It is our job, miss.' He waved to her as they

drove off.

Sarah walked into the hotel. She still felt a bit foolish. Her mother would scold her if she knew, but she wasn't going to tell her. Sarah had learned her lesson. She would stay clear of people and clubs she didn't know for the remainder of their holiday.

She went up in the lift. She had decided to go straight to her own room, but as she left the lift on the third floor she saw the door of her mother's room open. She was preparing her excuse for being late when she saw a man emerge and caught a glimpse of her mother. She was wearing a pink silk dressing gown, which had opened at the front, revealing her breasts. Her lipstick looked smeared and her hair was untidy. The picture told its own shocking story.

Sarah stood absolutely still as the man leaned forward to kiss her mother and then walked past her and pressed the button for the lift. Mrs Jenkins had become aware of Sarah now and the look on her face said everything. She looked startled, then guilty, and finally ashamed.

'Sarah,' she called as the man disappeared into the lift. 'It isn't what you think. Come in, please, we have to talk.'

Sarah followed her mother into the hotel bedroom. The bed was rumpled, the pillows bearing the indentation of someone's head. It seemed obvious that the bed had been used for sex and she could smell something – a man's cologne mingled with sweat.

'Sarah, what you saw...' Mrs Jenkins broke off as Sarah brought her gaze back from the bed. 'It is no use lying to you. Besides, you are old enough now. Your father and I ... we go our own separate ways. Our marriage hasn't been what it should be for years. He has his lady friends when he goes away on business trips. I had an affair a year or so back, but this is the first time I've ever picked a man up in a hotel bar. I'm sorry you had to see it.'

'You've always been so strict with me,' Sarah said. She stared at her mother and felt sick. 'All the time you were lying...'

'No, Sarah!' Her mother moved towards her, hand outstretched to touch her, but Sarah jerked back, anger and disgust in her eyes. 'Don't be like this, dearest. I care about your father but I'm not in love with him. He started having affairs soon after we were married. I wasn't unfaithful for years – not until you were nearly old enough to leave school. We've stayed together for you; we don't live as man and wife any more, but we're still friends.'

'All the things you said to me, about saving myself for marriage – all the warnings...' Her eyes glittered. 'It makes me sick. You make me sick!'

Her mother flinched as if she had struck her. 'Maybe you'll understand one day. Please don't condemn me, Sarah.'

'You condemned Connor. It was because of all the things you said that I sent him away. I knew he wouldn't rape that girl, but I wouldn't listen to him, because you kept saying there was no smoke without fire. I doubted him – and that's your fault.'

274

'Blame me if it makes you feel better,' her mother said. 'It was your own decision to send him away, Sarah. I dare say he will come back if you ask him.' Sarah turned away. 'Where are you going?'

Sarah paused and faced her. 'I want to go home tomorrow. I know we have another few days booked, but I don't want to stay here. I'm going to pack my case, but you can stay here if you want. You might find someone else you fancy.'

'Don't you dare talk to me like that!' Mrs Jenkins lashed out, striking Sarah across the face.

Sarah put a hand to her face but she didn't say anything. She didn't need to because her eyes said it all.

'I'm sorry, I shouldn't have hit you. Please don't look at me that way,' her mother said. 'I may have tried to keep you too innocent, Sarah, but I didn't want you to be disillusioned with life too soon. I've never been happy. I wanted you to be happy. Please believe me.'

'I believe you,' Sarah said coldly. 'But I'm not sure I can forgive you.'

She left her mother staring after her. She regretted going to the club with Rod and she regretted letting him kiss her. She wished she had stayed in the hotel with her mother – perhaps this might not have happened if she'd been here.

Sarah felt disgust turn in her. She was angry with her mother. She couldn't come to terms with what she'd been told about her parents' marriage. She had thought it was all so perfect,

275

but all those times they played happy families on birthdays and Christmas – they had all been lies. Her father had a mistress. When he went away at the weekends it was to see another woman. He had lied to her for years. Both her parents had lied to her so many times.

Sitting on the edge of her bed, Sarah looked at herself in the mirror. Did she look any different? She certainly felt it – older if not wiser. She must have been stupid not to see the signs: all those nights her father had been late home, she'd imagined he was working hard. It was a sham, a front kept up for her sake – and perhaps because it suited them both.

Would they get a divorce now that she knew what was going on? Or would they still keep up the respectable front for the sake of appearances? She felt angry and betrayed. Why hadn't they told her the truth ages ago?

Maura opened her eyes and shivered. She was lying on grass and she felt frozen. How had she got here? She sat up, blinking as the blinding headache struck her. Just how many gins had she had the previous night? She struggled to her feet and looked down at herself. Her dress was stained with something and her stockings had holes in them. She must look like something the cat dragged in! She tried to remember what had happened. She had been with a man ... Pete. He had suggested they go outside and she'd gone willingly, but then his friends had followed. What happened then was a blur in her mind, because she had been so drunk, but her body felt sore and she could vaguely remember being thrust down on the ground as one after the other they raped her. She wasn't sure how many, but it must have been at least five...

Maura tried to block the pictures of her humiliation. They had raped her and laughed as she struggled and screamed, begging them to stop. Shame washed over her. She knew she had brought it on herself. They had called her a whore and the rape had been a form of punishment; she vaguely recalled Pete standing over and urinating on her as she lay in a daze, telling her she'd got what she deserved. Oh, God, what had she done? How low had she got that a man would do that to her?

She staggered a few steps and then vomited. Glancing round, she realized she was on the playing field where the football matches were held in the season; they held the schools athletic championships here, too, and sometimes fêtes. She wiped her mouth with the back of her hand, tasting the bitterness on her tongue. She needed a drink of water.

She heard a church clock chiming somewhere in the distance. Eight strikes of the bell. It was eight o'clock in the morning! Suddenly, Maura remembered her promise to David. She had gone out for one drink and left him alone all night...

She started running as the panic swept over her. She was such a fool. She had got drunk and then let those men she couldn't even remember properly abuse her. Shame and remorse swept through her as she dashed into the street. She had to get home before David got up and realized

277

that she had been out all night.

She never stood a chance. She didn't see the heavy lorry speeding through the back street, and he didn't see her until it was too late. As it hit her, Maura saw her son's face and that of his father. David would be all right. Please, please, let him be all right...

Daniel walked into Maura's hairdressing shop. He saw that two customers were standing at the counter talking to the girl who worked there. Their faces were serious and it was clear they were shocked. He hesitated as they looked at him, then asked for David.

'He is upstairs. The police are with him.'

'Police?' Daniel frowned. 'What is wrong? Has something happened?'

'Maura ... she was killed early this morning,' Shirley said, her face white and shocked. 'She ran in front of a lorry near the Paradise football ground and it killed her.'

'I'll go up,' Daniel said. 'Is it the stairs through the back?'

'Yes.'

Daniel knew that they were staring at him as he went through to the back. The gossips were bound to pick up on his arrival and make four into five, but he couldn't leave David to face this alone.

At the top of the stairs he saw an open door. A police constable and a woman were standing over the boy, who was shrinking into his chair and staring at them, his face white and scared.

'You have to go with Mrs Briggs. You can't

stop here alone,' the police officer was saying.

'No. I won't!'

'David, are you all right, lad?'

The officer turned his head as Daniel stepped into the room.

'Who are you, sir?' he asked, but a small tornado went past him, throwing himself at Daniel, burying his head against his side as he clung to him and sobbed.

'Mum's dead. They want me to go to a home and I won't. I won't go!' He looked up at Daniel, his face streaked with tears. 'Don't let them take me, Dad. Please don't let them.'

Daniel stroked his head. 'Calm down, son. Let's hear what they have to say. You can't stay here alone.'

'Are you the boy's father?' the police constable asked.

Daniel looked down at the boy clinging to him and nodded. 'Yes, he is my son. I knew Mrs Jacobs years ago. We never married, but David is mine. He stayed with me a couple of weeks back. He was upset at the time and I came over this morning to see how he was getting on.'

'Is that true, David?'

'Yes. He's my dad. I want to go home with my dad.'

'Your name, sir?'

'Daniel Searles. I think it might be best if David came home with us. My wife was anxious about him and we wanted to help him. She will take him in until his future is decided.' He looked down at David. 'Do you still want to live with your grandmother and uncle in Ireland?'

'I don't want to go with her.' David sent a look of dislike at the woman standing near the chair where he'd been sitting. 'She wants to put me in a home.'

'We called Mrs Briggs,' the constable said. 'The boy can't be left on his own in an unfortunate case like this.'

'He isn't alone,' Daniel said. 'He can live with us until he decides what he wants to do. He has relations in Ireland. I am sure there must be an address for them. I'm not sure about Maura's husband. I think he walked out on her a while ago. I'll see to the funeral arrangements – if that is all right with you?' He glanced down at David. 'Do you know where your grandmother's address is?' David nodded. 'Go and fetch it then, lad.' As David ran off, he looked at the police officer. 'Would you rather contact the family – or do you want me to?'

'We'll do that, sir.' He took a notebook from his pocket. 'Could you give me your address?'

'Greenfields, Acre Drove, Stretton. It's a farm. I have four children besides David and he will be fine with us until this business is cleared up.'

'What do you think, Mrs Briggs?' the constable asked.

'We've only his word that he is David's father...' She hesitated but then nodded. 'I suppose it is all right – but you may receive a visit from a council officer to make certain David is living in a suitable home.'

'That's all right by me,' Daniel said. David brought him an address book, opening it so that he could see the address in Ireland. He handed

280

the book to the constable, who copied the address into his notebook and then returned it to the boy.

'Do you want to go with Mr Searles?' he asked David.

'Yes. I'm not going with her.' David took shelter behind his father's body and clung on to his jacket. 'You can't make me. I'll run away.'

'I think it's best you take the boy for the moment,' the constable said and smiled. 'He seems to know what he wants. We shall be in touch, sir. You should be able to start making arrangements for the funeral in a few days, but perhaps Mrs Jacobs' relations may have something to say on the subject, so don't be in too much rush.'

'I'll wait to hear from you.' He looked down at David. 'Do you want to pack a few things? You'll need some clothes – underpants and socks, shirts. Do you want me to help you? Has your mum got a suitcase?'

'I'll get it,' David said.

'It was lucky that you came along when you did,' the police officer said. 'We'll be on our way now – but someone will come and talk to you in a few days.'

'Whenever you like. I'm usually about the yard, but if not I'll be on the land somewhere nearby.'

'If your wife isn't happy to take the child, let us know and we'll fetch him,' Mrs Bates said and followed him out.

David came back into the room a few minutes later. 'Have they gone?'

281

'Yes.' Daniel smiled at him. 'Let's pack some clothes and anything else you want to take – you'd better bring the address book. We will need to contact your grandmother.'

'Can I stay with you until Mum's buried?'

'Yes, of course. You can stay until your uncle or grandmother sends for you.'

'What if they don't?'

'We'll think about that if it happens,' Daniel said as he followed the boy into his bedroom. 'What do you want to bring with you?'

Daniel hoped Alice would be all right with what he'd done. He had acted on impulse, because he couldn't let his son go to an orphanage.

'Of course you did the right thing,' Alice said when she came down from settling David into Connor's bedroom. 'You couldn't let David go to a home. Some of those places are all right these days, but I should have hated to think of him there being looked after by strangers.'

'I thought you would say that.' Daniel felt the relief sweep over him. 'If you'd seen his face and the way she was standing over him – old battleaxe! I couldn't let it happen, Alice.'

'Of course you couldn't,' she agreed. 'Poor kid. It's an awful mess, Dan. What do you think happened to her? I mean, why did she run in front of that lorry?'

'Her bed hadn't been slept in. I think she must have gone out drinking. Maybe she slept it off somewhere and then tried to rush home before David got up.'

'How could she go out and leave her son alone

282

all night? Supposing something had happened – a fire or...' Alice shook her head. 'What will happen to the shop now?'

'Shirley asked me what she ought to do. I told her to carry on as normal for now. I suppose Maura's husband is entitled to anything she had, though I think it should go to David. If his family come over for the funeral, they can decide. I think Shirley might like to take the shop over, but that isn't for me to say.' Daniel looked thoughtful. 'I said I would arrange the funeral, but David told me his grandmother and uncle are Catholics, so they may want to do it differently.'

'We shall have to wait and see if they come for the funeral,' Alice said. 'I'm sure one of them will come, because of David. They are sure to take him back with them to Ireland.'

'Yes, I suppose so. I know it is what he wanted...'

'You sound unsure?'

'Do I? I'm just shocked. It was all a bit sudden, Alice. Maura promised she wouldn't drink – and now she's dead. David is stunned. He hasn't cried properly yet. I don't think he really understands what has happened.'

'I am sure he knows, he just can't take it in,' Alice said. 'Poor little love. It is awful to lose your mother – even if she wasn't as good a mother as she might have been. He will be all right with us, Dan. He can stay for as long as he needs to.'

'You wouldn't mind if he stayed for good?'

'Not if it was what he really wanted,' she said

283

and looked thoughtful. 'We might have to tell the children that he is their half-brother in time, but we'll leave that for now.'

Sarah could hear the sound of raised voices downstairs. She knew that her parents were arguing. Her father wanted to know why they had come home earlier than planned. She heard the telephone shrill in the hall and then the sound of her father picking it up.

'Sarah,' he called from the bottom of the stairs. 'It is for you.' Sarah went down the stairs. He handed her the receiver. 'It's Connor.'

'Thank you.' Sarah took the receiver, her heart thumping wildly. 'Connor, where are you? I want to see you!'

'I'm staying with Emily. Are you all right? You sound upset.'

'Yes, I am. I'm sorry I didn't believe you,' Sarah said. 'I love you, Con. I know you would not do anything like that. Please forgive me.' She gave a little sob. 'I am so sorry...'

'Don't cry, darling,' he said. 'I shouldn't have said those things to you. I was angry and I didn't know what I was saying. I love you, Sarah.' He hesitated, then said, 'The police want to see me again. I have to go back to London today. If I can, I'll come down as soon as I finish there.'

Sarah felt cold all over. 'Why do they want to see you? They can't arrest you. You didn't do anything. I know you didn't!'

'No, I didn't,' Connor said. 'I didn't speak to them myself. I just got a message that they needed to see me. I'm sure it will be all right, Sarah.

If they were going to arrest me, they would have got the local police to do it. Besides, my lawyer told me that he had taken them some new evidence about the girl – so maybe it is that.'

'Yes...' Sarah could hardly keep the tears from her voice, because they were trickling down her cheeks. 'I love you. I'll stand by you whatever they do.'

'Sarah, I wish I were with you. I've missed you.'

'I've missed you.'

'I thought you might still be away.'

'We came home early. I hated it there. I hate it here without you. I just want to be with you wherever you are.'

'I've had some thoughts about the future, but I'll tell you when I see you. I have to go. I've got to get to London.'

'Love you,' Sarah said and put the phone down.

As she turned, she saw her father looking at her from the doorway into the sitting room.

'Sarah, I should like to talk to you. If you could spare a moment, I have something to tell you.'

'Is something wrong, Dad?'

She went into the sitting room. Her mother was sitting hunched up in a chair, her face like stone. Sarah sat down on the edge of the sofa. Her father went to stand by the fireplace.

'I wanted to tell you the truth a long time ago,' he said. 'It was wrong to hide the way things are from you, Sarah. Your mother and I have stayed together for your sake but that is over. I think you will be getting married quite soon now. As soon as the wedding is over I intend to leave this house...'

'Dad!' Sarah stared at him. 'What about Mum?'

'She will have the house and enough money to live on, but I've wasted enough of my life living in a sterile marriage. I'm going to stay with a friend, but I'll visit from time to time and I'll definitely be there for your wedding, Sarah.'

'Mum...' Sarah looked over but her mother was staring into space. 'Why now, Dad?'

'Because you know the truth and there's no point in continuing this sham. You've made it up with Connor. I'll give you my permission in writing before I leave and you can arrange the wedding for whenever you like. Naturally I'll pay the bills and I'll give you five thousand pounds as a wedding present.'

'Dad, that's a lot of money!' Sarah felt the tears pricking. Impulsively, she went towards him, putting her arms about him, her head against his chest. He smelled so familiar and dear, and it was breaking her heart. 'I'm so sorry ... sorry that you've been unhappy all this time ... both of you...'

Her mother got up and walked out of the room without looking at either of them.

'Mum!'

Her father caught her arm as she would have followed. 'Let her go, Sarah. Don't you understand why she didn't want you to get married – why she has tried to keep you a little girl all this time? It was because she knew that once you got married I would leave her. She blackmailed me into staying and into keeping it from you. I think we should have told you when you were sixteen.'

'Dad...' Sarah caught her breath because his words struck like a knife. She knew that he was telling her the truth and it hurt. Her mother had deliberately tried to turn her against Connor because she wanted her to break it off – to stay at home a few years longer. 'You shouldn't have let her.'

'I didn't want to hurt you, princess. I've always loved you even though...' He shook his head. 'Marry Connor and be happy. He really loves you.'

'Yes,' Sarah said. 'I know.'

She was thoughtful as she went upstairs. She prayed that the police weren't going to arrest Connor, because she wanted – needed – to be with him. All the doubts and the uncertainty had gone. She didn't care where they went or what they did; she just needed to be with the man she loved.

Eleven

'I wish I could come with you,' Emily said as she said goodbye to Connor. 'Remember, if they arrest you, get a message to me. I'll make certain you have the best lawyers.'

'I have a good lawyer. He is going to meet me in London and we're going to the police station together. You don't need to worry about me, Emily. I'll be fine.'

'You're still my little brother and always will be,' she said and kissed his cheek. 'Bring Sarah here for a holiday if you can – unless you want to get married immediately? You could always have it here if you like.'

'I'll talk to Sarah. At least she has forgiven me.'

'So she should, because you didn't do any-thing,' Emily retorted. 'Drive carefully.'

'You look after yourself – and Alan,' Connor said. 'He needs you more than I do at this moment, so don't feel guilty because you can't come and hold my hand.'

Emily laughed. 'You never change, Con. All right, get off then. I'll see you soon.'

'I'll bring Sarah,' Connor promised. 'You know I have plans, but I have to ask Sarah if she will be happy here.'

Emily nodded. She stood back, waving as he drove off in his car. She had offered to lend him hers, which was bigger and more comfortable for a long journey, but he refused to be parted from the Austin that Daniel had given him. She smiled because fame and fortune hadn't changed Connor one bit.

Her smile faded as she turned back into the house. Alan was still clinging to life but he was very frail. He hated being confined to bed and disliked the fact that he needed to be nursed. Emily had engaged the services of a professional nurse, because she knew he would have hated her to be his nurse. She visited him several times a day, but he slept a lot and they were only able to talk for short periods.

She knew that she was going to lose him very soon. The doctor had told her that it was a miracle the massive heart attack hadn't killed him straight off. It broke her heart to see him the way he was, but she tried not to show it. There would be plenty of time for tears when Alan was gone.

She had been meaning to phone Frances again. She'd tried a couple of times, but each time there was some excuse. Frances was out or she was busy. It made Emily wonder if her sister were deliberately avoiding speaking to her. If Alan hadn't been so ill, she would have got in the car and gone down to Cornwall to visit her, but she simply couldn't leave Alan for the moment. If Frances wanted to speak to her, she could pick up the phone and ring her.

* * *

'We think she may have been raped – several times,' Constable James told Daniel as they stood together in the yard. 'I didn't want to say anything when you came to the shop, because it wasn't certain, but the pathologist has put in a comprehensive report – and he says she was raped more than once.'

'I'm glad you didn't say anything in front of the boy,' Daniel told him. 'It makes you sick to think someone could do something like that – have you any idea who did it?'

'I've asked the landlord and he says he remembers her speaking to some men, but he has no idea who they were. He says they weren't regulars. He thinks they may have been from a fishing club, but he can't tell us any more than that, I'm afraid.'

Daniel nodded. 'I suppose it would be difficult to prove she didn't consent even if you knew who the culprits were. Have you contacted the family in Ireland?'

'We spoke to the police over there, because the family don't have a telephone. They promised to contact Mrs O'Brien. I expect someone will come over. I've been told you can go ahead with the burial. You can collect a death certificate from the station – but I'm not sure if you want the bother.'

'I've arranged for her to be taken to a chapel of rest once you release the body,' Daniel said. 'David says she was a Catholic, though she hasn't taken him to church much and he hasn't been confirmed or whatever they do. I've contacted the Catholic church in Ely, and I'll fix it up for next week. Hopefully, Maura's family will have made contact by then. If they don't, I'll just go ahead with it.'

'It will be better than if the parish buries her – though it means you will have to pay.'

'It's the least I can do. This stuff about the rape – will it get into the papers?'

'I expect there will be a small paragraph, but with luck not many people will notice it.'

'I don't want David to know.'

'I can understand that,' Constable James said. 'It's hard enough on the boy as it is. How is he coping?'

'He seems all right. My wife is worried because he hasn't really cried, but he is fitting in well. The boys have a holiday from school at the moment. I'm not sure what to do about David. There's no point in asking if he can go to Chatteris School with my eldest boy if his grandmother wants him with her. Until I hear I'll just keep him with us. He likes watching me work on the cars. I think he is bright but it won't hurt him to miss school for a bit.'

'Well, I must get back. I just wanted to come and tell you myself.' Constable James wandered over to look at the sports car Daniel was working on. 'I've always wanted one of these. Does it belong to you?'

'I bought it to restore. I'm waiting for planning permission and then I shall open a garage in Stretton.'

'Is the car for sale?'

'Yes. I want seven hundred pounds for it,' Daniel said. 'It cost me three hundred and I've spent a couple of hundred on it. I've put in a lot of hours on this one.'

'It looks like new. Seven hundred sounds cheap to me,' the constable said. 'Don't sell it just yet, Mr Searles. I might be interested if I can get the money together. I've got most of it but I shall have to borrow a few hundred from the bank. It does run well?'

'Listen...' Daniel got in and started the engine. It purred to life. He smiled as the young police officer walked round the car. 'I always guarantee the engines – and this one had hardly any rust even before I started. It is a good buy.'

'I'll let you know in a couple of days.' The constable climbed on to his motorcycle. 'I use this for work, but I really want a car for taking my girlfriend out. I'll see what I can do.'

'I'm in no hurry to sell,' Daniel said. 'I shall put it in the showroom if it doesn't sell before I get the garage open...'

'I want it clear that my client has presented himself voluntarily for questioning,' Connor's lawyer said as they walked into the interview room. 'I shall be present at this and any further interview.'

'Well, it's good news,' Inspector Evans said and smiled, indicating that they should sit down. 'Miss Meadows has retracted her statement. She says that she was upset and told a stupid lie and she has made a full statement clearing Mr Searles of any blame.'

'May I see that?' the lawyer asked and took the paper he was offered. 'She is saying now that she wasn't raped at all but had consensual sex with a man she refuses to name?'

'She made up the story of rape because she was frightened her father would find out. Apparently, he walked into the bedroom and accused her of having sex and she panicked.'

'Is she aware how serious this charge was – what it has cost Mr Searles?'

'Yes, I imagine so.' Inspector Evans looked at Connor. 'Miss Meadows has done this once before at her school – accused someone of attacking her and then retracted her statement. Your lawyer discovered that she was expelled and when I questioned her house mistress, the truth came out. I visited Miss Meadows at her home and she broke down and confessed.' He sat back in his chair. 'What do you want to do about it, Mr Searles? We could bring a charge of wasting police time and of malicious slander – but you might do better to bring a private prosecution. I understand her father is a wealthy man.'

'I'm not interested in suing for money,' Connor said. 'What I want is a public retraction in all the newspapers.'

'I can arrange that,' his lawyer said. 'But she should be made to pay for what she has done.'

'I think Lisa will already be paying,' Connor said. 'I've been told that her father is a bit of a tyrant, which is why she runs off from time to time. If I get my apology in the papers, I'm willing to drop it there.'

'Exactly my own feeling,' Inspector Evans said and offered his hand. 'I had a feeling she might be lying from the start – though I do believe she was raped.'

'Then why is she saying she wasn't?'

'I think the man may be a friend of the family. You would be surprised at how often this happens. I'm sorry you got caught up in this, Mr Searles. Believe me; the leak did not come from us.'

'I know who went to the papers,' Connor said. 'I'm free to go now?'

'You can do whatever you wish. No need to let us know where you're going.' He offered his hand. 'I am glad this is over.'

'Yes, thank you.'

Connor walked out with his lawyer.

'Thanks for everything, Kevin. If you could inform the papers that it was all lies, I should be grateful.'

'Don't worry. As soon as I send them copies of the statement and threaten to sue they will mess themselves in their hurry to get an apology out. They've cost you a record contract and I could make them pay compensation.'

'They don't know it, but they did me a favour,' Connor said. 'I wanted out anyway, but now Moon Records have sent me a letter to say the contract is finished – and they sent five thousand pounds. I didn't even remember but it was a clause we had inserted at the start.'

'Chicken feed to what I could get you if you say the word.'

'Thanks, but all I need is an apology,' Connor said. 'I have plans for the future and I just want to forget this ever happened.'

'If that's what you want,' Kevin said. 'I shall

enjoy making the bastards sweat a bit.'

'Thanks for everything – and for believing in me.' Connor extended his hand.

'I would have defended you either way,' the lawyer said. 'Look me up when you next have a contract to sign.'

'I'm not sure that I want to sing again,' Connor said. 'Sarah will see those retractions and that is all that matters to me.'

'Are you going to see her now?'

'I need to make a few phone calls and then I'm on my way...'

'Thank God it is over,' Terry said when Connor contacted him on the telephone. 'I'll get straight back to Moon and ask them what they intend to do now.'

'Waste of time. I'm not signing for them again. I'm not sure what I want to do yet – but if I do sign another contract, it will be with one of the big companies. Decca or Columbia.'

'Yeah, you may be right,' Terry said. 'Keep in touch, Con. I'm not sure what I want to do. Some of the guys want Phil back in but I'm not keen. I think I'll give it a miss for a while – see what happens. Moon might release the album once they see the retraction.'

'I'll be in touch. I'm going to Sarah's now, and we'll probably visit my sister in a week or so. Emily wants us to spend a few days there before the wedding.'

'Right. Invite me to the wedding, won't you?'

'Of course. See you.'

Connor put down the receiver. He smiled to

himself as he checked out of the hotel. He couldn't wait to see Sarah.

Sarah left her ex-employer's shop. She had given notice that she wasn't coming back to work and it hadn't gone down too well. She knew it was short notice, but she wanted to be free to go with Connor when he came for her. She lingered outside the new shop further up the street. They had reduced the blouse she had liked when they opened to less than half price. Smiling, she went inside and inquired if it was her size. She was lucky. They just had the one left and it would fit her.

Sarah paid for her purchase and left the shop carrying the smart paper bag. She was being extravagant but she would need some new clothes for her honeymoon, and her father had promised to pay for her wedding dress.

Sarah hadn't seen him since he left the night he'd told her he was going to divorce her mother – or perhaps it was her mother who was divorcing him? Sarah wasn't sure, because her mother wouldn't speak about it. She had hardly spoken to Sarah at all since then. It was almost as if she were blaming her for the end of her marriage.

'Sarah!' Janice called to her and she stopped. She hadn't seen her friend for a few weeks. 'I wanted to tell you – I'm getting married next month.'

'That's lovely,' Sarah said. 'I'm so pleased for you. I'm getting married soon, too. Connor should be coming tonight – or tomorrow.'

'Good. I wanted to tell you that I didn't believe

what everyone was saying,' Janice told her. 'The papers ought to be sued for what they said – an apology isn't enough for what they did!'

'An apology? Have you seen this evening's paper?'

'Yes. I bought one just now.' Janice took it from her shopping bag. 'Do you want to have a coffee and read it?'

'Yes, thanks,' Sarah said. 'We haven't done that for ages. I knew Connor had gone to see the police. He wasn't sure what was happening, but it must have been because of this.' She smiled. 'Thanks so much for telling me.'

'Well, I was a bit mean to you a few times,' Janice admitted. 'I was jealous of you, Sarah, because you had everything and I was so miserable, but I'm happy now.'

'I didn't even know you were courting seriously,' Sarah said. 'Let's have that coffee and you can tell me all about it.'

She glanced at her watch. It was nearly six o'clock. Her mother might have started the tea, but she was just going to be late for once.

It was past seven when Sarah got home. She had enjoyed talking to her friend and she didn't particularly want to go home at all. She wasn't sure when Connor would come, because he hadn't said anything definite. She didn't think he would be with her much sooner than nine in the evening, because it was a long way to drive. Besides, he'd probably had things to do before he could leave London. He might have telephoned and she would find the message waiting when she got in.

She went round the back and tried the kitchen door but it was locked. Her mother didn't usually lock the door, but Sarah had a key to the front door. She unlocked the door and let herself in. The television wasn't on and nor was the radio. She couldn't smell anything cooking.

'Mum, are you home?' Sarah called. She checked the message pad beside the phone and found nothing, then turned towards the kitchen. There was no sign of anything cooking – no plate in the oven. She opened the refrigerator and saw some pork chops in a dish. Sarah frowned. It wasn't like her mother not to cook a meal, but perhaps she had gone out. She filled the kettle and put it on the gas hob, then took butter and bread and a pot of salmon paste from the cupboard. She would make herself a sandwich and a cup of tea. In the meantime, she would go up and change into her jeans and a jumper. She didn't want to be wearing this formal suit when Connor arrived.

She went into her bedroom and changed her clothes, then paid a visit to the bathroom. The kettle had begun to whistle. Sarah was about to go down when something made her look at her mother's room. The door was slightly open. A shiver went down Sarah's spine and she moved towards it, opening the door. Her mother was lying on top of the covers. An empty whisky bottle had fallen on to the floor, and as Sarah moved cautiously forward, she saw that a bottle of sleeping pills lay on the cover next to her mother's hand.

'Mum!' she cried. 'Mum – what have you done?'

She touched her mother's hand and gasped because she was cold. She shook her mother's shoulder, refusing to believe what her eyes were telling her. 'Mum! Wake up. Please wake up!'

Her mother's arm flopped limply. She couldn't wake up: she was dead. She had taken the whole bottle of pills and drunk a bottle of whisky. There was no doubt that she had wanted to kill herself.

'Oh, Mum, why did you do it?' A little sob escaped from Sarah. She hadn't realized how desperately unhappy her mother had been. Remembering their quarrel at the hotel, she felt awful. Had she contributed to her mother's desperation? 'Mum, you didn't have to do this!'

Tears stung her eyes. She bent down and kissed her mother's cold cheek, then went downstairs. She couldn't cope with this on her own. She would have to telephone her father. He had to come home and sort out this mess. She could not bear this alone.

Connor pulled up three doors away from Sarah's home. He couldn't get any closer because there was a police car and her father's Jaguar parked outside the front door. He frowned as he got out, because there was obviously something going on. Please God, don't let it be Sarah! He could take anything but that...

He rang the bell and a moment later the door flew open. Sarah had been crying. Her nose was red and her cheeks were wet. She gave a strangled cry and threw herself at him, sobbing as he gathered her close.

'What's wrong, darling?' he asked. 'Why are the police here?'

'It's Mum,' Sarah gulped. 'She killed herself with sleeping tablets and whisky!'

'She what?' Connor stared at her as she drew back. 'Why on earth did she do a thing like that?'

'She was miserable. She and Dad were going to get a divorce. He had already moved out, though no one knew about it yet. He was going to come back sometimes until the wedding...' She stopped and looked at him. 'Will you still want to marry me?'

'Of course I shall! Why wouldn't I?' He looked beyond her as her father came down the stairs. 'This is an awkward time for you, sir. If I'm in the way...'

'You're as good as family now,' Mr Jenkins said. 'I would be grateful if you could take Sarah off somewhere for an hour or two. I shall be here when you get back, Sarah. I know you haven't eaten. Get some fish and chips and eat them if you can. We'll talk about this later.'

'Are you sure? The police won't need me?'

'You mean you found her?' Connor asked. Sarah nodded. He looked grim. 'They can talk to you another day if they need you. Your father will manage and we'll talk to him later.' He took her hand. 'I've got some good news for you, though it isn't important now.'

'Of course it is,' Sarah said, taking her jacket from the peg in the hall. 'I saw the apology in the paper. Janice bought it and she showed me. We went for coffee. If I had come home sooner...' She broke off on a little sob.

'She had been dead for hours,' Mr Jenkins said. 'It isn't your fault, Sarah. It is no one's fault but her own.'

'Your father is right,' Connor said as he took her outside. 'She didn't have to do it, Sarah – even if she was miserable. She could have thought of you.'

'I think she blamed me for Dad leaving her,' Sarah said. 'Because I grew up and he wouldn't pretend any more.'

'There's more to this, isn't there?'

'Yes, quite a bit.'

'Do you want to go for a coffee or get some fish and chips?'

'Could we go for a walk – by the river? I just want to talk.'

'Of course we can. We can do anything you want, Sarah.' Connor bent his head and kissed her softly. 'We'll walk and talk. I've got things to tell you, too.'

Dan was sitting at the kitchen table eating his supper when someone knocked at the door. He frowned because it was almost dark and they seldom had visitors late at night. He put out his hand when Alice started to get up.

'You stay where you are, love. I'll answer that.' He went to the front door, turning the key. They never locked the back door but seldom opened the front. A tall, thickset man was standing with his back to the door, but he turned as

Daniel spoke.

'Can I help you?'

'I'm Paddy O'Brien,' the man said. 'I've come about Maura's son. They told me he was staying with you.' His dark brows met in a frown. 'They said you were his father – but you're not the man she married.'

'No. It wasn't like that,' Daniel said. 'Do you want to come in? David is in bed at the moment...'

'I haven't come to take him,' Paddy O'Brien said. 'I wanted to know about the funeral. Someone said it is tomorrow at the Catholic church in Ely. What time would that be?'

'It's eleven o'clock. I haven't arranged anything for afterwards. I didn't know who to ask and I wasn't sure her family would come.' Daniel led the way into the kitchen. 'This is my wife, Alice. I was just finishing my supper. I work late most evenings.'

'I'm sorry to intrude.'

'Sit down and have a cup of tea,' Alice said. 'Finish your supper, Dan. Mr O'Brien has time for a cup of tea.'

'Yes, I have, thank you kindly, ma'am,' he said. 'I should have been here before, but I was at another funeral yesterday – Mrs O'Brien was laid to rest, so she was, and we had a fine wake for her, too.'

'Your wife? I am so sorry.'

'I'm a single man, ma'am. Mrs O'Brien was my mother, so she was, God rest her soul.'

'David's grandmother is dead?' Alice stared at him as she filled the big brown pot with boiling water. 'How dreadful for you – to come from one funeral to another. I am so sorry.'

'I shall miss Mam and that's the truth. She was a good woman despite the tongue on her – but it will be a struggle without her. I'm busy on the land from dusk to dawn. You'll know that yourselves, being farmers.'

'Yes, of course. You don't have anyone else?'

'Nary a soul,' he said. 'Mam wouldn't have taken to another woman in her kitchen. I'm not much given to courting...' He took the cup Alice pushed towards him and helped himself from the sugar pot she offered. 'Do you see my problem? If Mam had been alive, I'd have taken the boy like a shot, but...' He shook his head. 'I just don't see how I can manage to look after Maura's lad.'

'He is going to be upset,' Daniel said and pushed his plate away; the food no longer held any appeal. 'He wanted to come and live with his grandma and his uncle.'

'Mam would have had him, so she would, but it wouldn't be right. In a year or two when he can work for his keep...'

'He is a child,' Alice said sharply. 'He needs love and care. Besides, he wants to be a mechanic like Dan when he grows up.'

'They were going to put him in a home,' Daniel said and got up, going to the foot of the stairs to listen. 'I wouldn't want any of the boys to hear this...'

'Mayhap he would be better off in a home – better than with me anyway.'

'No! I've listened to that boy sobbing when he thinks no one can hear him. He's missing his mother and he'll be devastated if he has to go into a home.'

'Alice.' Daniel looked at her. 'Are you sure about this?'

'Yes.' Her eyes met his. 'He is your son, Dan. I can't see him go into care. I haven't said anything, because I thought his grandmother would take him, but now it's settled – we're keeping him.'

'Yes, we are,' Dan said and put his arm about her shoulders. 'I'll be asking you to put it into writing, sir. You're giving him up to us, agreed?'

'He'll be better off with you,' Paddy O'Brien said. 'I'll see you after the funeral and I'll come back later to tell David that his granny's dead. I've got something for him. She wanted him to have his grandfather's gold watch and chain.'

'What about the shop?' Daniel asked. 'Maura put some money into a business in Ely. I think David should get anything that is coming from it, but you're her nearest relative, other than her son – and her husband, wherever he is...'

'I'll not be making a claim. I agree that it should be David's. Talk to the lawyers yourself.' He stood up and offered his hand. 'I'll get off. It's a bit of a walk back and I've a bus to catch.'

'I'll run you into Ely myself,' Daniel said. 'I think we should talk some more.' He turned to look at Alice. 'I'll see you later, love.'

'Do what you have to do,' Alice said. 'I'll be here when you get back.'

'Feeling better?' Connor pulled Sarah close to his side, his arm around her waist. 'I suppose we

304

ought to go back. The police will have gone by now and your father will be waiting.'

'I suppose we have to,' Sarah said. She glanced towards the river, which was dark and cold. They had walked for a while and then climbed into the back of Connor's car to get warm. He had kissed her and held her, and her feeling of horror had gradually faded. 'I'm not sure I can stay in that house any more.'

'You don't have to. You can collect some of your things when we've talked to your father and then leave. We'll take a couple of rooms at a hotel somewhere. I would take you to Alice, but it's late. Tomorrow we'll visit Dan and Alice – and then we'll go to Emily.'

'What about the funeral?'

'It will probably be a week or two before the police allow it,' Connor said. 'We can come back for it. Your father will let us know.'

'Why did she do it?' Sarah wailed. 'Surely she wasn't so unhappy...'

'Don't cry any more, darling. You can't bring her back – and perhaps she is better off where she is.' Sarah just stared at him. 'She would have been lonely when you left home.'

'Yes, she would.' Sarah blew her nose on the handkerchief he gave her. 'She wanted us to break up because she knew Dad would leave her once I was married.'

'She wasn't thinking straight,' Connor said. 'People say things they don't mean when they're upset. She must have loved you, Sarah. Think about the good times and forget the rest.'

'You're so good to me,' Sarah said and nestled

up to him. 'I was mean to you last time you were home.'

'You were upset and I got angry,' Connor said. 'It won't happen again, because we know each other better now. We had best go now or your father will get annoyed.'

'Are you absolutely certain you are prepared to take on another lad?' Daniel said when he got back that evening. 'It is going to make more work for you again.'

'I know that – and I know it means we'll need a bigger house when we move,' Alice said. 'I don't mind stopping here for a while until you get the garage running properly.'

'There's no need for that,' Daniel said. 'Connor doesn't need those fields on Stretton Road. I can sell those as well as this house and we'll be able to afford a decent place in the village. It won't be quite yet, because I am going to have it built. There is plenty of room at the back of the garage. You'll have a separate entrance but it will be just like it is here – I can pop in for a cup of tea whenever I feel like it.'

'Oh, Dan.' Alice gave an emotional laugh. 'You and your cups of tea! Are you going to tell David – or am I?'

'I'll do it in the morning,' he said. 'I'm going to have to tell Danny the truth, Alice. He's old enough to understand, and if David lets the truth out accidentally, it could cause trouble.'

'Yes, I know you're right. If David had gone away to Ireland, it wouldn't have mattered, but now that he is going to be a part of the family they should know they are brothers.'

'Half-brothers,' Daniel corrected, his expression thoughtful. 'There's not many women would have done what you have, Alice. People are bound to talk.'

'I minded that at the start,' she admitted. 'But it doesn't matter any more, Dan. We are a family and that's the way we'll be – and let the gossips get on with it. I'll tell my parents. They may give you some odd looks. You know my mother – but she won't say much when I tell her it was my idea.'

'She can say what she likes to me,' Daniel said. 'But I hope she will accept the boy. He has lost the only two people in the world who cared for him.'

'Well, he has a new family now. It may take a while for him to settle in, but we shall all have some adjustments to make. David will have to share a room with Danny when Connor comes to stay...'

'Did I tell you I picked up an evening paper in Ely? It was just lying around when I filled up with petrol at the garage. Someone had abandoned it – but there was an apology on the front page. Connor has been cleared of that rape.'

'I told you he would never do something like that,' Alice said and looked pleased. 'I should think there will be a wedding in the family soon. I am going to have a new dress from that posh shop in the High Street, Dan, and a big fancy hat as well.'

'You can have whatever you want,' he told her and reached out to kiss her. 'You deserve it,

Alice.'

'And so do you,' she said. 'Come on, let's go to bed...'

'How soon do you want to get married?' Mr Jenkins asked. He handed his daughter a glass of sherry and gave Connor a small whisky. 'I shall sell this house, Sarah. I wouldn't want to live here again.'

'I don't even want to stay here tonight,' Sarah said and drank her sherry straight down. 'I'm going to a hotel for tonight and then I'll stay with Con's family until we get married.'

Her father nodded. 'Will you go back into singing, Connor?'

'I'm not sure.' Connor glanced at Sarah. 'I am thinking of setting up a business of my own – restoring old houses. I might consider another record deal if the right one came along, but I shan't go back on the road. I've had enough and it isn't fair to Sarah.'

'So when did you think of getting married?'

'I think we should wait a few weeks,' Connor said. 'Sarah and I will be together, but I want her to be happy on her wedding day – and she needs a little time.'

'Well, let me know when you decide,' Mr Jenkins said. 'I'm going to set up a bank account for you, Sarah. I'll put some money in for you so that you can pay your way until you get married – and I'll pay for your wedding, clothes and anything else you need.'

'Thank you,' Sarah said. 'Did ... did they say when we...?'

'The funeral?' Her father frowned and finished his drink. 'I suppose a couple of weeks – they said something about a post-mortem and perhaps an inquest. Nothing for you to bother your head over, Sarah.'

'I'm not a child, Dad. I know the police may want a statement from me.'

'I didn't think you were a child, Sarah – that was your mother's idea.' He refilled his glass. 'I don't know why she had to be so damned stupid!'

'Daddy!'

'I'm sorry if it upsets you, but your mother was a selfish woman, Sarah. I'm not going to pretend I care. She has made things unpleasant for everyone.'

'I'm going upstairs to pack some things,' Sarah said, then jumped to her feet and ran out.

Her father sighed. 'I shouldn't have said anything, but I can't pretend to something I don't feel. I've wanted a divorce for years. I only stayed for Sarah's sake.'

'Sarah understands. It was a shock for her. She will be all right in a little while. I'm going to take her to meet my family in Stretton, and then we'll go to my sister. Sarah will feel better when she gets away from Ely.'

'Yes, I expect so. Give me your sister's telephone number. I'll let you know when things are settled here.'

Connor took the pad he was offered and wrote the number down. He stood up and walked to the door. 'I think I'll go up and see if Sarah needs a hand. We might as well take as much as we can.

It will save coming back again.'

'Anything she leaves I can send on.'

'Right, thanks. I'll tell her.'

Connor went up the stairs. Sarah had a large suitcase on the bed, but she had only packed a few things.

'There's so much – a whole lifetime...'

'Your father will send on anything you leave behind, darling.'

'Some of these things I've had since I was a little girl,' Sarah said, looking round the room. 'Mum kept everything – all my dolls and books...'

'Leave them for now. Your father can pack them into boxes. You might want to give them to our children one day.'

Sarah lifted her head. Her lashes were wet, but now she was smiling through the tears. 'Yes,' she said. 'I'll just take some clothes and my make-up and jewellery. Dad can have the rest packed and send it on to me at your sister's.'

'I hope you will like it there. I'm sure you will love Emily – and she will love you.'

'I am looking forward to meeting her.'

'We'll go down in a couple of days. I want you to meet Dan and Alice first. I lived with them for a long time.'

'We'll go there tomorrow,' Sarah said and then looked shy. 'About the hotel, Con ... I think we should take just one room...'

Twelve

Emily sat on by Alan's bedside as the light faded. He had slipped away from her an hour or so earlier. They had said their goodbyes and then he had just gone to sleep – peacefully, quietly, with dignity. In a few minutes she would have to call a doctor, begin all the process that went with death, but she wanted this gentle time first. Once the doctor arrived it would break the link and she would have to let go. For a few moments longer he belonged just to her.

'I am going to miss you so much, my dearest,' she told him. 'But I shan't be sad, because you wouldn't want me to be sad. We were so lucky to have that little time together. I shall treasure the memory, my love.'

'I loved you so much,' she seemed to hear Alan's voice as a breath of air in her ear. 'I wanted to set you free.'

'And you did for a while,' she said, a tear slipping from the corner of her eye. When she was with Alan, in his arms, wrapped about with his love, she had been young again. She had forgotten all the cares and the duties this house imposed on her. She had been just Emily Searles again. Now she was Lady Vane once more.

She bent to place a last kiss on Alan's cold lips.

311

It was her final farewell. A mantle of serenity had settled about her shoulders as she went down the stairs to her study. She picked up the telephone and rang her doctor. A few words and it was done. He was on his way. Everything would be done as it should be. Alan had asked to be buried here in the churchyard so that he could be near to her.

'When you need company you can bring me flowers,' he had told her with his gentle smile.

Emily got up and went to look at the portrait of her father-in-law. Vane glared down at her, colder in oil than he had ever been in life – to her at least. His portrait was a faithful representation of the face he had shown to the world.

'I'm going to do it, Vane,' she said. 'I'm going to do as Connor suggested. I shall open the gardens to the public on two days a week in the summer – and I'm going to convert the East Wing into a hotel.'

'Of course you are, Emily. And about time too...'

Vane's voice was so clear, so real, that for a moment she thought he had actually spoken to her. It was a long, long time since she'd had that sensation, but for a moment she thought his portrait was smiling at her.

'I'm going mad, of course,' she said and laughed. 'Even if it is only in my head, I am taking that as agreement, Vane. It is the only thing I can do. It would be difficult on my own, but Connor will help me – and perhaps Sarah will take an interest. I haven't met her yet, but I'm sure she will be nice if Connor loves her.'

Silence reigned. If Vane had an opinion on the matter, he wasn't sharing it. Emily laughed. She was such a fool! She should take the advice of those that loved her and cut free while she was still young enough to have some life – but she wouldn't. She wouldn't sell Vanbrough because she loved it as much as Vane had – and he had known it.

'You were a wise old devil,' she said. 'Sometimes I hate you, Vane, but you knew me better than I knew myself.'

'Are you sure about this?' Connor asked softly as he closed the door of the hotel room behind them. 'I can wait until we're—' He broke off as Sarah pressed two fingers to his lips and he kissed them. 'I love you so much. I've wanted this so much, my darling...'

'So have I,' she said and smiled at him. 'I don't know how you put up with me for so long, Con. I was a silly little girl. It was ridiculous to keep saying no when we both wanted it...'

'I wouldn't have you any other way,' he told her. His hand reached out, stroking her hair and then caressing her cheek and her throat. 'You are perfect, Sarah. The only girl I've loved – or ever will love.'

'And you're the only one for me,' she said, lifting her face for his kiss. She sighed as his lips caressed hers, tongue pushing inside her mouth, tasting her, and she melted into him, her body dissolving, becoming fluid in the heat of love. 'Make love to me. I want to be yours...'

'You are mine – now and for always.' He

reached out, undoing the button at her throat and then kissing the pulse spot. 'I'll be as gentle as I can, darling. I think it hurts the first time...'

'It doesn't matter,' she said. 'I just want it to happen now – with you.'

Connor took her hand and led her towards the bed. He unfastened her buttons and slipped the silky blouse over her shoulders. It slipped to the floor. Her jeans soon followed it, as did the pale pink bra and French knickers. He looked at her in wonder, touching her softly with searching fingers, cupping her breasts, licking at them delicately. Then he was tearing his own clothes off, impatient to feel the satin of her flesh next to his. They lay down together and he drew her closer, kissing her lips, her throat and her breasts. His hands caressed and explored her, making her moan with pleasure as she discovered unknown sensations that had her trembling. His hand slid between her thighs, touching her lightly and then more firmly as she arched beneath him.

When he slid his body over hers, Sarah stretched her legs wide, offering herself to him. He nudged at her with his urgent need, slipping into the warmth of her wetness, moving carefully at first and then thrusting deeper. He felt the resistance give, heard her muffled cry of pain which became lost as he kissed her. She clung to him with her legs and he knew that she wanted him to continue. Pain and passion mingled as he broke through and they became one, joined by love and their mutual need.

After it was over, Sarah lay pressed into him,

her legs still curled around him, her face against his throat. Tears trickled down her cheeks, but she held on, needing the warmth of his body. She was wildly happy and deeply miserable all at once. Con had given her something special, but the horror of her mother's death was still there. She couldn't have slept alone, because the nightmare would have haunted her, but wrapped in his arms she fell into a peaceful sleep at last.

Connor held her. He smiled as the night faded and the first rays of dawn crept in at the window. Sarah was his and the future looked bright. He knew she was grieving for her mother, but the pain would ease. He would make it go away, because he would give her more love than she'd ever had in her life. He would make her laugh and then she would forget the sadness in her heart.

Emily sat at her desk and reached for the glass of wine she had poured. Connor and Sarah were arriving the next day. She had been glad that they'd decided to go off on their own for a few days after they had visited with Daniel and Alice. She had wanted to get the funeral over before they moved in. The news that Sarah's mother had committed suicide was shocking and she had suggested that it would be better if they did not come until Alan was buried.

She had asked a few of Alan's friends and hers back to the house, but they had gone now. She was alone apart from her staff, but they would not intrude on her unless she rang for them. She had a mountain of work waiting for her, letters to write and people to telephone.

Business could wait for a moment. She would have liked to talk to Alice. Connor had told her about the amazing thing Alice had done in taking in Dan's illegitimate son. Dan had never told her what happened the night he took Maura home during the war. Apparently, he hadn't known that she'd had his child until recently.

It was tragic the way it had all happened, David's mother dying in a traffic accident and his grandmother dying of a stroke in Ireland. Alice might have said the boy had to go to a home, but she hadn't. Emily applauded her for that, because it couldn't have been easy to accept that Dan had a son – and she already had four children of her own.

Emily's hand moved to the telephone. It was time she rang Frances again. She needed to be in touch with her family. Sometimes she got caught up in work and it wasn't right to neglect those she cared for too often. Just as she reached for the phone, it rang, making her jump. She picked up the receiver.

'Lady Vane speaking. How may I help you?'

'Lady Vane, this is Tara Manners. I am very sorry, but I have to tell you that Mrs Danby died this afternoon. Her brother was with her. He called the doctor when she was taken ill, but it was too late by the time the ambulance arrived at the hospital.'

'Frances is dead?' Emily was stunned. It was as if all the breath had been knocked out of her. 'I had no idea she was ill. Why didn't anyone tell me? You said her brother was with her – do you

316

mean Daniel?'

'No, it was Mr Clay Searles. He came down with his wife a few days ago. I am so glad he was here, because it ... was not pleasant. She was screaming ... her head hurt so much and she had hallucinations. Mr Searles told me that she had a brain tumour. The doctors thought she would have longer, apparently, but it got worse all of a sudden; they don't know why. I suppose they will do an autopsy.'

'Oh no,' Emily said, feeling cold all over. 'You mean she knew she was ill but she didn't tell me? Why didn't someone tell me?'

'I don't think anyone knew,' Tara Manners said. 'Mr Searles may have had some idea, because he didn't seem surprised, but Mrs Danby certainly didn't tell any of us.'

'I can't talk to you now,' Emily said, because she couldn't think straight. 'I will telephone tomorrow about the funeral.'

'Mr Searles has that all in hand. He has gone to the undertakers now. He said he would let you know – but I thought I should ring you first.'

'Thank you, it was good of you.'

Emily replaced the receiver. She was too stunned and too distressed to take in what was happening. Frances was dead. She must have been ill for some time but she hadn't told her family – except that Tara Manners thought she might have told Clay.

'Oh, Frances...' Emily said brokenly. 'Why – why didn't you tell me?' Why hadn't Frances wanted her to know? Why hadn't she come to her so that they could be together? 'I could have comforted you...'

Could anything have comforted Frances? She had known that she was going to die within a certain time – and she must have known it wasn't going to be pleasant or easy.

She didn't deserve this! Emily was filled with anger. Why should it happen to Frances? Frances had always been so lucky when she was young. She had married a man who seemed to have everything. Emily had envied her at one time, but then it had all gone wrong for Frances.

'Hadn't she suffered enough?' Emily cried. 'Don't you have any pity?'

She wasn't sure who she was talking to, because sometimes it seemed that God didn't exist. How could there be a higher being when things like this happened? They said God was kind and gentle and good, but Emily didn't believe it. How could a loving God let this happen?

She felt the tears streaming down her face. She hadn't cried this way for years. She had felt sad when Alan died, but not this tearing, hurtful grief, this sense of bitter frustration.

'Oh, Frances,' she wept. 'Why didn't you tell me? Why didn't you tell me?'

Frances *would* have told her if she'd gone down to see her. But Emily had been too wrapped up in her own life. She felt a slashing regret that she hadn't made time to see Frances somehow. She would never forgive herself and she would never stop wishing that she had gone down when Tara Manners had told her that Frances had fainted that day.

Of course, it wasn't a simple faint. It was a

blackout, but Frances had kept it to herself – just as she had kept her problems to herself all those years before...

Alice opened the door to the boy and saw the telegram in his hand. She hated telegrams, ever since the one they had received during the war to say that Daniel was missing, believed dead. She took the telegram from the boy and went back inside the house. It was addressed to Daniel and she knew it had to be urgent, because no one sent a telegram unless it was bad news.

Daniel was out in the barn working on one of his cars. She went out to him, her stomach tying itself in knots.

'Dan...'

He looked up in surprise as she held the small yellowish envelope out to him. 'What is it?'

'A telegram.'

'Oh...' He took it from her and ripped the envelope open, a soft curse escaping as he read what was inside. 'This is from Emily – Frances is dead. Apparently, she had a brain tumour...'

'Oh no!' Alice felt sick, shaken. She stared at him in dismay. 'Dan, why didn't she tell someone? Why didn't Emily tell us?'

'She didn't know. She has asked me to telephone her straight away. I'd better find a phone box and ring her now.'

'Yes. I'm so sorry, Dan. I feel terrible. Frances asked us for Christmas and we didn't go...'

'If she'd said something...' Daniel shook his head. 'It's no excuse, I know. I should have made time to take you and the kids more often. I always thought there would be plenty of time in the future.'

'Everyone always thinks that,' Alice said with tears in her eyes. 'Sometimes time just runs out.'

Daniel was pensive as he drove into Stretton. Frances dying so suddenly had left him feeling stunned. He found himself remembering the times when Frances had been his big sister. She'd taken him up the street to buy sweets when he was just a lad. He'd come home from the war just after his father died and Frances had been about to get married. After that he hadn't seen her all that much – until Marcus died, and then he had thought she was behaving foolishly, but he hadn't known what Sam Danby was doing to her.

'Frances, I'm sorry.'

Daniel wasn't sure whether he was apologizing for not knowing what was going on when she was in trouble years earlier or not sensing something was wrong these past months.

She had seemed fine the last time he'd seen her, but, of course, that was months ago. He had meant to phone her but he'd tried once and been told she was out. After that he had just let it slip.

Daniel wondered what would happen about the money he had borrowed from Frances. She had said he could pay it back when he was ready, but it might depend on what the lawyers had to say ... But he shouldn't be thinking of that at a time like this! He was ashamed of himself for worrying about his personal plans when Frances had just died.

Emily would be devastated. She had been closer to Frances than any of them. Her telegram made it clear that she hadn't known either – so why had Frances kept it from them all?

'She wouldn't!' Daniel exclaimed into the mouthpiece, as Emily told him what Tara Manners had said about Clay. 'Frances was bitter over what he did to Margaret and the bankruptcy. She blamed Clay for taking all the best land – and me for not giving her the choice to sell her share of the farm. She wouldn't confide in Clay if she didn't tell us...'

'Then how did he know? I'm surprised she even had him and Dorothy to stay,' Emily replied from her end. 'I can't understand why she would tell him something like that and not me.' There was a little break in her voice as she said, 'I wish I'd known, Dan. I've been wrapped up in things here but I would have gone down if I'd known – and I would have brought her back to Vanbrough.'

'Perhaps that is what she didn't want – us making a fuss over her,' Daniel suggested. 'She used to write to Alice all the time, but I think there has only been one letter since Christmas.'

'I rang her several times but she was always out – or that's what I was told. I'm wondering if I was deliberately kept from speaking to her...'

'Who would do that – unless Frances deliberately cut herself off from all of us?'

'I'm thinking Clay,' Emily said. 'He had gone to see the undertakers without even consulting us. He did ring me last evening...'

'What did he say?'

'He said that it was my fault if I didn't know my sister was ill – and that Frances had asked him to take care of everything.'

'Do you believe him?'

'I don't know. I am going down there tomorrow and the funeral is on Monday. Will you come?'

'Yes, of course. I'm not sure about Alice. I'll see what she says.'

'Connor and Sarah are here. Connor says he won't come, because he hadn't seen Frances for ages. Besides, Sarah has had enough trauma for the moment and she may have to go home for her mother's funeral. I suppose Frances and Connor were never close.'

'I'll talk to him. Shall I come to Vanbrough, Emily? We could go down to Cornwall together.'

'Yes, perhaps that would be best,' Emily agreed. 'You really should have a phone put in, Dan. I wanted to talk to you last night.'

'Yes, I shall when we move into the village,' he said. 'I'll see if I can afford it sooner.'

'I'll see you soon, then?'

'If I'm coming on my own, I'll be there by this evening. If Alice wants to come, it will probably be tomorrow sometime.'

'I should like to see Alice, but I really do need to see you, Dan. I've been crying all night...'

'I knew this would upset you,' Daniel said. 'You were closer to Frances than any of us. I feel dreadful. She loaned me some money when we were down there and apart from a quick call at

Christmas I hadn't been in touch.'

'Don't blame yourself too much,' Emily said with a little sob in her voice.

'I don't. Neither of us imagined anything like this would happen.'

'But we should have done,' Emily said. 'Clay is right. It is my fault if I didn't know my sister was ill.'

'Of course it isn't Emily's fault,' Alice said when Daniel got home. 'She is busy, just as we are. Frances could have told us she was ill. It wouldn't have been easy, but you would have got there somehow if you'd known.'

'Perhaps she wasn't expecting it to happen so suddenly,' Daniel said. 'Do you want to come with me, Alice? I called in to see Mary. She says she won't go for the funeral, but she will have some of the children if you want to come.'

'Not this time,' Alice told him. 'You'll travel easier and faster alone and Emily needs you. I should like to visit her during the school holidays and take all the children. Send her my love and tell her not to blame herself.'

'I'm afraid she does,' Daniel said and went to put his arms about her. 'You will be all right here on your own? Shall I ask Mary to come and stop?'

'How can I be alone with five children?' Alice smiled and kissed him. 'You get off and don't worry about me, Dan.'

'I'm going to pack my things...' He laughed as he saw his wife's face. 'You've done it for me. I might have known you would. I'll send you a telegram when I get there.'

'No, just a postcard after the funeral. I hate telegrams. We should have a telephone put in, Daniel.'

'We will,' he promised. 'I'm going to get off straight away, because Emily wants to go down to the hotel tomorrow.'

'You said the funeral is on Monday?'

'Yes. I think Emily wants to confront Clay – and she needs me with her.'

'Don't get involved in another feud, Dan. It isn't worth it. You've been at odds with Clay for years.'

'I shall keep out of it if I can – but I have to support Emily. She wants to know what has been going on.'

'Are you sure you won't come with us?' Daniel asked his brother. 'I know you didn't always get on with Frances, but she is your sister.'

'Sarah has been through enough recently,' Connor told him. 'I'm sorry Frances was so ill and sorry that she died like that, but going to her funeral won't change things. I hadn't seen her for years. I rang her a couple of times but then she started refusing my calls...'

'She did it to Emily too,' Daniel said and frowned. 'I think she was too ill to know what she was doing. Emily thinks Clay had something to do with it, but I would be inclined to think Frances gave orders she wasn't to be disturbed.'

'Perhaps,' Connor agreed. 'I am surprised she even had him to stay, because she was bitter about what he did ... but if her mind had started to play tricks on her...'

Daniel nodded. 'It doesn't bear thinking about, does it? I'll get off then, because I know Emily wants to get there and hear what Clay has to say for himself.'

'Emily has told us we can have the wedding here and I think we may. Sarah says she would rather it was here – we're planning a few weeks after her mother's funeral.'

'That might work out well. Alice wants to come and stay during the school holidays. She is looking forward to your wedding.'

'Yeah? So am I.'

'You are still here, then?' Emily gave her elder brother a look of dislike as they met in Frances's private sitting room. She had never forgiven him for all the trouble he had caused during the war. 'It's just as well, because I want to know what has been going on here.'

Clay Searles met her furious gaze without blinking. He was a tall man who had been as good-looking as his brothers when he was young but had thickened and coarsened over the years. There were streaks of grey at his temples and red veins with purple patches in his cheeks.

'I visited Frances just after Christmas. She asked me to bring Dorothy down for a few days, which I did a week or so ago. Frances wasn't well. She hadn't been well for some months. She had terrible headaches and sometimes she was depressed – black moods that took her over. Tara Manners will tell you that sometimes she shut herself up all day and said she didn't want any calls put through.'

'If you knew she wasn't right when you visited the first time, why didn't you tell me?'

'Frances didn't tell me it was serious. I discovered that for myself when her doctor rang and I answered. She had missed two hospital appointments for treatment.'

'She was having treatment?'

'She was due to have a course of treatment that can be unpleasant. Maybe she didn't fancy going through all that trauma.'

'Frances hated hospitals,' Daniel said. 'It's a pity you didn't tell us, Clay.'

'Frances said she had asked you to stay repeatedly but you kept making excuses. If she didn't feel like telling you, that was her business.'

'You could still have given us some idea,' Emily said. 'What have you been up to? When did Frances ask you to see to the arrangements for her funeral?'

'It was in a letter in her desk.'

'You've been through her desk?' Emily glared at him. 'What else did you find?'

'A copy of her will, if that is what you want to know,' Clay said.

'Was there anything else?' Daniel asked.

'Like what?' Clay's gaze narrowed.

'Letters. I thought she might have left a letter for Emily or me.'

'No, just the letter asking me to see to the arrangements. I'm her next of kin – and that is what it says on the envelope.'

'She probably thought that was you, Dan,'

Emily said. 'If her mind was muddled, she wouldn't have been able to think clearly.'

'Well, whatever she thought when she wrote the letter, I'm the eldest and that makes me the one she wanted to see to things for her.'

Emily walked towards the desk and opened the drawers, looking through them. She found some receipts and a few Christmas cards but nothing else.

'Where is the will, then? What have you done with it?'

Clay hesitated, and then his hand went to his breast pocket. 'You're not going to like it – but don't blame me.'

Emily took the will and read it through. She was frowning as she turned the page and then she gave an exclamation of disgust.

'I don't believe it. Frances would never have done this – unless you had a hand in it.' Her eyes were accusing as she looked at Clay. 'How did you get her to change her will? This was made just after Christmas. I know it wasn't what Frances originally intended, because she more or less told me what was in it. She had left most of it to me and Dan, with a few thousand pounds to Connor and a bit for Mary.'

'It was all Frances's idea,' Clay said, his face stony. 'I know you think I'm a cheat and a liar, but I didn't guide her hand. She told me that she was convinced none of you cared for her. I knew she was going to make a new will but I had no idea what was in it.'

Emily passed the document to Daniel. He read through it and gave a snort of disbelief. 'Five thousand each to Emily, Connor and me – and three thousand pounds for Mary. "The rest goes to my next of kin, Clay Searles... "'

'Frances would never have left everything to you, Clay,' Emily said. 'She must have nearly a half a million in property and shares. She was so bitter about what you did. I know you've done this! I don't know how, but you persuaded her or forged it...'

'That is a damned lie! Frances was upset because you wouldn't visit her. Don't blame me. She was ill but she did it off her own bat.'

'At least we know why you didn't let us know she was ill,' Daniel said. 'You wanted to make sure we didn't come down here and queer your pitch. She might have changed it back again if we had.'

'You won't get away with this,' Emily said. 'She wasn't fit to make a new will in her state of mind. We shall take this to court and fight you every step of the way.'

'You can try,' Clay said with a sneer. 'It may cost you a packet – and I don't think you will enjoy the publicity.'

'I don't care what people think. I'm not going to let you get away with this!'

'You can speak to the lawyers on Monday,' Clay said. 'I've got things to do. Please make yourself at home. I've given instructions that you both have a room with a bath.'

'He thinks he owns the place already!' Emily burst out as her eldest brother left the room. 'He can't get away with this, Dan. Frances would never rest if she knew.'

'Maybe she forgave him,' Daniel said. 'If he came when she needed someone – and we weren't around. She forgave me for not being there when she needed me after Marcus died, so maybe she forgave him.'

'You don't really believe that?'

'What I believe doesn't make much difference. If the will is properly witnessed and signed, we could waste a lot of money trying to overturn it. We might get a fair hearing, but on the other hand we could look as if we are greedy relatives who didn't bother about Frances and are squabbling over the money now she's dead.'

'Dan!' Emily sat down, her face white. 'It isn't like that – you know it isn't. I'm angry that Clay should get all the money. You could do with some of it, don't tell me you couldn't.'

'Five thousand pounds is a nice sum for me,' Daniel said. 'I won't deny that I would have liked more – but I can't afford to go to court over this, Emily. I borrowed two thousand pounds from Frances. I thought the paper might be in her desk.'

'She probably tore it up while she could still think straight,' Emily said bitterly. 'If it was there, Clay would be asking for the money already. He hadn't seen it or he would say.'

'Don't be bitter,' Daniel said. 'I know you need funds for Vanbrough, but Frances was entitled to do what she pleased with her own money – besides, most of it was dirty money. I don't particularly want it.'

Emily sighed. 'It isn't really the money itself. Alan left me several thousand pounds in his will.

I'm not desperate – but I am sure Frances didn't know what she was doing when she signed that paper.'

'You can't know that,' Daniel said. 'She might have done it in a fit of temper.'

'She wouldn't have wanted him to have her money. He wasn't in the original will at all.'

'Well, speak to the lawyer after the funeral,' Daniel said. 'If he thinks you've got a good case, you can have a go – but be careful. You know what Clay is like. He would fight you every step of the way. You would probably see most of the money go in court fees...'

'And Mary could do with her share,' Emily said. 'It was a clever touch leaving us all something ... I know Clay did this, Dan. I don't know how he talked her into it, but I know he did.'

'I couldn't give a damn about the money,' Connor said when Daniel told him about the will three days later. 'I'm sorry you and Emily didn't get more. You can have my share and welcome.'

'I'm already in your debt,' Daniel told him. 'Five thousand in the bank will help me get the garage started, Con. I could have started anyway, but it will be a help to know I've got something extra.'

'Emily isn't going to take it to the courts, is she?'

'No. She calmed down after she thought about it. I think she agrees that the money came from a bad source. Money like that brings no one any luck. Clay is welcome to it. He is the loser in this.'

330

'What do you mean?'

'No one in the family will have anything to do with him in future. It seems money is his god, so I hope he is happy. Dorothy told me she is leaving him. She knows what he did – though she wouldn't tell me – and I think she is using her knowledge to get her freedom. He is giving her a house and some money – and he wouldn't do that unless she had something over him.'

'Well, I have some good news,' Connor said. 'My last two singles have been released and one of them has gone straight to the top of the charts!'

'You're number one?'

'Yes, I can hardly believe it, but it seems the stuff in the papers was good publicity in the end. The record sold out and they had to reissue. It may even go platinum. Moon Records want me back on their books, but I shan't sign with them again.'

'One of the big companies?'

'Maybe. I haven't discussed it with Sarah yet. I've got an idea but I need to talk to Sarah and Emily first...'

'That is fantastic news,' Emily said when Connor told her later that evening. 'What does Sarah think?'

'She doesn't mind if go back to recording but she doesn't want me to go on the road, and I shan't.' He hesitated. 'I'm thinking of starting my own label. I might make some records myself, but I'd like to give some other groups a start – and I know a group I could use on my own records. They could do with a break...'

'Do you think you could make a success of it?'

'I've talked to some people I know and they think it might work – but I need somewhere to set up a recording studio...'

'And you thought this might be a good place?'

'If I could use a part of the West Wing ... I know it is a lot to ask, but I'd be here most of the time and Sarah is keen to live here.'

'I would be happy for you to make your home here, and I think your idea is wonderful.'

'I'll pay you rent, of course, and if the label is successful, I'll give you a share of the profits.' Connor grinned. 'We'll be a family business, Emily.'

'Yes, a family together,' Emily said. 'Dan is bringing Alice and the children for the wedding and I have a feeling they will be visiting more often in future.'

'Sarah told me she would like to help you with your charity work.'

'A family firm...' Emily smiled and suddenly the shadows were lifting. 'It is what Vane hoped for, I am sure. He wanted to keep the old traditions but move forward into the future. This is exactly the way forward. The artists who come to record with you can stay in the hotel, and the people who visit the gardens will have an added interest if they see a few famous faces arriving.'

'I know it is going to work out for us all,' Connor told her. 'You don't really care about Frances's money – do you?'

Emily shook her head. 'I was so angry when I knew what had happened. Frances wouldn't have done it if she hadn't been ill, but Dan is right. If we go to court to contest it, we're the ones who look greedy. He would come out of it smelling of roses, because no one who didn't know about things that happened in the past would understand why I know my sister would not have wanted Clay to have her money – but I don't care. I just wish she was still here. I didn't see her much but I am going to miss her.'

'Yes, of course you will. We all wish she was still here.'

'Love is more important than money.'

'Dan says it is dirty money. It didn't bring Frances much luck, did it?'

'No.' Emily looked thoughtful. 'If she hadn't had that money, she might have come to live with me. Dan is right, as always. It is dirty money. Clay is welcome to it.'

'Clay is a loser, despite all his money,' Connor told her. 'Everyone loves you, Emily. Daniel has his family; they take all his time and he works all hours for them, but he has the important things – and so do I now Sarah is going to marry me.'

'You are leaving tomorrow for the funeral?'

'In the morning. We shall come straight back and start planning the wedding and the future.'

'Take care of yourselves, then,' Emily said and kissed him. He hugged her back. 'Go and find Sarah. Tell her I shall be delighted if she wants to help me with the charity work.'

After Connor had gone in search of his fiancée, Emily stood looking out at the view. It was all so beautiful and she had been right to keep her promise. For a while she had felt trapped, worn out by the constant need for more money, but the feeling had gone now. All the plans she and Connor were making for the future would ensure that she could afford to keep the house and estate running. She would be able to pass Robert's inheritance on without selling land or treasures from the house.

The hurt of Frances's death was beginning to ease. She would always regret that her sister hadn't come to her – hadn't told her she was dying – but it had been Frances's choice.

'At least you're at peace now, love,' she said softly.

'You are at peace too, Emily, my love.'

Emily turned. For a moment she felt his presence, wrapping her about with loving arms.

'Vane,' she said. She went to gaze up at his portrait. 'Vane, it is all going to be wonderful.'

'Yes, of course it is. I always knew it would be.'

For the briefest moment she heard his laughter.

'I am certainly mad,' she said and laughed. She felt as if she had shed years in an instant. The future held a shining promise. It was up to her and her family to make of it what they would...